"Almost certainly Ward Just's best novel . . . He writes of the mind and of the heart and of the soul. . . . An important writer."

Chicago Tribune

"There are few American novelists who successfully fuse political depth and literary achievement. . . . To this short list should be added the name Ward Just."

Seattle Times/Post-Intelligencer

"With his 10th novel, [Just] has earned a space on the shelf just below Edith Wharton and Henry James. . . . His characters are uncommonly alive. . . . Just also knows the quirks and undertows of official Washington."

Newsweek

"Compelling . . . Just proves he is the reigning master of the political novel."

Booklist

"Fearlessly explores some of Just's distinguishing preoccupations: the rage between fathers and sons, the arrogance of power, conservative WASP uptightness, the mediocrity of academia . . . A Washington novel of rare psychological penetration and literary craft."

ly

D0802075

JACK GANCE

Ward Just

IVY BOOKS • NEW YORK

To Sarah

PART ONE

'Forties and 'Fifties

1

VACATIONS were automatic and followed a pattern. The day after school ended we left the apartment on the Near North Side and drove to the Little Fort River Valley, where we rented a cabin on Big Lake near the Wisconsin line. This was during the war. The trip took two hours in the red long-hooded Buick, my brother and I in the back seat and our parents up front. In those days the country began just north of Chicago.

We rented the same cabin, tucked away in the woods beside the lake, smelling thickly of pine and mildew. We cooked our meals on a wood-burning stove and slept under Hudson's Bay blankets the color of milk with wide red stripes. From the narrow porch we could see the dock and the dinghy with its two-cylinder Johnson, and the royal blue lake beyond. Even at the end of June the ducks were still about and we could hear their calling. There were many canvasback ducks and a few geese, big and unwieldy beside the sleek canvasbacks. My father was always up first and from my bedroom window I could observe him on the porch, huge in flannel shirt and heavy twill trousers, a steaming mug of coffee in his hand. I watched him put the mug carefully on the railing, raise his arms, and take imaginary shots at the ducks wheeling overhead.

"Bang," he said softly. "Die, you sucker."

Big Lake was one of a chain of lakes, all of them connected by the Little Fort River. It was always fragrant and chilly in the mornings, the sun still low on the horizon, slanting through the high firs, glittering on the lake. The cabin was situated in the trees across the water from a high point of land that rose sharply a hundred feet or more above the lake. That was where the big bass and muskelunge were, in the deep water. There were no other cabins in the vicinity, so the days were eerily quiet and slow-moving. It was as far from the helter-skelter of the Near North Side as you could get.

My mother, my brother, and I always played killer Parcheesi after dinner. My father sat reading in a chair by the fireplace, the radio turned low. He listened for bulletins of the war, and when one came he would put his book down, turn the volume up, signal for us to stop rattling the dice cup, and grimly listen to the news. He was thirty-nine in 1944, too old for the war. He said they didn't need old men, they had enough young men; and the war wouldn't last forever, unless they were even more stupid than he thought. Never underestimate their stupidity, though. They thrived on it, so don't expect an end to the war any time soon. The politicians were corrupt and the generals vainglorious.

After Parcheesi we all went onto the porch and lay down, head to head so that our bodies looked like points of a star. We watched for meteors and falling stars. I tried to divine the thoughts of my mother and father. My father never liked these evening séances, but Mother made him do it; it was nice, touching heads in the darkness and pointing at the Milky Way, listening to the rustle of night creatures. Then my brother and I would be sent off to bed and my mother and father would stroll down to the dock and sit in canvas chairs in the darkness, drinking highball nightcaps. I knew they were there by the red glow of the cigarettes, the smell of the tobacco, and the clink of the ice cubes, though that may have been the wash of wavelets against the stony beach. The night was always still and secret. My mother and father talked in tones so low that I never heard what they said to each other.

Their oldest friend lived nearby in a large house on Egg Lake, the largest of the chain. He had been best man at their wedding but had moved away from the city, north to the Wisconsin line, where his life was simpler and not so raw. I didn't like Chicago's rules, so I moved to the sticks, Carl said. He maintained that he was a country boy, "just a country lawyer trying to make a living," but he didn't look like one or act like one. Carl Fahr looked like a man of the world, as debonair, buoyant, and lithe as Fred Astaire.

On the second or third day of our vacation he would come to call in his Gar Wood speedboat, arriving with a mighty roar around the point of land, the boat skidding as he slid it around in a wide dramatic turn, the water flying in a huge fan. Approaching the dock, he would cut his engine and the boat would heave on its stern, pushed by the swollen wake. Then he would reverse gear and the boat would halt, roaring, agitated water all around it, the wake curling now onto the small beach next to the dock. We all cheered and applauded. Carl had his white yachtsman's cap low over his eyes, so he had to lift his chin to see properly. He was as tall as my father but slight; he went with the boat as other men go with a pipe or a fedora. He tied up expertly at the dock and hopped from the Gar Wood with an almost dainty step, shaking hands with my father and embracing my mother. They all talked at once, laughing and firing questions at one another. Then my mother went inside to prepare a pot of coffee. The three of them sat on the canvas chairs on the dock, drinking coffee, catching up.

My brother and I were there to say hello, and to admire the speedboat, whose lines were lovely and economical and curvy as a bull's horns, and as lethal. The brightwork was polished and the mahogany varnished to a luminous shine so that you could see your face in it through the tiny weblike cracks. The leather seats were soft, like the well-worn seats of an English sports car. The leather smell mixed with gasoline fumes was intoxicating. In a machine like that you could go anywhere, north to Mackinac or south to St. Louis, always attracting attention. It had been built years earlier in Sheboygan, and built to last.

When my mother and brother left to go to the store for provisions—Carl would stay for dinner—I remained in the boat, sitting in Carl's place, slowly turning the wheel and making engine noises, *vroom vroom*, until my father told me to stop it and Carl said never mind, it didn't matter, kids loved the Gar Wood almost as much as he did.

"He'll screw up the mechanism," my father said.

"No, he won't," Carl said.

"It's your boat," my father said.

Carl smiled at my father and slapped him on the back. "How are you, old Vic?"

My father moved his shoulders as he habitually did when he felt hemmed in. He looked at me moving the steering wheel and scowled.

"They giving you a hard time?"

"No more than usual," my father said.

"Look at it this way," Carl said. "They're bastards. The hell with them."

I was listening carefully, trying to discover the meaning of the conversation. My father and Carl Fahr seemed to inhabit a twilight world where shadows distorted the meaning of things. It was a world of innuendo and sudden darkness, often formless. Just then I was worried that they were talking about us, my mother and me, though I was certain that couldn't be it. Their "they" was another and more remote "they."

"Easy for you to say; you're here in the sticks. I'm there. I'm where the money is." My father leaned back in the canvas chair, his legs straight out, his hands drumming on his thighs.

"That's why I got out."

"Maybe too soon," my father said.

"What the hell," Carl said. "I have enough."

"Bastards, give them an inch—"

"Victor, you know what I think? I think you shouldn't fight City Hall quite so hard."

My father sighed. "That's what they're there for." Then, looking around, "Where's whatshername?"

That would be one of Carl's woman friends, blond, long-legged, dressed in floppy shorts and a cotton shirt and wearing a baseball cap, always friendly to my brother and me. The baseball cap was the real thing, a gift from a Cub outfielder.

"Arlene," Carl said. "Didn't like the sticks. Went back to Aurora."

"The bright lights of Aurora," my father said.

6

"That's right, Vic. She left me high and dry." Carl smiled again and turned to look at the water. There was a little silence. "Do you want to go fishing?"

My father squinted at the sky. "It's bright as hell."

"I saw one jump on the way in," Carl said.

"Let's go then," my father said.

"What about Jack?" Carl said.

"Do you want to go?" My father looked at me.

"Sure," I said.

"Then let's saddle up," Carl said. Dad went into the cabin for our rods and tackle. Carl had live bait and plugs in the Gar Wood. It seemed to take them forever to transfer the gear to the dinghy, Carl being slow and careful stowing the rods and tackle. He handled them with respect and I watched him attentively, knowing that he was doing things properly, the way they should be done, the way a man did them, taking his time, making certain everything was secure. I was sorry to leave the speedboat, and Carl laughed and said you couldn't fish from a Gar Wood. It wasn't done. It wasn't allowed. It wasn't de rigueur. It was against the law. They catch you at it, you've had it.

"Whose law?" my father said.

"Mine," Carl said.

"Christ," my father said. "I thought you were serious. They'll make any damned law, interfere with your fun. Make things difficult. I figured they made one against your boat."

Carl shook his head. "They don't give a damn up here."

"For the time being," my father said.

Carl looked at him. "By the way. You and the boy have licenses?"

"No," my father said. We were in the boat and Carl was standing on the dock holding the dinghy's painter. "Shit, I forgot. What difference does it make? Up here where they don't give a damn." Carl said nothing, just stood and shook his head. He wound the end of the painter around his wrist, reached into his back pocket, and took out two pieces of paper and a pencil. He said, "I figured." He leaned against the piling, asking me my vital statistics—age, place of birth, color of hair, color of eyes, weight—writing as he went. Then he asked my

7

father the same questions. My father grumbled that he had never seen a warden at Big Lake, had never seen an unfamiliar *boat*, for Christ's sake, but Carl just smiled and went on writing. "You owe me a buck," he said when he was finished. "Jack's my guest. Here you are, Captain," he said to me. "Sign it, make it legal." I took this prize, the first official paper I had ever seen with my own name on it, carefully printed my name, Jackeson Gance, and put it away in my pocket.

So we went off in the dinghy, Carl manipulating the two-cylinder Johnson. He was in the stern and my father in the bow and I was amidships, on the small seat. When we were in the middle of the lake, Carl cut the engine, allowing the boat to drift in the direction of the deep water below the high point of land. The surface of the water was calm and unruffled as milk in a saucer, nothing moving except for water bugs and the huge Wisconsin black flies, sluggish in the heat. There were no ducks or geese. It got warm and then hot, and I trailed my finger in the heavy water, watching its minute wake, imagining a great fish below, attracted by my fingernail. I imagined the lake teeming with fish, unseen, scavenging the bottom. I thought, Jack Gance, licensed fisherman. The men were casting with small plugs and I was trolling, daydreaming because there were no strikes. Carl had taught me how to pierce the worm with the hook so that the worm would be firmly fixed yet appear natural. The fish had to believe it was real, a fact. I moved the rod back and forth in a lazy swing, hoping that the worm's movement below was factual enough to catch the eye of a bass.

Carl and my father were talking about Chicago and the changes in the six years Carl had been gone. My father said that Chicago was a boom town and there was no telling how big the boom would get. Given time, Chicago would be a greater city than New York, if they didn't screw it up. That was a big "if," because they had always screwed it up in the past; it was the civic sport. My father talked about his real estate business. He was guessing that the growth—the way he said it, it sounded like underbrush—would be west and north. But probably it didn't matter where he bought property, because the growth would be everywhere, given time. There were

8

only four or five people who decided things, and you tried to follow their lead; everything cost money. Then Carl was talking about the Little Fort Valley and laughing because the wiseguys had brought in slot machines and in one of the roadhouses there was "a wheel," all of this for the amusement of the summer and the weekend trade. Damned Syndicate, he said, you couldn't get away from them. And the authorities couldn't do anything about it, or didn't want to, or were afraid to. They're all the same, my father said. Carl said, They've come up here with a ton of money and muscle. He said that he'd done some legal work for one of them before he knew who they were and what they represented but, hell, they paid on time and in greenbacks. They scare you to death, Carl said. The one who was his client talked out of the side of his mouth like Cagney and it looked as if he was carrying, too, but he was so damned fat it was hard to tell. But no one cared, the one-armed bandits appealed to the tourists—can you imagine, tourists in the Little Fort Valley? Just the other day it was a wilderness. What did you do for them? my father asked. Carl didn't reply right away, and then he said they were buying property for summer cottages, themselves and their friends, and they needed title searches and the like. They were buying land piece by piece in order to keep the price down.

"No big deal," Carl said.

"Watch out for them," my father said.

"Yeah, Vic," Carl said. "I will."

In a minute they were talking politics, or my father was talking politics and Carl was listening while he snapped his rod, effortlessly sending the plug into deep water near the high point of land. My father said, God damned Dewey is a loser and Roosevelt is a winner and that's all there is to it. Dewey doesn't know anything about the country and that was why he'll lose and Roosevelt'll win. Roosevelt has the answer, tax and spend. And he has the power that comes with virtual dictatorship. And the booming wartime economy. That's his edge, my father said. Everyone has one. That's his. Might as well crown him King Franklin I. He and loser Dewey, what a great choice for the American people. God damned Easterners.

9

"There's nothing out there," my father said.

"Patience, Victor," Carl said. "Patience. Look at your son."

"Jack?" my father said.

I looked at him.

"What are you doing?"

"Nothing," I said without looking up. I wanted to ask Carl what a Syndicate was, and what a one-armed bandit looked like. I was bored, dozing, watching my rod bend and dip. It seemed to me that we had been fishing for hours.

My father said, "There are a hell of a lot of fish in this lake, but they don't like us. They're opposed to us."

"They knew you were coming, Vic." Then, after a little pause, very quietly but with a fisherman's authority: "Jack, reel in a little. Victor, don't cast for a minute." Carl put his own rod down and leaned close to me. "I think you've got one." I began to protest, No, but when I started to reel in there was a sharp tug, as if the line had caught on something. Carl put his hand over mine, a cautionary gesture. Easy, he said softly. Just reel in, slow but not too slow, and easy. Don't jerk; pull. The fish made one little run, almost pulling the rod from my hands; it was amazing to me the way the line went out straight, as if it were alive, then stopped dead. The fish dove, loitering a moment near the bottom; and that was it. Reeling him in was like collecting an inanimate object. When I saw him at last, a foot below the surface, silvery and limp on the line, I began to smile. My fingers hurt but I forgot about them. After the first great rush of surprise, a tremendous calm seemed to come over me, and I knew this was just right, the way it was supposed to be; and now when I actually saw him, the excitement came back. I was filled up with it, with the satisfaction and the complete veracity of the moment, mine and mine alone. Carl maneuvered in behind me with the net.

"Do you want to bring him in?"

"You can do it," Carl said. "Bring him in a little."

"All right," I said.

"Good boy, son," my father said.

"Watch out, everybody," I said.

10

"You did real well," Carl said, sliding the net through the water, trapping the fish and bringing him to the surface so that we could look at him.

"Well," Carl said.

"I really caught a fish," I said.

"You sure did," Carl said.

"Is it a muskie?" Muskelunge were the fiercest fish in the lake and everyone wanted one.

"No," Carl said. "It's a little bass." He turned to wink at my father. He was moving the net back and forth in the water, the fish trapped in the net.

"We can eat him tonight?"

"Sure," my father said. "You catch him, you eat him. That's a universal law."

I laughed. "And Ma cleans him."

"We'll see," my father said.

"It's great," I said.

"Bring him in, Carl," my father said. But Carl made no move to boat the fish, only continued moving him back and forth, trapped under water but alive. I felt rather than saw them look at each other.

Carl said, "He's a little small."

"What the hell," my father said.

"Under the limit," Carl said.

"What's the limit?" my father said.

"Believe me when I say that this one is under it."

"I don't care," I said.

"It's the kid's fish," my father said.

"It doesn't matter," I said. This was not the exact truth. I both wanted him and didn't want him; he was the evidence, but it didn't necessarily make him mine. Or did it? The fish itself mattered less than the excitement of catching him, making no mistakes, doing it the way it was meant to be done. Or so I told myself, watching him move sluggishly in Carl's net, the line moving with him. I struggled with this thought, not knowing what I really felt or wanted. I knew that I didn't want to hear them arguing. Their argument ruined everything. I had a vague idea that since Carl was the skipper of the boat it was his decision. I looked at each of them, waiting for an answer; but they were concerned with the argument

11

and didn't notice me, so I turned back to the fish in the water.

"It's small," Carl said.

"Let the kid have his fish," my father said.

"Even if it's under the limit?"

My father laughed. "*Especially* if it's under the limit."

"Whatever the kid wants he gets," Carl said quietly. "Is that it?"

As Carl spoke he raised the fish clear of the water, I think without meaning to. The bass was gasping now, its mouth making little O's and its gills pumping. The hook glittered in the bass's lip and the snell tightened as it made a jerk. The fish was already beginning to lose its vitality, its eyes glazing and growing pale.

"Carl, it's a god damned *fish*," my father said.

Carl said, "It's a fish under the limit."

I said, "Dad, I don't mind. Really I don't."

Carl said something I didn't hear, and then my father said, "You're the guy who doesn't like the rules. Wanted to move to the sticks, make his own rules."

I looked at the fish, dying a few inches above the water.

My father said, "Is it that important?"

"Victor," Carl said.

"He's just a kid," my father said.

That seemed to settle it, and not to my advantage; either way it was not to my advantage, but for the past few moments I had known that it would be this way. Without another word, Carl boated the fish. We sat looking at it in the bottom of the boat, barely breathing now. It had lost none of its color. The underside of its gills were blood red and the hook was still in its lip, and the worm on the hook. The worm was dead, I noticed; and the fish was about to die. The fish had suddenly become the center of everything. Much later, remembering the events of that day, I thought of my bass as the anonymous person suddenly thrust onto the front pages of newspapers, a gangster or a lottery winner or a political hostage. In the bottom of the boat the fish looked smaller, as if it were diminishing before our eyes, belittled.

12

"Let's throw it back," I said. That seemed a fine solution, bury the evidence. I looked at my father and then at Carl, trying to discover what it was that had set them against each other, and against me. They were very old friends. My father once said that he would trust Carl with his life, screwball though Carl was. I knew suddenly that whatever the trouble was, I did not have the power to set it right. The fish stayed, the fish went; somebody lost, and I was responsible. Carl lost or my father lost and I did not want either of them to lose. It seemed that everyone wanted a piece of my fish, and in their desire it was necessary to exaggerate its insignificance and my insignificance; it seemed to me later that the struggle was like an obscure war fought by conscripted armies over anonymous terrain. Yet at that time I also knew, knew instinctively and with absolute certainty, that Carl was right and my father was wrong, and that my father knew that I knew and that Carl didn't know.

"You did fine," Carl said to me. He put his hand on my shoulder and squeezed, a little harder than he needed to. I looked up at him, at his thin, handsome face and his yachtsman's cap pulled low over his eyes. He said, "Did you have fun bringing him in?"

"Never anything like it," I said.

"You're a fisherman now," Carl said.

"I guess so," I said.

Carl started the engine. "What do you say, Victor?"

My father said, "Let's go in. Cook the god damned fish."

Carl brought the boat around in a wide arc, then throttled back suddenly. He was looking behind him and smiling in a dreamy way. I turned to see a boy scrambling down the high point of land to a little ledge perhaps twenty feet above the water. He paused, then flung himself into the air, arms wide in a perfect swan dive; he seemed to hang a moment, then straightened, plunging, entering the water with hardly a splash. It was thrilling to watch. I turned to say something to my father but he was staring at the fish in the net. Carl gunned the engine, heading for the dock. I looked away from the spot where the boy hit the water and saw my mother and

13

brother, sitting on the end of the dock, their feet dangling. My mother was shaking her fist and I thought for a minute that she saw what had occurred between my father and Carl, either that or she disapproved of the boy's flamboyant swan dive. But then I saw that they had the Parcheesi board between them and she was shaking the dice cup.

Carl stayed to cocktails and dinner. As far as anyone could tell from the conversation around the table, everything went well; that is to say, Carl and my father pretended that nothing had happened in the boat; but all that may be a false memory, or a dream or hallucination. I fell ill that afternoon and by midnight was running a high fever. I heard shouting and laughter, and then I was with the diver, both of us poised on the ledge, raising ourselves on tiptoe and launching into space, miraculously rising and then falling, we two entering the water with barely a splash. Then I was in the boat with my father and Carl, realizing I never saw the boy surface. I imagined him under water, living in the restless lake reeds, communing with the fish. He was a renegade, one of those who scorned human society. I tried to talk to him but he was mute, silently turning this way and that on the bottom of the lake.

My mother came into the bedroom, put her hand on my forehead, and went to call the doctor. Carl went away to fetch him in the Gar Wood. The doctor gave me an injection of some kind, after taking my pulse and listening to my chest. Everyone in the Midwest was worried about infantile paralysis, but the next morning the fever had vanished. I was wrung out, having passed the crisis. No one knew what had caused the fever or the hallucinations, but everyone agreed that I had been very fortunate, and I must have been for I have remembered the incident for more than forty years.

I told a version of that story to Tap Gobelin once. He had come to Chicago to interview me during my campaign. He asked me to recall an early memory, some G-rated memory he could write about, teasing his readers. We had been talking about ethics in public life, the rules and regulations that gave stability to our world.

Tap was a famous reporter who had become confessor to Washington magnificoes in political trouble, something like Bishop Sheen to fallen-away Catholic industrialists in the 1950s. It was good insurance to be a secret source to Tap, whose newspaper was a kind of *Daily Tablet* to the federal government. Confessing to Tap was absolutely safe, since he never, never burned a source—any more than Fulton Sheen would have denounced a wealthy penitent on network television. Gobelin was a connoisseur of greed and ambition, Washington's Tweedledum and Tweedledee, the capital's divine afflatus.

Perhaps a story about money, he said.

Money? What about money?

Money, he said again. Money's fascinating.

In prosperous middle age, Gobelin had turned from scandal to psychology. His investigations often turned on the misuse of money, but since he had become rich himself, he discovered that money was more subtle than it seemed when he was poor. A dubious investment had led to an inquiry by the Internal Revenue Service. Tap paid up at once, but the incident had left a bad taste. He had been misled by his accountant—so often the case with wealthy individuals whose affairs were complex. Was there not a razor's edge dividing "evade" and "avoid"? And that blade was called "intent." Serious reporting, he concluded, was less an exposure of the facts than the ambience of the facts. Not the fact itself, but its pentimento; its provenance, no less. The truth was a forest of facts, and the facts were in shadows, and if you could describe the shadows, you had the truth. Gobelin looked on his newspaper as a great canvas, and himself as a master impressionist.

Since Tap was a very old friend, and had proved reliable in the past, I told him about Big Lake. I wanted to avoid any discussion of money. He listened listlessly and observed that it was a terrible lot of significance to invest in one poor fish. One poor small-mouth bass, he said, and laughed. He had not taken many notes during my monologue, a sign that he was bored, though you could never be sure; he had a superb memory, and loved to stack the deck.

Tap sighed and changed the subject. He talked for a moment of this and that, the stock market and the various deficits. This was October 1986. He confided that he was doing very well, having bought deutsche marks the year before. The German economy was a wonder and of course the dollar was falling like a stone. On the advice of a friend he had also gone into gold, although he didn't like it because of the damned Boers. However, this was Swiss gold, guaranteed Swiss .997 fine. And he had his properties, the Connecticut property and the pied-à-terre in New York. His next assignment, after he finished with me, was a youthful arbitrageur. Terribly bright but unscrupulous. The little prick, he said, smiling wolfishly.

I'm going to cut him a new asshole, Tap said.

Oh dear, I said.

He burned some friends of mine, Tap said, mentioning a diplomat and two congressmen. He looked at his empty notebook, and then at me. Perhaps it was an attack of nerves, he said. Your fever.

I think I was scared to death, I said. So much violence in one small boat.

That's what I mean, he said. Nerves.

This is a political campaign, I said. Nerves are off the record.

Trust me, he said.

I always have, I said, and we both laughed.

Tap said, I like it, Jack. It's an interesting story, even if there's nothing in it about money. You've got an interesting background, and an interesting turn of the mind. But the story won't read very well—too many loose ends, too ambiguous. Can't we tidy it up a bit? Can't we get something in there about the day the dog died or the sound of train whistles in the night?

I could do that, I said. But it would be wrong.

Jack? How much did you leave out?

About half, I said.

Which half? he asked.

The half that's mine, I said.

I still don't get it, he said. I'd like to be helpful. Give me the rest of it. Or is there a cover-up here?

I told him there was nothing specific to "get" from

16

this succinct story of Chicago and north of Chicago, provincial America in the 'forties and 'fifties. It was life in the foundry, that was all; the world that was the foundation of my political career. Chicago and north of Chicago were to me what Trier and London were to Marx, or Kafka's father to Kafka.

2

We could see Lake Michigan from our apartment on the
Near North Side and most days, winter and summer, it
was as flat and placid as a prairie. The cardinal's mansion
was around the corner. We looked down on it from the
den, watching the cardinal leave in the morning and return at night, always with a briefcase in hand; his assistants carried briefcases also. They looked like Venetian
businessmen as they tumbled out of the gondola-shaped
Cadillac and hurried into the mansion, the doge and his
consiglieri, as my father said. Every morning and every
evening my father watched them, a dour smile on his
heavy lips. Of course there was a police escort, two ro-
bust sergeants, Irish from the look of them. My father
had names for the cardinal's assistants: Marshall for the
slender older one, Field for the dough-faced younger one.

In the mornings he watched them while drinking coffee
and in the evenings with a dry martini, playing Broadway
show tunes on the phonograph.

All the houses and apartment buildings were solid affairs of brick, concrete, stone, and iron, presenting an
exacting face to the world. That part of Chicago had and
has a Northern European look, perhaps a port city on the
margins of the German plain. Grandfather Gance said it
reminded him of Hamburg, except for the innocuous lake.
The lake was a feature of the flat terrain, bearing no
resemblance to the riotous North Sea or the Baltic, cruel
bodies of water with distinguished histories: murderous
naval engagements, conquest, and exploration, for cen-
turies portals to the world for the thriving cities of the
Hanseatic League (and what were Chicago, Detroit, and

Duluth but a Northern American Hanseatic League). Lake Michigan had no past that anyone spoke of. There was little commercial fishing and only moderate commercial traffic, mainly ore boats from the Mesabi Range. At that time Chicago was still foundry to the world, the goods moving mostly by rail; the lake seemed less gateway than barrier.

They can say what they want, my father said, but this city is landlocked. We might as well be living in Grand Rapids.

A prodigious Grand Rapids. South and west were the sprawling neighborhoods laid out in a monotonous checkerboard, to the north the lakefront communities, docile as the Cotswolds. The city was then a collection of well-defined nations—here Estonia, there the Ivory Coast—where outsiders never thought to go. Our apartment was analogous to the city. My brother and I each had our own rooms, to which the other was not welcome. My mother had her sewing room and my father his study. Lincoln Park began at our front door. My parents had a few close friends, businessmen and their wives. I grew up among large, good-humored businessmen talking about commerce and sports, and their mysterious wives, whose conversation was too subtle to grasp. It was difficult to understand how and where the businessmen and their wives fit. I thought of them as elementary machines of interchangeable parts. It seemed that the men manufactured things for money and the women spent the money, always hilariously, while the men looked on approvingly. There was plenty of money to go around. They drank cocktails and talked about money, ate dinner and talked about money; and it was only much later that I understood that a culture was at work before my eyes, a culture as dense and as consequential as any I would ever know, infinitely subtle, complex, and emotional. Their chatter, which seemed so aimless and shallow, was a cover for their actions. Talk was cheap. Actions were not cheap.

In our apartment the afternoon silences were heavy, my mother reading in her sewing room and my father working in his study, or in his office on South Wabash Avenue. Occasionally Eddie Snethan, my father's ac-

countant, came to the apartment to talk business, the two
of them disappearing into the dark square room, Snethan
as animated and excitable as my father was taciturn.
Mother said, Mr. Snethan's here, be quiet and don't disturb your father. The liege man and his lord, talking
business, inspecting the numbers, correcting the accounts. No sound escaped from the study. The city's noise
was inaudible behind thick curtains, its blue foundry haze
unseen. It seemed in a certain way that the city was inside and we were outside. The world behind the curtains
was as turbulent, dangerous, and unpredictable as a man's
heart, and as unknowable.

I was eighteen when my father went to prison. The
trial lasted two weeks and I was in court every day with
my mother. At breakfast we read about the previous day's
testimony on the front page of the *Tribune*, long gray
columns of quote and counterquote—the *Trib* was our
Izvestia, and how strange now to find it belligerent; was
this how a newspaper repaid a subscriber's loyalty? My
father poked at his grapefruit, reading the financial section and the bridge column, working Bidder's problem in
his head. The meal was eaten in silence, and then with
a sigh my father stepped to the sideboard and poured
himself a shot of Hennessy cognac, sipping it thoughtfully, moving his jaws as though he were chewing it. This
had nothing to do with the strain of the trail. He drank a
shot of cognac every morning of his adult life.

The lawyers met us each morning in a black Chevrolet
sedan, one lawyer driving and the other in the seat beside
him; we three squeezed into the rear seat, my mother
always in the middle, her handbag in her lap. The stop-
and-go ride took twenty minutes, during which time the
lawyer discussed what would happen that day, the prosecutor's strategy, the witnesses from the bank and from
the Internal Revenue Service, and whatever documentary
evidence there was, and there was always a surfeit, one
piece of paper after another that proved that my father
had had, for five years, a very large income and that he
had paid no federal income taxes on it. While the lawyers
talked, he looked out the window, often humming a Cole
Porter song.

20

Victor, are you listening?

Every word, he said.

Give us a hand then.

Nothing to say, he said.

We hurried up the steps of the courthouse past a throng of reporters and cameramen. I came to know the cameramen by their shapes, since I never saw their faces. All of them were using the big Speed Graphic cameras with the flash attached. We said nothing to the reporters, not even "No comment." The lawyers told us to look cheerful and confident, but in the circumstances that was not possible, so the captions to the photographs always described us as "grim-faced" or "unsmiling."

My father sat at a table with his lawyers. He was a large man, physically imposing; his back to us, his shoulders looked as powerful as a wrestler's. Toward the end of each day's session he would turn and stare at us, his expression vacant and distracted. Then he would turn back, eyes front, and his shoulders would sag. He was looking for my brother Sam, but Sam was not there.

Brother Sam was in his final year at law school in the East, and the trial—the worst year of his life so far, he said—had caused him to turn his back on the family. Loyalty worked both ways. I don't understand the principles of this family, he said to my mother, whom he believed an accomplice. He was appalled by the consequences of my father's crime, the carelessness of it, the disgrace, the publicity; it was the publicity that guaranteed the disgrace. Private disgrace was an inconvenience, but public disgrace a calamity. To Sam, the details were unimportant. Causes were unimportant. The old man was guilty and the details were only—details.

So much was out of sight in my family; we seemed to thrive on rumor and supposition. So I was obsessed with the details. I wanted to know everything, what my father thought, and what he did, and when he did it, and how, and why. I wanted to *know*. It was an inexplicable event—he was rich and in good health, with a wife who loved him and two sons who obeyed him—but at eighteen I did not believe that events were inexplicable. Events had causes, and if you know the causes you could explain the events; and to understand was to sympathize. I thought I could discover how the world worked. I mean, how things broke down. My brother wasn't interested in the world; he was interested in himself, how the disgrace would affect him, his prospects, his position in the world, his blameless reputation. In his eyes, my father—*our* father—was no better than a common criminal, and not as bright as a common criminal, and not as resourceful, nor as needy.

Who does he think he is? my brother demanded.

After two weeks in court, I thought I had a partial answer. In his absolute contempt for authority, my father chose not to fight the charges of the government. He refused to defend himself but he also refused to plead guilty. He gave his lawyers rein to do their work, but he would not testify in his own behalf. My father's hatred of the government, any authority, was fierce and without compromise. He thought the state beneath him. The usual rules did not apply. The rules belonged to the powers that be, and vice versa. He allowed his lawyers to make a defense—ludicrous in retrospect, it amounted to "inadvertence" or "misadventure," the carelessness of a busy and successful business executive—because in his prideful discontent he could not allow the state the satisfaction of absolute power. He refused to speak in his own behalf; and he would not express regret, and would not plead for mercy.

His evasion of federal income taxes was a political act; I was certain of this, and to me it had an anarchic appeal. It was a kind of defiant mania that in anyone else might have produced sexual chaos or the rapture of a crusade, Alcoholics Anonymous or Moral Re-Armament. I put this notion to the lawyers, who rolled their eyes; no, there was nothing political about it.

"He couldn't get around to doing it," one of them said to me.

"I don't believe that," I said.

"He thought he could stiff them," the lawyer said.

"Absurd," I said. "He knew he'd never get away with it."

"Yes," the lawyer said. "I think that's the point."

Of course my father's crime was conspicuous. And he was not an attractive man nor an admirable outlaw; in

22

person, he frightened people. There was nothing in his background to elicit sympathy. He had grown up with all the advantages, yet had behaved like a scoundrel. There were newspaper cartoons and even editorials of the no-man-can-set-himself-above-the-law variety. His few friends did not call to offer their support; they were mortified. So much for class solidarity (though after he had done his time they were generous, believing in the redemptive value of punishment). My father was an embarrassment, a traitor to his class worse even than Roosevelt. His crime seemed to confirm everything that the left-wingers said about businessmen, their rapacity and selfishness. The publicity inspired my brother's permanent retreat to the cosmopolitan East Coast, where no one knew or cared abut the disgrace of a Chicago businessman. Sam couldn't handle him, this hot potato of a father. One by one his friends abandoned him, and then his first-born son abandoned him. My father lived in an airless world of his own manufacture, absolute monarch in his own country—an attitude, or psychosis, he passed along to Brother Sam. It was only a particular feature of their personalities and the changing times that my father became an outlaw and my brother a prig.

Much of the time he did not seem to understand what was happening in the courtroom, though the expression on his face—when he turned in his chair, slowly crossing his legs—was the same sour look he reserved for the cardinal and his suite. Owing to his refusal to testify, his version of the story remained a mystery. He listened carefully to Eddie Snethan's testimony concerning the firm's double-entry bookkeeping, how he had tried to argue against it, and how my father bullied him.

"You fought against it," the prosecutor said.

"I did," Eddie Snethan said.

"But there was nothing you could do," the prosecutor said.

"Mr. Gance is a hard man, and very persuasive," Eddie Snethan said.

"Why didn't you quit?"

A look of shocked surprise. "And leave Mr. Gance in the lurch?"

"Yes, exactly," the prosecutor said.

"The business was in trouble and Mr. Gance was trying to save it. God, he loved the business. Just loved it."

This was the first hint of motive, and now the prosecutor moved closer to the witness; he knew enough never to ask a question to which he did not know the answer, but his curiosity got the better of him and he said, abruptly, "Explain that."

"It's obvious," Eddie Snethan said—and his face froze. My father was looking at him with an expression so malevolent, so contemptuous, that the little man halted, then began to ramble, a wordy discourse on generally accepted accounting procedures and the difficulty of financing a business . . . The prosecutor listened, then let it go, uncertain where this testimony was leading. And my father's lawyers were no more successful, and at length the judge cut them off and dismissed the witness, who left the stand with a hopeful wink at Victor.

My father's sullen dignity infuriated the court, but I found it admirable. At the end he submitted to the rules, but he did not surrender his personality, his own view of things. When he walked out of the courtroom manacled to a federal marshal, he did not look back, at me or at my mother or at the judge or at anyone, until he reached the side door. Then he turned to glance over his shoulder, his haughty presence causing a little rustle in the courtroom, spectators and bailiffs shifting nervously on the hard mahogany benches. He stared hard at my mother, whose eyes filled with tears. I am certain that he was searching for Sam and somehow held her responsible for his absence, though his face was expressionless and he did not speak. The door opened and he and the marshal passed through it into the darkness.

My father remained inside himself, a perfect mystery or riddle, like the Sphinx. I had never known him well and now I felt I did not know him at all—what was the cause of his anger and contempt? When I asked my mother why he had not defended himself, she said there was no defense; he had neglected to pay his income taxes. But why had he made no move to enlist the aid of people? He knew people who could help, put a word in the right ear; there were people in Chicago who specialized in ear work. She offered only the ghost of a smile: Your father

24

doesn't like to ask for favors, she said. He loved his business, it was his business and his responsibility, no one else's. Its affairs were private, personal and confidential; his linen, clean or dirty. There was no difference between them, him and his business. He made a mistake, poor darling. And they came after him.

They? I asked her if he *wanted* to go to jail, and she shook her head slowly; she didn't know the answer to that, but he hadn't done anything to avoid it, had he? She looked at me sadly and said, Please remember that people aren't alike. People are strangers to each other and to themselves, and what is true about one person isn't true about another; and sometimes it isn't possible to *know*. Things happen. You do not do some things that you should. You do some things that you shouldn't. How hard it is to discover motive, Jack. Yet that's the important thing. Your father is a superior man, she said. As you are. In any case, we belong to him and he belongs to us. He is very particular, that's true. He only wants to be himself.

Your father is not a happy man, she said.

Sam, I began.

Sam can go to hell.

Ma, I said.

Sam wants to be someone else, she said.

Well, I said. And to myself I thought, Wasn't that true generally?

He thinks he'll be happy if he's someone else, she said.

Maybe he will be, I said.

After a fashion, she said.

Listening to my mother, I was doubtful—not about Sam, who was far from my thoughts at that time, but about my father. Certainly he was not a happy man, but many men aren't. It occurred to me then that he was simply a son of a bitch—as some men are said to be nice guys—a stubborn, spoiled, careless man, a man heedless of consequence. When leaving the courtroom he turned, everyone was watching him, waiting for some demonstration, a gesture of reconciliation. When he did not give them what they wanted, the spectators turned to look at us, the wife and the son, conspicuous on the front-bench. Even the lawyers turned, momentarily neglecting their studied nonchalance. The faces were mostly sympathetic, for the Midwest is a sentimental place. Behind its Teutonic façade, Chicago has a forgiving nature, and fraud was a civic sport.

Sit up straight, my mother whispered to me.

Yes, I said.

Give them *nothing*, she said fiercely.

We were objects of pity. The judge's charge still echoed in the great high-walled room, the Stars and Stripes and the state flag of Illinois hanging limply either side of the judge's dais, the only splashes of color in a background of brown. He had excoriated my father as a brigand, an irresponsible businessman, arrogant and corrupt, who had struck at the American ideal no less than the thug who robbed the corner grocer; worse, because he was a man who had grown up with all the advantages, graduate of a distinguished university, recipient of a substantial inheritance, grandson of a great Chicagoan, a fine citizen, therefore a man with an obligation to the community, to the American dream . . .

Look him in the eye, my mother said.

I am, I said.

I am making an example of you, the judge said. He was a small gray-faced man, almost bald, with a sharp beak of a nose. He banged his tiny foot against the dais for emphasis, *bang* an example of you *bang bang*. Then a dramatic pause.

Two to five at Joliet. Stateville, to those inside.

At that time the public memory was a damp sponge. It was before the deluge that drenches it today. In those days a scandal was here today and here tomorrow and the day after tomorrow. A good reputation was durable and notoriety was forever. I knew that I would always be known as the son of the man who had neglected to pay his taxes, and had gone to prison without apology; indeed, without comment. Of course in some quarters this made him a stand-up guy, no whiner, a guy who took on the system and got licked (he wasn't the first and wouldn't be the last), taking his punishment like a man.

My father would never allow me to visit him at Stateville, though we exchanged letters. His letters to me contained detailed descriptions of his bridge triumphs with an embezzler from Winnetka. The day they bid three-no and made six; the day they doubled and set their opponents; the finesse that worked; the cross-ruff that was pretty as a picture. My letters to him were concentrated chiefly on my life at the university. I, too, was going from triumph to triumph as the protégé of a senior professor in the department of political science, the university's best. I let my father know that I was well and happy and that the atmosphere was congenial (he had always thought it a haven for Reds and their fellow travelers). Once in a while I gave him news of Brother Sam, graduated from law school and now with an old-line firm in Boston. The varsity, Sam said. He specialized in wills and trusts, a fertile field in Massachusetts. Sam was a solid citizen who voted Republican and paid his taxes and was shortly to be married to a debutante, the daughter of the senior partner of his firm. The wedding would be private, family only, in France, where the bride had connections. I had been invited but declined; midterm examinations, I explained. My father received the news without comment.

It would be pleasant and uplifting to report that prison did not change my father, but it did. I hardly recognized him when he walked through the gates at Joliet (and that was how it was then: the gates swung open and the free man walked through them). He seemed to have physically shrunk. His face was beet red and lined as an artichoke, the face of a derelict. His clothing hung on him in folds and he shuffled when he walked. It was an odd shuffle, as if he did not quite know where to put his feet. I suppose it came from standing in lines, or pacing his cell, or being ordered about. But I almost didn't recognize him. His voice was thin and hesitant. It took him a long time to make up his mind about anything.

Someone had lent my parents a house on the west coast of Florida. I drove them to the airport, handled the bags, and checked them in. My father had said very little, and now stood at the window staring at the airplanes on the tarmac. I watched him fumble absently in his jacket pocket and withdraw a pack of cards. He began to shuffle them deftly with one hand. They were frayed cards, held together with Scotch tape. I watched him manipulate them in his huge hand, then quietly excused myself and once out of their sight ran to the cigar stand. I bought a pack of Bicycle cards and ran back. He was still standing at the window silently shuffling the cards. When it was time to board the plane, I kissed my mother and shook hands with my father. All this with no words between us; my father looking out the window at the airplanes maneuvering in the cold. It was very warm in the waiting room, the sun streaming through huge plate glass windows. I handed him the fresh deck of cards. He took it, hefting it, then turning it over in his hands, expertly splitting the cellophane with his fingernail. The cellophane fluttered to the floor, and my father picked it up and carefully put it in his pocket. He took the pack from the box. I heard him wheezing, a kind of lumbar whistle. The expression on his face was one of infinite confusion and the baffled kindliness one associates with the very old and down-and-out, to whom any show of attention is a benevolence. His eyes filled with tears. I held out my hand and we looked each other over. I wanted him to give me his old deck, and for a moment he seemed about to comply. He turned it over in his hand, looking at it as one might a wallet-worn family photograph. The cards were thick, repaired as they were with tape. He lowered his eyes. He could not surrender them. His hands were trembling and slowly he put both packs into his jacket pocket. The gate attendant motioned at me and at my mother.

She moved to my father's side, supporting him.

She said to me, Thank you, dear.

I wished them a good flight to Florida.

She looked at my father and said, Victor . . .

He did not hear her, or gave no sign of having heard her. His tears were beginning to spill, but he did nothing to stop them. It was as if he didn't notice. My father looked at me, opening his mouth to speak; but he didn't say anything. He squeezed my elbow, a manly gesture, Chicago stuff. I knew he was deep in his memory somewhere, perhaps back in Joliet, perhaps somewhere years before that, his own youth, an awkward encounter with his own father. I watched them slowly descend the stairs, their chins tucked into their coat collars against the evil wind. Even in his diminished state, he towered over her; but now he had his arm around her waist, holding on. She was his crutch. My God, I thought, what had they done to him?

Suddenly he wheeled, stumbling on the final step. He let go of my mother and his coat flew open, revealing how thin and white and shabby he truly was. The expression on his face was terrible to see. His wet eyes burned with malevolence. He shook his fist and yelled something I couldn't hear, and then he reached into his pocket and with a tremendous effort threw the deck of Bicycles back up the stairs. They went every which way, caught by the wind, sailing here and there, red and white confetti pasteboard, almost festive. But he didn't see any of this because he had turned to shuffle off across the sunny tarmac in the direction of the DC-6, its port engine already beginning to turn.

The hell with you! I shouted after him. *Go to hell, you son of a bitch!*

And so, many years later, as I remember this—the scene returns to me from time to time, each detail vivid and complete—I am appalled at my presumption and pathetic sentimentality in the presence of one whose life I could only dimly know. He had been abroad to a country I knew only from books. I knew that prison was not benign; it did not ennoble. It did not make a man wise; it made him cunning. It crowded and darkened the memory. I reproach myself for interfering, and it is no good to argue that it was not my intention to humiliate him. To do such a thing unintentionally, to know one's blood kin so slightly . . . But as my mother said, we were all strangers.

A good son should have more sense. It was right for him to keep his battered cards, his dark memory, his evidence of life. And it was right, too, for me to tell him to go to hell, because he had not troubled to learn of my life either. And there was more to it than success in the brilliant political science department at the university; so we had both been witless. We were sovereigns of warring nations, my father and I, each with his special agenda,

29

his plan of campaign, and his policy of unconditional surrender.

To hell with you, I said. But it will come as no surprise when I report that he was a surrogate, my broken-down old man. He had no power to hurt me or anybody. The face I saw before me as I yelled into the roar of the engines was Brother Sam, sanctimonious Sam, Sam and his chaste debutante and his château honeymoon, his law degree, his spotless reputation, Sam-who-didn't-understand-the-principles-of-this-family. Wills-and-trusts Sam. Beacon Hill and Nantucket Sam. Sam the prig. The hell with him.

3

A few months later my parents returned to empty the apartment, pack their things, and leave Chicago for good. Sarasota had been a success and they had bought a small apartment in a new co-op building near the water. Late one afternoon I drove up from the South Side to help them sort through things, what they would take, what I would take, what would be sent to Sam, what would be put in storage, and what would be sold. I had not spoken to Victor since the incident at the airport, and was naturally apprehensive. But when I arrived he was in his study, the door closed.

My mother was surprisingly cheerful, supervising the chores. Yet from time to time she would walk to the big window overlooking Lincoln Park and stand there silently, tapping on the glass as if summoning someone. The apartment, hushed and gray in the pale light of a winter afternoon, reminded me of a museum. The guide would say, This is how the bourgeoisie of the Middle West lived at midcentury. Note the appointments, the furniture vaguely French provincial, the carpet beige except for the red and blue Moroccan with its asymmetrical design, a comfortable room once you got to know it. In the corner a sturdy bridge table with its lamp, four chairs, scorecard, and sharpened number two pencil. A room with a certain formality: end tables with their bulbous lamps, wing chairs either side of the tables, a davenport facing the ebony coffee table with its burden of thick magazines, the bookshelves floor to ceiling—novels mostly, and the *Encyclopedia Americana*, matched sets of Whittier, Dickens, Defoe, and the Indiana bard, James

Whitcomb Riley—the glowering ancestor over the fireplace (this family, or one side of it, was rich before 1900), the hearth and andirons spotless. Little elephants, two dozen or more, marched left to right on the narrow mantel over the fireplace. Family history: Grandfather Gance had been a Republican first, last, and always. He believed in God, the Gold Standard, and the GOP. One of the elephants was said to have been a gift from Warren Harding. My mother's great-grandmother knew Mary Lincoln and there is today in the Chicago Historical Society a fat bundle of letters between the two, the letters concerned with money—getting and spending in postwar Washington. All the letters are in the archives save one, framed and hung inconspicuously over the Duncan Phyfe extension table in the foyer. Mary Lincoln to Iva Jackeson in the fall of 1869: *Thank you so much for the shawl from State Street. You never forget my birthday, dear Iva.*

My mother's family had lived in Chicago since the 1830s, and my father's since the Civil War. His grandfather is the one glowering over the fireplace. He was a delegate to the Republican National Convention in 1920, one of those who was in and out of the original smoke-filled room at the Blackstone Hotel, hustling votes for Senator Harding. Of course the museum guide would not know this, nor that the porcelain elephant arrived inside a box from Peacock's that also contained a gold brooch for my Grandmother Gance, the brooch never worn but tucked away in a safe deposit box at the Harris Trust and discreetly removed a week or so before her death. Victor always maintained that it was the brooch that belonged in the Chicago Historical Society, an artifact more resonant than the letters from poor daffy Mary Lincoln. Victor was fond of drawing a visitor's attention to his grandfather's enormous hands, hairy as a bear's, thumbs stuck in his waistcoat, gold chain drawn tight as a noose around his belly. Things stuck to his hands, Victor said; his hands reached out and things stuck to them, money and people. He had read law and styled himself an attorney at law but never opened a law book; never had occasion to. His specialty was commodities, grain and—hell, in and out of barley, tomatoes, precious metals, mortgages. An acquaintance of Yerkes, Victor said.

Charles T. Yerkes, along with Insull the region's greatest confidence man and patron saint; their ghosts were still floating around La Salle Street and the Hall. Every time the bell sounded on the Exchange, Yerkes and Insull answered the call and commenced to float, hovering overhead, whispering, *bzzz bzzz*. Trouble was, Victor said, Donald Gance never got truly rich. Story was that he loved the game more than the prize, so he never—consolidated. Oh, he was rich enough; but not Yerkes rich, nor Insull rich. On the other hand, he never went to prison either. Loved politics. *Loved* it, loved *dealing*. Never learned to say No. And for that reason his son, my father, never learned to say Yes. The poor bastard.

Only a few old-timers remembered Donald Gance, who lived to a great age, outliving his son by twenty years; scarcely anyone remembered Donald Jr., an inconspicuous salesman of musical instruments. Of the women in the family, scarcely anything was known. Grandmother Gance, invariably described by Victor as "long-suffering," lived also to a great age. Donald Jr.'s wife, Victor's mother, died when Victor was twenty-one. Emily Rose Gance gave piano lessons from their house which, as it happened, was but two streets away from Jackeson Place.

My mother had never lived out of sight of Lake Michigan, first on the South Side and then, after her marriage, on the North; the lake was her anchor, she said, along with a fine building on South Michigan Avenue, a property that had been in her family since the turn of the century. Her grandfather had bought it as a hedge against inflation. Little was known of Grandfather Jackeson, who went quietly about his business, accumulating property; even the family did not know whether his hands were large or small, or what stuck to them. A photograph reveals a middle-sized gentleman with broad shoulders and a walrus mustache, a trace of a smile on his lips, formally dressed, handsome after a fashion; the pose indicates he is wary of the photographer, or perhaps only of the phosphorous flash. An excellent man with numbers, a Presbyterian. His son, my mother Iva's father, carried on his father's business until the crash of 1929 ruined him. The building on South Michigan Avenue was the

33

only property that survived, and that was now on the market to finance the move to the west coast of Florida.

Your father and I, my mother said, there's an awful lot of Chicago history between us. Not that it matters today. Not that anyone cares. Why should they, for heaven's sake? And all that's left is my building and grandmother's brooch. And I'm selling the building. Your father refuses to sell the brooch. A souvenir, he calls it. He says that if the old rascal had been as smart as he pretended to be, he could've been in for a piece of Teapot Dome. He knew Harry Daugherty, you know. It was supposedly Harry Daugherty who arranged for the brooch, and tied the GOP elephant to the package. He was a great kidder, was Harry Daugherty, according to your father.

She was talking about Florida now, standing by the window in the pale light. I could hear Victor in his study listening to "Miss Otis Regrets." She had been sorting books, wondering what to do with the unreadable Whittier and the popular novels from the 'thirties and 'forties. She said I could have the encyclopedia. I coveted the fine first editions of Fitzgerald and Aiken and Mann, but she said she wanted those; she reread them from time to time and she wanted them in Florida. It was hard, and she wanted something of Chicago with her. Florida was a peculiar environment; the humidity, everything so new. It's as if they started yesterday, she said. But she thought she would be content with the Caribbean—turbulent but warmer, and the sunsets were spectacular; lovely, really, to have a drink and watch the sun go down. It wasn't Lake Michigan but, hell's bells, water was water. Victor had bought a skiff and fished in the evenings.

We have a drink, watch television, and are in bed by ten. And I read until two, sometimes later. Sometimes it's hard to sleep in the humidity. But still.

Chicago has changed so, she said. I hardly know it anymore.

So many friends have moved away.

She spoke with her back to me, staring out the window over Lincoln Park to the lake. There were no boats to be seen, only the great placid plate of blue.

Their few friends had moved to the suburbs. She reminded me of the four or five friends, good, close friends, living now in Winnetka or Lake Forest. They love it there. They love the country clubs. They play golf with their sons and their sons-in-law on Sundays, and watching the foursomes come in, you think it's the last act of a corrida. The sons and the sons-in-law are all apprenticing to their fathers and fathers-in-law. You don't always know who's the toro and who's the matador except that the boys look beaten.

I began to laugh. My mother had a wonderful droll side to her.

I watch old Dad take out his putter and I think it's a sword. You ought to watch them around the greens, the boys are walking on eggshells and the dads and the in-laws are watching them as if they're going to steal the silver. Oh, well. Poor boys.

Which ones? I said.

The whole kit and caboodle, she said. She laughed suddenly. They do love it there, in Winnetka or Lake Forest. They never come in to town for a play or a concert, or even for dinner, though they're always promising. Meet at the Barclay, go to Orchestra Hall, stop at the Palmer House for a nightcap and maybe a little dancing; but they never do it. They're like White Russians who moved to Paris after the Revolution, living now as émigrés, feeding on rumors from the occupied capital city. And such rumors! Noise, dirt, crime, corruption, taxes. The jigs, the Machine, the Syndicate. She laughed again, turning from the window. Difference is, she said, there's no urge for a counterrevolution. They're happy where they are, well out of it. They love the North Shore and their cookouts and Sunday foursomes. And their money.

They're welcome to it, I said.

Let the city stew in its own juice, she said.

Are you worried about money? I asked.

She did not answer directly. She said instead, You don't know this, Jack, but we almost moved to the suburbs the year of your father's troubles. It was before I knew anything about that. I was in the dark. I thought we could buy a little place by the lake. It'd be nice in the country. Sam was gone and you were about to go; this place is so big, Victor and I just rattle around in it. But he wasn't enthusiastic. He hated commuting and didn't play golf and if he lived in Winnetka or Lake Forest he couldn't spy on the cardinal, which he loved doing. Drinking his martini, listening to show tunes, and spying on the cardinal. Your father is such a funny man in his habits. And then he was arrested and we had the trial. So that was that and we didn't move to the suburbs.

He wouldn't've gone, I said.

Oh, yes, she said. He would have done it for me.

That's right, I said.

He never denied me anything I really wanted.

Well, I said. I'm glad you didn't move.

I am, too, I guess. I've lived so long in Chicago. It would've been a real adjustment, living on the fringes. No car horns or Lincoln Park, no Field's downtown. No Art Institute. Who needs a park when you've got the back lawn? And of course no cardinal, though your father would've found someone else to spy on. The banker across the street, probably; or the banker's wife.

I laughed at that.

You're right, my mother said. She'd be fat and uninteresting. She wouldn't even play bridge. Or she *would* play bridge but she wouldn't be very good at it, always talking while she missed the trick.

I said, What's he doing in his study?

Arranging his papers, she said. We listened a moment to Fred Astaire singing "Cheek to Cheek"; very faint but the voice and rhythm were unmistakable.

I said, I've got to get back.

No, Jack. Don't. He feels bad about—the last time. He wasn't himself. He's much better now. Of course, he won't bring it up. And you shouldn't either.

I thought, Why not? I said, Okay. How does he feel about Florida?

He's getting used to it, she said. Everything takes a minute, you know. You can't just jump into things. It's worked out so far, though there's no question we're transplants. Most people are, down there. When people ask me where I'm from I'll always say Chicago, as if next year or the year after that we'll be back. As if we're down there for our health. But we won't ever be back, that's understood. Still, we're Chicago people. Move to the suburbs, that's where you are. *That's* where you're from, Winnetka or Lake Forest. Did you see the story in the *Trib* a while back? An earthquake somewhere you never heard of and the Red Cross moved the inhabitants, primitive people, from their land and resettled them. And very soon they began to die, one by one, for no apparent reason at all. They're still dying. The Red Cross thinks they're dying of broken hearts, leaving their ancestral places. Their souls rebel and they die. And that's what would have happened to me, probably; died of a broken heart in Lake Forest. Knowing that Chicago was just over the horizon and I couldn't go back to it to live. From Lake Forest at night you can see the city's lights. On a still night you can hear it, even. Driving back to Chicago at night through the Skokie peat bogs I got the creepiest feeling: all that soft earth underneath, the peat burning, the smell, the smoke and the fog, but still I rolled my window down. It was like crossing a no man's land. We used to go for the parties in the summer and I couldn't wait to get back. Everything's so quiet in the suburbs. Even when the band's playing, it's quiet. When I smelled the burning peat I knew we were only twenty miles from the Near North Side, home.

Yes, I said.

Florida's different. Everyone in Florida's from someplace else. It'll work out all right. Your father and I'll have a little bit of money after the building's sold, and his health is coming back. Together we'll be fine. And there's a place, not too far away, where we can buy the *Trib*.

The hell with the *Trib*, I said.

Well, she said, and paused. She took a step toward me then, and spoke with sudden urgency. We had to leave, Jack. We couldn't stay here. All the bad memories crowded out the good ones. We understood that without even discussing it. Too hard on *him*, on Victor, do you see? I didn't know how dreadful that year was for him, the year he was arrested. It was bad before he was arrested. Something happened to him, I don't know what. He gave up. I don't think he knows what it was. And he doesn't want to find out and I don't want to find out, either. But he just went to pieces. I hate it, but he had to get away from here. Just had to.

I'll miss you in Florida, I said.

Oh, and we'll miss *you*! But you'll visit.

Always, I said.

I'm glad you're staying in Chicago, she said. I'm sorry we're not here with you, that we can't be together as a family. But you're grown up now. And I'd hate to think of Chicago without one of us. I don't know, taking part somehow. Not that it means anything except to *us*. People don't care about families in that way anymore, who they are and where they come from. And everything changes so. Jackeson Place used to be one of the nicest streets in town.

Yes, I said.

And who knows? she said brightly. Maybe it will be again.

Well, I said. I'll be here. I'll never leave.

Really? she said.

Never, I said.

She looked at me doubtfully, and I saw at once how well she fit in the room, indisputably a Near North Side apartment. She fit in like the subject of an artist's carefully composed portrait, in her beige slacks and furry sweater, her eyeglasses in her left hand, her cigarettes and lighter on the windowsill; in the fading light her features were indistinct except for the doubting expression, a pretty woman on the threshold of fifty, still trim; she was framed by the window, the lake just visible, there in the right-hand corner of the glass. She was motionless, her head cocked, waiting.

I said, I'll hold the fort in Chicago. The last Gance.

And the last Jackeson, she said. Let's not forget the Jackesons.

The last Jackeson Gance, I said.

She said, I think you'll leave Chicago, Jack. It'll become inhospitable. Not now, but sometime. And it makes me sad to think about it, our family has lived here for so long. When my great-great-great-great came here from Pennsylvania, it was Indian country. They called it Fort Dearborn, itty-bitty trading post.

That's what it still is, I said. A trading post.

More than that, Jack. Much more. Why—

I laughed and said I was joking. I said I liked Chicago. I liked the South Side. I liked the university and, as a matter of fact, I had met a girl . . .

Oh, she said.

Nice girl, I said. I was thinking about bringing her today, but she's packing. Making a quick trip south with friends. But there'll be other times.

From Chicago?

No, I said.

An Eastern girl, she said, trying to keep the disappointment from her voice.

No, I said, and was about to explain when the room was suddenly filled with music, Ella Fitzgerald's Cole Porter. Victor was striding through the dining room, a thick sheaf of papers in his hand. He stopped when he saw me, and for a moment I thought he would turn about and retreat back to his study. He looked ten years younger than when I had last seen him, at the airport. His face was tanned and his bulk seemed to fill the room as we stood staring at each other. I could tell he was in good humor.

Jack, he said, and we shook hands. I didn't know you were here.

I just arrived, I lied.

You look well, he said.

You too, I said. Very well.

Come here, he said. Look at this. He stepped to the window where my mother was and began shuffling the papers until he found the one he wanted. He held it up to the light, a certificate printed on creamy parchment. No document I ever saw looked more official or trustworthy.

Look at this god damned thing, he said.

It's a security, my mother said.

Security, my ass. He laughed, nudging me with his elbow.

All right then, Victor. What is it?

It's worthless, he said. One hundred shares of stock in the Blackstone Mining Company, Incorporated. Look at the date, eighteen ninety-one. The year of the panic. Panic to hell and gone, the year the economy went el foldo.

This is one of the reasons why, watered, worthless stock. They were probably mining gold in Indiana or diamonds in Wisconsin. Come to Green Bay, see the diamond mine!

Pretty piece of work, I said. There was a wonderful engraving of a muscular laborer brandishing a pickax. I asked him who the stock belonged to.

My grandfather, Donald the Great. Look at the god damned thing. Worthless. Not worth the paper it's printed on.

The Historical Society might want to have it, my mother said.

They'd like to have the brooch, too, he said. But they're not getting either one. This one I'm keeping. This one goes into my archives. Jesus, he was something, old Donald.

Victor turned and strode to the center of the living room, still staring at the certificate.

My mother said, A lot of people bought bad stock, Victor. Donald wasn't the only one. You know, there weren't any regulations—

My father wheeled, smiling broadly. Then he laughed, a sharp bark.

Iva, for Christ's sake. Donald wasn't buying it, he was *selling* it. Blackstone was his company. This is his name, next to the god damned date. Donald H. Gance, President and Treasurer.

Then, with a huge guffaw, he was gone.

The room was suddenly quiet, and somehow close and humid; the storm had passed. My mother took a long look around, up and down at the bookcases, and left and right at the familiar end tables, and at Victor's leather armchair. In the silence we could hear show tunes, but I could no longer make out the melodies. Victor had closed the door to his study.

Your father, she began.

I know, Ma, I said.

No, you don't, she said.

Well, I said. I think I do.

He won't let it alone.

I think he's himself again, I said.

She gave a shy smile and shrugged. She lit a cigarette, the smoke pluming in the heavy air.

We had such good times here, she said.

I said nothing to that.

And now it's time to leave, she said softly. It's time to get all this stuff together, pack what we want, leave the rest. I hate it, I hate it more than I can say. But that's what we have to do because Victor and I are going to live in Florida.

Ma, I said.

I wish you had known my father, she said.

I do, too, Ma.

Such a fine man. And he would've been a wonderful grandfather. He would have loved *you*. A wonderful father, a wonderful husband to my mother. She didn't appreciate him, though. You know Mother. He could read me like a book, know what I was thinking before I thought it. A modest man. We were a wonderful family!

Are, I said.

Oh? She smiled. I didn't mean us. I meant my father, my mother, and me. All gone except me, and now you. Sam. Of course we're a wonderful family, too. I was just thinking about my father and our building on South Michigan Avenue that I'm selling.

She pulled on her cigarette, the coal glowing, and exhaled a thin stream of smoke, turning again to look out the window at Chicago's haze, the foundry at dusk, the engine winding down. There were pinpoints of light on the lake, ore boats from Duluth. Lights were on all over Lincoln Park, people returning from a day at the office. You could imagine the kitchens all over the Near North Side, men in shirtsleeves washing the city's grime off their fingers and turning to the refrigerator for ice cubes or a cold beer. What a hell of a day. Bitch of a day. Let me tell you about my day.

But this room is still, except for the sounds of show tunes, muffled behind a heavy door. My mother's hands were suddenly on her cheeks, and I turned away, pretending to look for something. What I found was Donald Gance, implacable over the fireplace. I stared at him a moment, trying to connect him to Donald Jr. and Donald Jr. to Victor and Victor to me.

We are such a conservative family. She did not want me to see her tears, as if tears were not the most natural emotion. When I turned back to look at her, she was staring out the window into the gray dusk and her lips were moving to Victor's faint music. She sighed, smiling, and then made a little circular motion with her fingers, as if to roll down a car window.

4

Two years earlier I had moved to an apartment on the South Side, immersing myself in the life of the university, the alluring Bohemia by the lake. I traveled to the Near North Side only to see my mother, and each visit served to estrange me further from bourgeois Chicago, drowning in a sea of money, mindlessly made, mindlessly spent; on the South Side we allied ourselves with the blacks, a community as vivacious as we were sullen. The Machine, the Syndicate, and the banks controlled things as completely as any colonial office in nineteenth-century Paris or London. I was infatuated with the university, a great Gothic industrial park for intellectuals, esthetes in the board room, anarchists on the factory floor. Herr Kafka, meet Colonel McCormick. The Midway was always on edge, in the city but not of it; yahoo Chicago began at the Loop. We reviled it, plotted against it, laughed at it; and it went its own way, surging, driven by furious capitalist energy, absolutely indifferent to our contempt, to our existence, even. The students took their politics from middle Europe and the St.-Germain-des-Prés and were acutely self-conscious, and always apprehensive, like good children at mischief. At any moment there might be a knock on the door and a thunderous voice like Dad's, or Ike's: *All right, you two, break it up. Turn off the lights and go back to sleep.*

And if we didn't, he'd cut off our allowance.

This was the time when you saw a philistine under every bed. The university turned in on itself, camouflaged, removed from things, these being the days before universities were subsidized branches of the federal government, colonels and CIA analysts and foreign service officers reviewing the scholarship because they had commissioned it, paid for it, and owned it, as they owned the scholars who created it. But this time was not that time. At the university in the nineteen fifties, political theory was—political theory, not political practice. And that was the trouble; in Chicago, theory took you so far, practice took you so much farther. To discover how things worked actually, you needed Karcher.

I met Katrina Lauren in Professor Karcher's political science class, where she listened hard but rarely spoke. Where she came from, students were not encouraged to speak. Professors spoke, students listened and took careful notes. This was a course in mechanics, the organization of political parties in the United States, with emphasis on city machines. There was a full shelf of Great Books: Wittgenstein, Canetti, Dreiser's Cowperwood novels, Conrad's *Youth*. Katrina and Karcher had a sardonic rapport. When he spoke of Hague and Pendergast and Kelly-Nash he would often look at her, his eyebrows slightly elevated; she would return the look, on her part a barely suppressed smile, sometimes a grimace. This was a seminar, only nine of us around the table, and she was the only girl. When they looked at each other like that it made the rest of us uncomfortable; whatever the joke was, we wanted to share it. It never occurred to us that there was anything personal between them; and in fact there was not, outside the classroom. And what they shared was no joke.

Do you know what Mayor Kelly said about Chicago, Miss Lauren?

No, Professor Karcher. What did he say?

He was a great municipal philosopher, our Ed Kelly. And by no means the worst of our mayors. He said that Chicago was a place where bulls and foxes dine very well, but lambs end up head down on the hook.

Not only Chicago, Professor.

Just so, Miss Lauren. Can you explain?

I beg your pardon, Professor Karcher. I am not prepared.

And with a slow nod, evidently disappointed, Professor Karcher would continue with his lecture, trying to bring the rest of us into it and succeeding insofar as he dealt with mechanics. Canetti, Conrad, and the others seemed to us beside the point, though *Crowds and Power* was salient. We would watch for his eye to catch Katrina Lauren's and wonder about their silent understanding. We had the queer sensation that they, professor and student, had an agreement that excluded us and that this involved a specific experience, or memory.

Katrina was a historian by specialty but mostly she was a comedian, one of many at the university in those days who gathered after hours at the Proletariat Bar. For a time there was an ensemble called the Proletariat Players, "Proles." Katrina's métier was monologue, much of it inspired by Bertolt Brecht, "Bert," "BB." She would take a few lines of authentic Brecht,

PADUK: How did you like it?
CHAPLAIN: Excellent. That is— Why, it's hell on earth!

and then improvise, applying Brecht's sensibility to university life, Brecht as visiting fellow at the Committee on Social Thought, Brecht as chairman of the economics department, Brecht as university hygienist. She was breathtaking to watch, in part because through Brecht she become herself; at the end of her monologue Brecht was forgotten and there was only Katrina, compact, arms folded, head cocked to one side, a motionless woman in a bright spotlight. She rushed through her routines, savoring the hush of the audience, caressing them and then lacerating them with the sound of her voice. Of course onstage she was a different character from the diffident student in the classroom. Everyone predicted a great career; she was unique, so funny, funny as hell. On those nights when she was scheduled for a monologue the Proletariat was crowded and rowdy and not only with students; the faculty had heard about her, too. Karcher was a great fan.

She was German by birth, small and lithe with eyes black as onyx, black hair cut unfashionably short; she habitually wore black tights and a bulky black sweater, conspicuous even on the Midway, where half the girls

45

tried to look like Rosa Luxemburg (and the other half Gene Tierney). An American army colonel had found her in Berlin's rubble at the end of the war. She was ten years old. The colonel found her a place to live, fed her and clothed her, and when his tour was up brought her to the United States. The colonel and his wife adopted her and in due course enrolled her at the university. They were the only family she had. Her father had been killed on the Eastern Front and her mother had disappeared—both these events in 1944—''like that,'' Katrina said, snapping her fingers. Her mother's disappearance was a mystery; perhaps dead in a bombing raid, perhaps arrested and imprisoned, perhaps gone mad, perhaps—anything. No one knew. People disappeared all the time. Perhaps she'd just scrammed.

We were together six months, living sometimes at her apartment, sometimes at mine. Her friends could not understand what she saw in me, so studious and buttoned-up, so often melancholy, obsessed with the political life of the precinct. My friends couldn't either, though they were too polite to say so. I had a certain local celebrity, as the son of a jailbird; but that was a provenance attractive to the rebellious daughters of stockbrokers and dentists, not Katrina Lauren, refugee, wittiest woman at a university filled with witty woman, so very pretty and Bohemian. Maybe, they said, maybe it's because Jack is such a great listener.

She thought it was miraculous that she had survived the war, miraculous to find herself in Chicago, and miraculous that we had ever met. How normal it would have been to miss each other and spend our whole lives not *knowing*. That was the usual thing, life a series of missed connections, false identities, disappearances, pratfalls, like a French farce; take off one mask to find another beneath it. (Except it wasn't always so farcical, no.) Hence her miracle on the Midway, a thing to be protected at all costs, and never taken for granted, since it could so easily be taken away. Adolf Hitler and his SS had seduced an entire nation, the most talented in Europe, held it in thrall for thirteen years; he was *welcomed*, even by many Jews. Very much a Middle European view of things, allowing me to remind her, to insist, that she was in Germany no longer. She need not fear a knock on the door at midnight. The war was over and the fascists defeated; she need never go hungry again. This was Chicago, where things could be taken from you in other ways, more subtle ways, and would be, for certain, unless you took care. You could be eaten alive in Chicago but it was on the square, mostly—

Jack, she said. I think you are an innocent.

Anyhow, I said, the authorities did not interfere with romance. They didn't give a damn about boy-girl stuff so long as you did it indoors and had a decent respect for community standards, ha-ha; didn't *flaunt* it, flaunt sex, flaunt desire.

She was still very much a European and it took her a moment to adapt to the heartland and its conservative culture. She was amazed that bathers at the beach were always covered, that even modest bikinis drew stares. There were articles about them in the newspaper and discussions on television. Priests spoke from pulpits, and the Park District announced that there would be no nudity in city parks and beaches, period, end of sentence. Chicago is not St.-Tropez! She asked me why they cared so much. It is not healthy, so much cover. The skin must be allowed to breathe, and the sun to reach hidden places. This is healthy. Maybe it is sexy, also. But that is our own affair.

Not in Chicago, I said.

We were new to each other. And our friends were not entirely wrong. With me, Katrina began to pry open her memory. She claimed she had forgotten the war years in Berlin, from 1942 onward when things had gotten so desperate that even the rats were hungry. She had practiced inner migration, she said, exiled herself to a region of her mind where she could live without memory, and submit to whatever presented itself, in Chicago or anywhere else, in the present moment. She began to talk one night and talked all night long, ending at dawn in tears. At intervals she would speak as if in a trance, her eyes narrowing as she fought to remember each detail.

At first I listened casually, interested of course, but listening as if it were a story, a yarn, something that had happened to someone else. I had no point of reference,

47

nothing known at first hand. Because I was a child of privilege, danger was infinitely remote, theoretical in its way. I am not certain that in my own inner migration I refused to take her entirely seriously, as I did not take seriously her theories of physical culture; instead, I found them charming. The Middle West then was an isolated place, self-sufficient as any city-state of the sixteenth century, and proud. The prairie did not open the horizon, but closed it. News was brought by travelers, but unless you knew the travelers you did not believe the news; it was unverified, and you did not take it to heart. The world was regarded with suspicion, outlanders were liars and men of sharp practice and you had to be on your guard, never gullible or seen to be gullible. The war had occurred on the front pages of the *Chicago Tribune* and on the radio, and that made it not quite real; or real in the sense of the earthquake in Bolivia, THOUSANDS PER-ISH. One did not know Bolivia, nor the thousands who lived there.

So I listened, casually at first, and then avidly. Katri-na's details began to fill my mind; and there was plenty of space. Noise, smoke, and dust. Homeless people, field kitchens, makeshift hospitals, hunger and thirst. All the Jews were gone, and people closed their eyes and ears to the stories; no one spoke of it, but everyone believed. She and her mother maintained themselves in a flat near Spandau. The walls were brown and the room crowded with heavy furniture. (Pointing to a Morris chair in the corner of the apartment: Like that one, except bigger and not piled with dirty clothes, and an armoire twice as tall as I am, and a red plush sofa, and a crimson carpet.) Her mother worked at one of the ministries. Katrina remem-bered the salty taste of pork once a week and potato soup the rest of the time; they were sacrificing for the war effort. That was all there was in Berlin, the war. She went to school as always but each day there were fewer chil-dren; they died in the bombing or were sent to parents or friends who lived in the countryside. Germans have always believed in the safety of the forests, the redemp-tive pastoral life. Every night there was a bombing. Once, she couldn't remember which year it was but it must have been 1944, there was the most fantastic rumor: Hitler

48

was dead, killed by German traitors. The city held its breath, until he came on the radio with a passionate speech. She remembered her mother listening and then breaking down, weeping uncontrollably. The German nation would fight as it always had, would continue fighting to the last citizen; the war would go on forever because the Germans were great fighters, a warrior nation wanting only its rightful place at the table. Then one afternoon an officer arrived to give them news of her father, dead, heroically, proudly dead in Poland.

On Sundays her mother took her to the zoo, and once to hear the Berlin Philharmonic, von Karajan conducting. Someone at the ministry had given her a ticket. Brahms, Beethoven, Wagner. It was thrilling, the audience applauding wildly at the end, applauding as if this would be the last music they would ever hear. The English and American pigs would ban Brahms, Beethoven, and Wagner when the war was lost, as surely it would be. And she, too—she was on her feet with the others, banging her hands together as the final notes still hung in the cold air of the great hall. And then of course the national anthem, because the bombers were due.

Memory after memory, and I listened to all of them, hypnotized; sometimes. If it was late enough and Katrina far inside herself, she would lapse into German, then quickly correct herself. Once she saw a man and a woman making love in a doorway, standing in the shadows, the woman with her skirt hiked up over her thighs, the man with his trousers around his ankles. Berlin street scene, she said. In the last year of the war she was alone, living here and there, seldom more than a week at a time in any one place. There was bombing every night and when she heard the siren she would begin to tremble, tremble making her way to the shelter, trembling inside the shelter, trembling sometimes for hours before the klaxon sounded and she and the others moved up the stairs to the surface, where fires were burning, firemen and soldiers rushing about, bodies in the streets, and the cries of those trapped alive in the rubble. She had nowhere to go but she was terrified of being underground, buried alive, no one knowing or caring where she was, nothing to mark her grave. She would not be an anonymous victim, so she never remained in the shelter no matter how foul the weather. She knocked on doors and people took her in. Or not. For a while she lived in an army barracks, then with a doctor and his wife. In the spring the weather improved; and then the Russians came.

She did not ask me about the war years in Chicago but I told her anyway. They were nothing like Berlin. Only the tiny pocket aircraft carriers on the lake reminded you that there was a war on; everyone's explanation, "There's a war on." There was no bombing nor any serious rationing. Gas masks were issued but no one took them seriously. Victor arrived home one night with four gas masks, placing them just so on the mantelpiece, two on each end, flanking the elephants. We all tried on the masks, inhaling rubbery air. Families with casualties hung little ensigns with stars in their windows; those were taken seriously, to the point that you lowered your voice in the street when you saw one. No one went hungry. Gasoline was rationed, but it was still possible to drive to the lakes for a vacation when school was out, and plenty to eat when you got there. There were more people hungry now than there were during the war. The war brought prosperity and a momentous sense of purpose. Describing the war years in Chicago—toys at Marshall Field's, a dance band at the Edgewater Beach—I felt unaccountably guilty. It was unaccountable because the European war was Hitler's war, Germany's war, and if the Germans suffered, it was a suffering brought about by themselves, for their obedience and their appetite for revenge, and for delivering their country into the hands of a maniac. However, Katrina Lauren was not "the Germans"; she was Katrina, four when the war started, ten when it ended; orphaned, or anyway abandoned, and now an American citizen and undergraduate even as I was. She was the star of the Proles, so lucky to have survived a natural disaster.

Look at this, I said one night. I handed her a copy of the famous Jex Bardwell stereograph.

Yes, she said. Of course. I recognize it. Berlin, 1945.

No, I said. Not Berlin, 1945. Chicago, 1871. The view from the southwest corner of Dearborn and Monroe Street, the macabre wreckage of the Grand Pacific Hotel in the background. The Gothic fenestration was reminiscent of Berlin, was it not? The romantic style of the Dark Ages was visible even in the rubble of the Near North Side. The Great Fire was a holocaust no less complete than the saturation bombing of the Second World War. The center of the city ceased to exist. It literally melted.

She listened, nodding.

Hundreds died, I said.

Hundreds? she asked, her mouth moving in a Brechtian grin.

Her memories thickened. She peeled them away with difficulty, one by one, holding them up to the light, turning them this way and that to see them from all angles, and then putting them back where they had been, now near to hand. She called them ''my valuables.'' She listened politely to me, but as I spoke I recognized the inequality of experience, the density of hers and the lightness of mine; in the context of the war in Berlin, my father's troubles were nothing. Listening to her, I began to understand how little I knew of the world and its terrible odds, how people behaved, what they wanted and what they would do to get it, and what they had to do to survive, and how to imagine the unimaginable. In Chicago we went to bed and got up in the morning and went about our business, each day much like the one before; in a little while the war would be won. I learned this lesson: that, truthfully, some did survive despite all odds. Katrina sensed my confusion and accepted it; my life was mine and hers was hers. What a miracle it was that we had found each other.

In the spring we quarreled. She was going to Florida with friends for spring break. Everyone thought this amusing. Katrina Lauren in Fort Lauderdale, Brecht's doppelgänger on the beach where the boys were throwing up on their shoes. I wanted her to stay in Chicago, where I remained to finish up a project for Karcher. But she wanted to get away with her friends, to see Florida. Thinking like a lover, I found it disloyal; but she would not be diverted. I got a postcard from some place in Kentucky and another from Georgia. They were casual postcards, written at gas stations and roadside diners. Then I received a long hilarious letter from the Sun 'n

51

Surf Hotel. She was having fun and being good, though her friends weren't being good, drinking beer like Germans and necking like French. Late one night a boy arrived at their door. They had been with him on the beach. He wanted to sleep with one of them, it didn't matter which one. He was so drunk and excited. He took off his clothes and lay down on the bed. We were laughing, it was all so corny and disheveled. But we had to get him out of the room, even though he was playful and no harm to anyone. He was excited and wanted to make love and my friends were teasing him, being provocative. I miss you, darling. Why did you stay in stupid Chicago? The boy left finally and we laughed all night long. So I am looking after my friends, darling, and being good, *Schwester* Lauren, Mummy Courage in Fort Lauderdale. There was no reason for you to be jealous and angry. We will never quarrel again. I kiss you.

Driving north toward home at night in the rain their car apparently swerved to avoid a truck; all dead, they didn't even known for certain who was at the wheel. Not Katrina; she didn't drive. It was after midnight on the lonely stretch of coast road south of St. Petersburg. What was a girl from Berlin doing in Florida? I learned about it in the *Tribune*, which misspelled her name and omitted her age. It took me a moment to grasp what I was reading, to give life to the words on the page. My head filled until I thought it would burst, splitting like ripe fruit. Then it emptied, leaving my dry and suffocated. So she was dead in Florida. I could imagine them laughing, remembering their week on the beach, driving too fast. There were always accidents involving college students in those years; and there still are. I was sitting at the bar of the Proletariat drinking coffee, and involuntarily I turned to look at the door. The paper slid from my lap onto the floor. A friend was standing in the doorway staring at me. I looked quickly away, at the tiny stage on which she and the others had performed, the stage vacant and silent, a single chair empty in the center; it was inviting. I heard music from a radio and suddenly I thought of her as music, straining to the breaking point, so full of life's turbulence—and in a moment, by word and gesture, turning her music into something benign and almost pretty. Berlin and the war, Chicago and the peace, the last *Dreigroschenoper* in Florida. We listened to music all the time in her apartment, the music moving as we did; so I thought of music now. Then I felt a hand on my arm, and began to break down.

Katrina's favorite story was Goethe's *The Sorrows of Young Werther*. It is impossible to read today, but the radiant misery—the rapture—of the boy who killed himself mourning his lost lover had had a terrible effect on the Germany of the 1780s. Boys were killing themselves by the score, by gunshot and sword and poison and by throwing themselves off bridges and mountain peaks. Goethe's reaction to all this is not known, exactly; but he was complicated about everything else, so I suppose he was complicated about that, too. I had never had a suicidal impulse, so when she read the story to me, its language thick and clotted, dense as jungle, I put her enthusiasm down to dark German romanticism. Or perhaps the story did not translate. But I had more of moony Werther in me than I thought or could have imagined, because I shut down my life after she died. I did it first out of simple—simple!—self-pity, then defiance. Defiance can become a way of life and its own miserable reward. And after a while my solitariness became habitual, a means of moving forward with security. I rusticated myself in my apartment and committed a kind of ritual suicide, erasing all traces of my former life. I thought that was done by throwing away a few sticks of furniture, some posters, and well-loved paperback books. I thought I could reinvent myself, as boys were supposed to do in America. Boys did it all the time; there was a whole literature devoted to the subject. But she was always there, moving around inside my skull, her voice at my elbow, cracking jokes, explaining about Berlin during the war, her voice low and musical, strings, horns, the bang of a drum, and at the end—her voice rising now, insistent, the words tumbling, falling over themselves in their urgency and heat—at the end a shrill kazoo. It was a whole-souled connection between us, as if we were blood kin, but Berlin had its own specific gravity. She brought the evil world to me, touched me with it, and I was better for it, and would never lose it. Her valuables were known to me alone, existing now only in my memory, potato soup, a flat near Spandau, lovers in a doorway, a little girl trying to survive the bombs, hazard every hour of every day.

Her life was there along with my work and after a while my work edged her out, crowded her into a corner. It was obvious that this would happen. My work was what I had, having her no longer—except of course for the valuables, now in my sole possession, unless you believed in the afterlife, as Young Werther did.

My affair was no schoolboy crush, and perhaps if it had happened two years earlier or two years later, the shock of it, its utterness, would not have been so great. The memory of the courtroom, the trial and its aftermath, was still with me, and now all the time I thought about inadvertence and misadventure, and the ethical life. Lambs ended up head down on the hook; that was obvious. But my father was no lamb, and neither was Katrina. A human being needed a good spirit, and to plunge deeply into the heart of things. But I had come to see Chicago in a new way, as a dark and dangerous city, a city of killer nightmares no less than Berlin. Its furious commercial spirit produced a kind of moral vertigo; and I had to figure that out for myself.

Katrina's life seemed to me more real than my own, and more felt, and more consequential. It was a life of daring, and it is astonishing to me now that she trusted me with it. I do not believe it is possible to know another human being. Loving them in not knowing them. You love what you see and you hear. You are thrilled. You share memories, for whatever they are worth. You share dreams and plot the future, for whatever it is worth. She says, I kiss you. You say, I kiss you. One simple act of love is worth a young man's decade of daydreams. You say, I know her better than I know myself; scant praise. You sleep together and say, My one and only. We will be together always. We will have children together. I want to have children with you, you alone, only you; we will make life together.

I was fortunate to have had what I had. I was fortunate to have her valuables, and my memory of our own valuables. It was like being given a great library assembled by an ancestor. You have it on loan. It will always be his, even when you give it to your children and they give it to theirs, and by then it is dispersed, a book here and a book there, books from another time and place altogether, books read in specific circumstances at particular times, books that aged well and books that didn't. Katrina Lauren's Berlin story was indelibly part of my life, being oral. I had heard it with my own ears, but there was no verification for any of it—except from the moment she was found by a compassionate American army colonel. It was like any great story heard or read at an impressionable age—*Gatsby* or *Youth* or *Young Werther*. You never lose it and years and years later you'd hear someone say "Sport" and you'd look up and smile and for a moment you would be in a mansion on West Egg in 1922, yellow cocktails and saxophones, and later a man floating face down in a swimming pool.

5

My last year at the university I discovered the world outside, and it was not as dangerous as I had feared. The world was approachable after a fashion, badly needing reform and reconstruction. I buried myself in work, American elections, a man's work in a man's world: politics. The symmetry of the arithmetic appealed to me, the various combinations of states that could go up or down, depending; I thought of them as states, not as people. The Solid South, the Farm Belt, the ideological affinity of Wisconsin, Minnesota, and Michigan. Southern Illinois a state of the wool-hat confederacy while parts of Virginia were as Republican as Vermont. The particular meanness of Indiana and the plain style of Iowa. Louisiana as a region of the Mediterranean and Mississippi as provincial France. The transparency of California, Pennsylvania's Rhineland, New York's shtetls. New Jersey so opaque, as opaque as the state of Maine. Assemble coalitions, marry one region to another, cut and splice the map, rewire the circuits; that was politics.

I had become interested in psephology my freshman year. It was then an infant science, and not so much a science as a technique. I had a theory that if you could identify the most basic aspirations of the population, then the campaign would write itself, so long as you had a hero to give it voice, and a villain to supply romance. Hope, not fear, animated America at that time; and a campaign needed a narrative as much as a movie did, and for the same reasons. I was attempting to devise novel polling methods. A man's dark heart was incomprehensible, but his mind was not. A dream was easier to discover than a nightmare—if your questions were agile. A successful campaign exploited the dream and suppressed the nightmare. My senior thesis on the subject attracted attention in the political science department, and shortly after graduation Professor Karcher offered to introduce me to a lawyer downtown.

City Hall is looking for someone, he said vaguely.

I was surprised. Karcher was a senior man in the department, a mathematician by training, a demographer by specialty. He was the leading authority in the world on population movements in Spain in the Middle Ages. A dry, aloof intellectual, he was not at all the sort of academic who would know a lawyer "downtown." Downtown was shorthand for lowlifes and grafters. On the other hand, he had been a regular at the Proletariat, and that, too, was surprising.

He explained that occasionally he met with the lawyer, who was very well connected with the Machine, being an alderman's brother-in-law.

I made a knowing remark about the professor's civic spirt, generously sharing his knowledge with practical politicians. It proved after all that there was a place for eggheads in public life. At least Adlai had gotten that much right.

There was a moment of silence as Professor Karcher's eyes narrowed. He sighed and said, "It doesn't have anything to do with civic spirit. It isn't pro bono. I'm not doing them any favors. I'm paid for my time. As a matter of fact, we learn from each other." He watched my confused reaction and went on. "It's a business arrangement, Jack. Downtown they call it a sweet deal. I have something that he wants, so he pays me for it. And his questions interest me, so I learn something. I learn what's on their minds, at the Hall and downtown."

When I was in high school three friends and I had approached an English teacher and asked if he would teach a course in the modern poets for us, after school. Welllll, he said, perhaps; of course there would have to be "a consideration." I remember recoiling; my God, he wanted to be paid for his time. My reaction now was similar; I was startled and then intrigued. It was as if I had learned that Oliver Wendell Holmes had begun his career as an ambulance chaser. *Professor Karcher moonlighted as a consultant and wasn't ashamed to say so.* This was not an academic dilettante proposing himself for a presidential commission or as a speech writer for a high-minded Democrat. This was a full professor, an eminent scholar, taking money from the Chicago Machine. And frank to say "We learn from each other."

"What about it?" he said.

"I don't think so," I said.

"What will you do then?"

"Travel," I said. "And then graduate school, I suppose." We had talked about that many times and he had always been noncommittal. "These theories I have," I said.

"Yes?"

"Need more experiments, fieldwork."

"That's true," he said.

"I want to get out of Chicago," I said. "That's the truth of it."

"Miss Lauren," he said.

"Yes," I said.

He nodded. "I understand."

"Maybe California."

"Fieldwork in California?"

"Why not?" I said.

Professor Karcher looked at me a long minute; I knew that he hated California. Then he spoke very slowly, his words thick and cold as ice, with the tang peculiar to Chicago. I had misread him completely, misread his classroom manner, mistaken his public face for his private face; that was the one turned to me now. He said, "Don't be a damned fool. Listen to me carefully and try not to be a damned fool, Jack." He was standing in his office window looking at the Gothic spires across the esplanade. He began to speak of the university, sounding now like a Syndicate hard man. His erudite classroom manner vanished.

He despised it, he said. Despised its privilege, its isolation, its security, its authority without responsibility. Its exquisite liberalism, lib'rul lib'rul lib'rul, sitting around a common room late at night drinking wine, talking about the Abraham Lincoln Brigade, and listening to

Paul Robeson sing "Water Boy." Its license, its distance from the streets, its cradle-to-grave hypocrisy, its mediocrity, its irrelevance to the real life of the world. Fussy academic journals, subsidized sentences on subsidized blackboards—written in chalk, easily erased. It was a scandal. We should be ashamed. There was injustice everywhere. He said to me, "Get out of this cocoon before it's too late. Get into the world. The world's a nasty place, and that is what makes it so interesting. City Hall is your graduate school. That's where the fieldwork is." He looked up, his face distorted suddenly in the glare of the light. His voice had the flat accent of back-of-the-yards Chicago, the turf of the Machine.

He said, "I arranged for Katrina Lauren to come here. I lived in Berlin before the war. Born there. My father was a professor, as I am. A scholar of the German language before they killed him, as they would have killed me. We did not understand them, what they were capable of. We did not trouble to learn, our minds did not admit the possibilities. We were asleep." He stared at me fiercely. "Life is quarrel and struggle. Life is imagining the worst, and then finding your imagination deficient. You knew Katrina. You knew about her life, what it was, what it taught her, what it should have taught you. Did it teach you anything, Jack? It should've." He looked at the floor, sighing. "We thought we were secure. Our beloved Germany, even after the Great War, with its terrible consequences, the *Entzauberung*."

I looked at him.

He said, "Disenchantment. Disenchantment was general; we all felt it. We understood it causes, this weariness of the soul. How disappointing, and how normal, to learn that we Jews were being held responsible. Well, that would pass. It had passed before, though the consequences were not always pleasant; still, the Germans were a different people from the pig Poles or the Russians. It did not occur to us that we would have to move on. This was the modern world and even with the *Entzauberung* people would discover that the Jews were no more responsible for the humiliation of Germany than anyone else. The ruling classes, for example. So we went

59

on as before, in our universities and our businesses, marrying, having children, living our bourgeois life, practicing our faith. We did not look around us. We did not listen. We did not investigate the streets, and we did not draw conclusions. So much the worse for us. Have you read Isaac Babel? You should. *You must know everything.*"

I looked closely at him. I was listening and trying to translate his life to my life. Chicago in 1959 was not Berlin in 1934. I did not see the connection. Professor Karcher's hard, squat body had curled in on itself. I could imagine him bent at prayer or at conspiracy, over a book or over a gun.

He smiled dryly. "I have made my life's work the study of population movements. Pestilence, famine, war, and religion. This place reminds me of Heidelberg."

I said, "And Katrina?"

"A child in Germany," he said. "She learned a great deal."

"Yes," I said.

"How to survive," he said. "She watched her country disintegrate around her. She wondered how the Allies could continue to bomb Berlin when there was nothing in Berlin except civilians and *der Führer*. Perhaps that was reason enough. It was total war after all. She heard people talk about it. Why? She decided that there were no limits to—call it what you will. Depravity. Excess. In a war, the word 'excess' has no meaning."

"Yes," I said.

"So she would always be insecure. Even in Chicago she would be insecure. Hence her 'act' at the Proletariat, a thick smokescreen, no one would ever penetrate it. Except you. Perhaps you did."

We were silent a moment.

"Never underestimate them," he said. He jerked his square head at the window. "Never underestimate what people will do to advance themselves at the expense of others. Even here. Perhaps here most of all." He moved his head from side to side, a gesture of distress. He was trembling, and I thought of the vast differences between us, of age and nationality, and of memory. I knew almost nothing about him. I knew he was married, but I had

60

never met his wife. I did not know if he had children, or in what circumstances he lived. Yet I was drawn to him. He was giving voice to my own inchoate beliefs, the things that kept me in such tension with the world, and that I feared would always keep me at a remove, apprehensive over what would happen next.

He said, "Sometimes I think the university is the enemy of humanity."

I said, "You don't believe that."

He said, "Don't I?"

"A university is not a church," I said.

He said, "They want us to be thought naïve. Woolly-headed, innocent of the world. Too often we fulfill their expectations. We are very far from the people we should serve. We know nothing of ordinary life, and therefore they are right; we *are* naïve, and it is a scandal." He paused, thinking, and when he looked at me again his expression was more kindly, as if he knew he had gone too far, or had somehow intruded. When next he spoke, his voice was neutral.

"I want you to see a man, my friend the lawyer."

I said, "All right."

"Nice fellow," he said. "A man of the world. We've already had a conversation."

"I'd like to meet him," I said.

"I told the lawyer about you. As a matter of fact, he knows who you are anyway. He's an old Chicagoan; he goes way back. He's interested in your background, your family, your father. And your work in my department. I told him about that, a little, not too much. He isn't interested in everybody, but he's interested in you, because I told him to be interested. He's always on the lookout for a pretty face, someone who can help him out, someone who knows a thing or two that he doesn't know. But he wants to meet, have a chat. Ask a question or two. Answer your questions. He wants to know whether you're as professional as I told him you were. Wants to know if you're straight. That's why he's more interested in your questions to him than your answers to his questions. He wants to know if you can be trusted, Jack. If you're a man of your word who can keep his mouth shut. So you visit with Mr. Bayley at the Morrison, noon Tuesday. I told Mr. Bayley that you work hard and that you're reliable but young; he can correct that. My Bayley has work, Jack, real work. Important work, in the world. I think you can do it. You can give Mr. Bayley what he wants and he can give you what you need. If you'll just grow up a little and be"—he paused, sighing, and turned from the window to look at me directly—"a mensch."

So I had lunch with Mr. Patrick Bayley, Esq., a long, productive lunch at the Morrison. He was fat and red-faced, and very polite. He had the fat man's fastidious manners. He looked like a cartoon of a ward heeler, which he was; and he was also a shrewd and subtle man. He began by praising Professor Karcher, so well educated, so thorough in his work, so *practical*. It was a wonderful thing to be educated, and in a position to teach the young, who had so much to learn of the practical side of life. Professor Karcher was a great asset for Chicago. And he had spoken so highly of me, the original work I had done, my enthusiasm, my personal modesty, my affection for the city, my discretion.

He said, "I know your father."

I looked up, surprised and wary. Most people, when they mentioned my father at all, used the past tense, as if when you went to Joliet you died. I could not imagine where Bayley had met Victor.

Bridge tournament, he said. A few years ago, the South Shore Country Club. They had faced each other in an early round. My father was a fine bridge player, very bold; occasionally reckless, not a man to consider the odds. Perhaps he was overconfident, more interested in the cards he held than in the cards his opponent held.

"You have to know your own cards," I said.

"True," Bayley said. "But except for extraordinary circumstances your cards are defined by your opponent's cards. Your hand is playable or not depending on what's across the table." He smiled. "And of course in your partner's hand. You have to know what support you have. To know whether or not you can make the contract."

I nodded. I was listening carefully.

Bayley said, "They blind-sided him." He watched for my reaction, and when I said nothing, he added, "And he didn't help himself." You had to do that, he said. You had to help yourself, go the last mile in your own behalf. There were too many enemies as it was, in any life. You could not be your own worst enemy as well.

"My father's arrest and trial," I said, incredulous. "Was it political?"

Bayley put up his hands. "I didn't say that," he said. "They had him cold, and when it's the Federals . . . But it always helps when you have *friends*, good close friends you can count on. When a man's a loner, it makes things difficult."

"I see," I said, though in fact I didn't see.

Bayley continued as if he hadn't heard. "Your father was not widely known. In his business he did not get around, try to make friends. Perhaps that was misinterpreted. You could imagine that it showed contempt for the rest of us, who're trying to make things go as best we can, get on with things. It's an imperfect world, Jack, and the successful guy's imperfect, too, not setting himself above the rest. Do you see what I'm saying here?"

"Yes," I said.

"We take care of our friends," he said.

I looked at him and shook my head. Victor was no friend of the Machine.

"Some of the old-timers remembered Donald Gance, great character, always around the Hall in the old days. He'd buy and sell any damned thing. A few of the old-timers still remember him. Everyone liked Donald Gance. Your father was of a different world, that's true. And natural. The apple keeps falling farther from the tree. But there are people who would've helped if they'd been asked. But they weren't asked, so they didn't help. The point about us is that . . .." He paused, watching me.

"You have long memories," I said.

"Damned right," Bayley said.

"And you take care of your friends."

"Absolutely," he said.

"And your enemies?" I asked, smiling.

"No," he said. That was the point. "Our enemies have to take care of themselves and that's hard to do, sometimes, in this city."

The food arrived and we busied ourselves with it. Bayley ate slowly, all the while describing his vision of Chicago, a city hustling, hard at work, the races harmonious, everyone with a job and enough to eat and a little set aside. The point was, there didn't have to be any enemies. The organization did not want enemies; it wanted friends. It did not want controversy. It did not want to stir the pot. There was enough for everybody. Chicago was a city of plenty. And it would grow, God how it would grow. The organization's tent was large; it was large enough for the whole city. No one was excluded, except for the sons of bitches who refused to contribute, who wanted a free ride. And they excluded themselves by their behavior. The hell with them.

Tell me about your polls, he said. Phil Karcher says you're a whiz.

So I told him about my theory of polls, what you asked, who you asked, where you asked them, and how you analyzed the results.

He listened very carefully; once or twice he shook his head when my explanations seemed to him overcomplicated. And when I had questions of my own, he was attentive and did his best to answer completely.

I may have something for you, he said at last.

I'd like that, I said.

I thought you would, he said.

Who would I be reporting to? I asked.

That was apparently a question he liked, for he smiled broadly. Me, he said. Me alone. Later, maybe others. For now, me.

At the end of the lunch I had found my future. The Machine would henceforth be my natural home. Loyalty given, loyalty received. My safe house, protection against natural enemies.

A week later I received a telephone call from Mr. Bayley. He had work if I was interested. A man he knew wanted some polls because in case I hadn't heard there was an election next year. The Man needed timely intelligence, worried as he was about John F. Kennedy's supposed weakness with the union rank-and-file, and worried also about the experience issue, the senator's youth, and about religion, anti-Catholic bias. Chicago was in the thick of things and the Man wanted his own polls, not

Kennedy's or Humphrey's or Symington's polls and, naturally, he wanted them done quietly, under the arm. These were not polls he wanted to read in the *Chicago Tribune*. The Man did not have great faith in polls; he trusted his own instinct and the instincts of a few close friends. But he had been persuaded that private polls, done by a disinterested professional, and done quietly, wouldn't do any harm and might help. The Man had not agreed immediately; he was suspicious by nature, and needed reassurance of absolute loyalty and discretion on the part of you, Jack. And I said that we had spoken and there was no problem on that score.

"And of course there won't be," he said.

"No," I said.

He mentioned a sum of money and I said fine.

"We're agreed then," he said. "And so far's an office is concerned, forget it. Work at home."

"I plan to," I said.

"Good," he said.

"I'll need help from time to time."

"You can have what you need, within reason," he said.

"Two field men," I said.

"We'll see," he said. And then he cleared his throat, the sort of audible signal that a father might make: Listen up, son. "And Jack? Buy yourself a new suit and some shirts and a nice pair of shoes. You don't want to walk around looking like a bum."

It was in that way that I was hired by the Man. That is to say, I was hired by the lawyer Bayley. I was on his payroll and my reports went to him, and from him, by hand, to City Hall.

6

Don't you love it? Tap Gobelin said to me once, years later. *God, I love this business.* We were lunching at the Hay-Adams. He meant the ambience, a dark rich room filled with men talking in low voices, everyone aware of everyone else. In the corner of the room a Supreme Court justice wagged his finger at the former vice-president, the vice-president dispirited and weary, the justice athletic and cheerful; and why not, Tap said, since the justice was a justice for life while the vice-president was a footnote, a parenthesis inside someone else's sentence. An army general was tête-à-tête with a political lawyer. Two congressmen were quietly drinking at the next table, saying little for fear of being overheard; one of them glared venomously at Tap. A wind of desire was in the room, a kind of disorienting mistral sweeping the bazaar; every man at every table wanted something.

Tap and I were dead center, with a view of pretty Lafayette Park. We were Paris, when Paris ruled Europe, and Europe ruled the world. Listening to Tap, I had been remembering Chicago, the Hall and the Morrison, my introduction to civics. Gobelin wanted something from me and I had given it. Now, satisfied, he sat back and scrutinized the room, a tailor taking measurements. He watched me drink a cognac, and signed the check with a flourish. He yawned, moving his chair back from the table. The two congressmen had left, the army general and the political lawyer were leaving, and the vice-president and the Supreme Court justice were about to leave. Tap's afternoon was arranged. A phone call or two back at the office, an hour at his typewriter, ten minutes' conference time with an editor—and socko, his column would be off to the composing room, page three in tomorrow's paper. And then the reaction, and the reaction to the reaction. That was work! Next week there would be something new, something altogether fresh and unexpected.

And then we can have lunch again, Jack.

Any time, I said.

God, he said. I do love it. I do love this business. Then he was rising, a broad smile on his face, shaking hands with the vice-president, who wanted him to know that the column was excellent, really first rate, with bite and—he sought the word—*texture*.

Pat Bayley and I lunched every other week and from time to time he would take me to an office in the Morrison Hotel to talk to his friends, all older men, very correct in manner, distinguished by a particular physical stillness. They sat on one side of a refectory table and I on the other. They asked me questions and I answered them. In the beginning they were skeptical because my data sometimes contradicted their instincts, and they were men who had come to trust their instincts. But they were open-minded, relatively, so long as my findings "panned out." They called it prospecting.

Mid North, Far North, I said. Humphrey. Some Adlai nostalgia.

Bullshit, one of them said.

Yesterday's figures, I said, and passed a piece of paper across the table.

Look at the numbers, Earl, Pat Bayley said. Interesting numbers. Maybe bullshit, maybe not bullshit. For right now, let's pretend it's not bullshit and see what we can do about it. If we're fucking up, let's find out where. That's your precinct you're looking at there, Earl. So it's your problem if it isn't bullshit, and I don't think it is, and as a matter of fact, the Man doesn't either.

Bullshit, Earl said, folding the piece of paper and putting it in his pocket.

I was careful never to be too glib. They hated cleverness of any kind, as if cleverness were a form of disrespect. In the young it was unforgivable. All very patriarchal, yet they listened to me with growing fascination. And perhaps there was envy, too, along with the inevitable suspicion; perhaps they saw that they were falling behind and were being overtaken; the modern era was at hand. In time they began to use my shorthand acronyms, "difs" (double-income families, of which there were not many in 1959), "bems" (black employed males), "bums," "befs," "bufs," and the rest. They used these terms, and the sociological jargon that went with them, reluctantly—but they used them. When I saw one of the acronyms in a newspaper piece one day I had an Orwellian thrill: Control the language and you control the thought, its rhythm, and tempo. It was the advantage of the composer over the musician. I began to believe I was inventing a new tongue, an Esperanto for the political aficionado. It surprised me that Bayley and Bayley's friends accommodated themselves so willingly, and then I concluded that they were apprehensive. I had something that the Man wanted. Therefore, they had better learn what it was so that they would never be on the outside, in the cold.

I liked the company of these older men and looked forward always to meeting them. They reminded me of huge cats, not in their indolence, but in their economy of movement. There was always something in reserve, and everyone was expected to contribute. They always had gossip, skeletons tumbling out of closets I didn't know existed. I was careful to follow Professor Karcher's advice: Listen to their questions and you'll know what's going on, what's worrying them, and more important, what isn't worrying them. This knowledge was exhilarating, the equivalent of the spy's purloined letter or broken code. I was living inside my own *Bildungsroman*, each day learning more about how things worked in the city that worked. I was interested in what was ordinary and true, not what was splendid and virtuous. I thought that if I learned the first, I could surely understand the second. I could deduce it. And then I would be able to make my own way. And when I was so foolish as to ask an indiscreet question—about money, or anything at all about the Man (I see him now with the authority and mystery of Stalin, about whom no questions were ever asked, and no information volunteered except as to the state of his health, always excellent and improving)—one of the cats would move its heavy shoulders, yawn, flex a hairy paw, and change the subject, but not before a glance that in its icy contempt would have frozen, and withered, the summer sun. It goes without saying that I was proud of what I was doing, thrilled with it, the work slightly sinister and a little off-key. I was as happy as I had ever been.

At the Hall and the Morrison I was known as the scholar, young Jack Gance, nice kid, no smart aleck, does the damnedest dance with numbers, Jack and his crystal ball, 'course when it comes time to shovel the bodies into the polls and count the votes later, when it comes time to do the arithmetic, well, that's *our* business, but if you're interested in what the jigaboo on the street corner's thinking about a man, say a certain United States senator, you want young Jack on that street corner doing his shuffle and asking questions, about the price of pussy or the time of day . . .

That summer was an Illinois masterpiece, soft, warm, filled with light. The days seemed never to end, dusk running on and on, pearl gray and then grayer, dusky at last; the days refused to surrender, holding the light as one holds one's breath, finally sighing sweetly, smiling, and holding on a little longer. It was warm all day and warm at night, with no breeze to move the trees. The lake water was as warm and heavy as gin, steely in the moonlight.

I rented an apartment near Lincoln Park, solid burgher country, the Mid North Side, quiet, respectable, and anonymous, the ideal hideout for a scholarly political agent. I was following Flaubert's advice: Live like a bourgeois in order to create like a god. My domestic nest: two bedrooms and a living room, a fine kitchen with yellow walls, a black and white television set, and my books. I had some furniture from my parents' apartment, and if I craned my neck at the kitchen window I could see a little sliver of lake, to remind me where I was, not very far from the neighborhood I grew up in. I bought filing cabinets and the most modern Burroughs calculator and a telephone with a headset. A friend of Bayley's supplied a recording device but I rarely used it. I was doing some polling by phone, although I preferred face-to-face on the street corner or the doorstep (never a bar except informally, and then you counted the ones who were silent as the consensus formed and listened to the loudmouths forming it and tried to judge if they were the kind of loudmouths people respected and followed). I placed my desk at the front window so that when I worked I could look into the street, so plain, quiet, and unassuming, so reassuring, a swing street that in a close election could go either way. It was a street where people knew each other, like Dr. Bovary's street. With its bushy elms and red fireplugs and Good Humor trucks, its cop on the beat and kids playing hopscotch, my street could pass for any middle-class street in the Midwest. The election would be decided on those streets. People would go to the polls on the first Tuesday in November with a hangover or an overdrawn bank account or in love or worried about their health, and vote their prejudices. What scared them the least? Exactly how dissatisfied were they, how profound the Middle Western *Entzauberung*? And how specific were the complaints? Who was responsible? Was it reason for a change in Washington?

Flaubert hated the bourgeoisie so, hated their pretensions and small spirits, pronouncing them the bane of civilization, narrow people living narrow, frustrated lives, always on the outskirts of the beautiful city. Flaubert, so dour and cynical; he preferred Egypt. It was important not to take Flaubert too seriously. Expectation was the enemy of prediction.

I observed the life of the street during the long days of early summer, the postman moving crisply from door to door, his movements at each mailbox as practiced as a veteran actor's. The postman swung up the walk to the mailbox, fetched the letters from his bag, and inserted them into the slot, giving a little tap to the letters so that they would fall cleanly, just so; and then on to the next. Up the street he shook hands with the cop on the beat, both of them standing head to head, nodding; government men, *uniformed* men, they owned the sidewalk and were at ease on it, as any official is at ease in his office.

What a great thing, I thought, to wear a uniform, the uniform putting distance between you and civilians, brass buttons and polished leather a signal of authority no less than a sword or an ermine cape.

I waited for my neighbor and at last she appeared, wheeling her baby carriage. She held the carriage handle with one hand and sorted the mail with the other, carelessly tossing all but one letter inside on the table in the vestibule. A letter from her mother, no doubt; she and her mother exchanged two or three letters a week, long newsy letters of life in Chicago and in Blackford, Virginia. The baby carriage was an English model, huge wheels and a veil over the top, a "pram" in Field's advertising; and Carole looked as English as the pram, with her fine blond hair and high color and short skirt. The city had forsworn its customary Anglophobia because the Queen of England was arriving, first visit ever. Michigan Avenue stores displayed little British flags, British woollens, British leather, and of course the prams. The newspapers were full of it; royalty in the Windy City, time to sweep away history. The bad old raffish Chicago was an antique, a quaint relic of the past. The Chicago of 1959 was a city of sophistication and nonchalance, rich, confident, big shoulders in a bespoke suit. The commercial establishment was worried that the mayor would blunder, commit a ghastly malapropism or an oafish attempt at humor. The *Trib* printed a pointed account of the etiquette appropriate to the occasion.

A bright smile lit Carole Nierendorf's face as she met the day, a soft Wednesday in June. With the window open, I could hear her whistling as she ambled down the street in the direction of Lincoln Park. Suddenly she wheeled and looked up at me. I smiled, and she waved. She motioned to me to come outside, the sweep of her arm childlike: Come out and play! I shook my head and said not loudly, "Work." The word carried easily across the street, it was so quiet that morning. She made a face and said, "You'll be sorry," walking on.

Watching her go, swinging up the street in the sunlight, I was beguiled, a schoolboy looking out the win-

71

dow at the playground while the teacher droned on. I spoke again and she turned, waiting; in a moment we were walking up the street together.

The park was filled with young women, most of them with small children. I was the only man in the vicinity, and from time to time one of the young women would look over at us and smile. It was a smile of envy. Carole had her baby and her husband; that was who I obviously was. She could sit on the park bench and stretch her legs, flirting with her husband. She could be as sexy as she liked in the park with her husband. Carole rose and peeked into the carriage. The baby was chattering gaily. She made motherly noises, then turned back to me.

"Do you like it?"

"It's fine," I said.

She lifted her chin, showing off her new haircut. "Charles doesn't like it. He says it makes me look like a boy."

"I don't think so," I said.

"Charles doesn't like change."

"And you do," I said.

"I sure do," she said. "They took off an awful lot of hair, though."

"Well," I said. "It looks good."

"I wish Charles thought so. Do you think you could ever like each other?" Charles Nierendorf and I were not close; it was obvious we would never be friends. He worked for a small law firm downtown, the most secretive of the political firms, Estabrook, Mozart. Whenever I saw them together, on the street or in the park, I wondered how they had ever found each other. He was tall and raw, with a brusque side-of-the-mouth manner. She was slight and provocative, always grinning. She described her husband as a small-town boy in the big city, having trouble adjusting. She was from a small town, too, but it was different. Blackford, Virginia, was a happier place than Du Cass, Wisconsin. And Charles worked so hard, he had no time for anything else.

"He doesn't have any friends," she said. "And you

72

don't look as if you have any, either. You should have a girl friend,'' she said definitely.

"I look but I don't find."

"That one over there." She nodded at the young woman who had smiled at us, thinking we were married. She was stretched out on the grass, her hair curled around her neck. Her blue skirt was hiked up to her knees. "She's very pretty," Carole said.

I nodded. More than pretty.

"That's what I mean," she said. "Maybe if you had a girl, you could get on with Charles, and then we could be a foursome." She watched me absently wrap a rubber band around my wrist, tighter and tighter. "Watch out, Jack. You'll cut off your circulation." The girl rose and brushed a few blades of grass from her blouse. She took her time doing it, dipping her shoulders left and right, concentrating. Suddenly she turned and gave us both a brilliant smile, and strolled off.

"Well!" Carole said, indignant. "That wasn't very nice."

"Why not?"

"She knew we were together. She thought you belonged to me. It's so—brazen," she said.

I laughed. Carole Nierendorf had a rich fantasy life in the Southern gothic mode. Perhaps it was what bothered her husband.

She looked at me. "Do you think we seem like a married couple, sitting here in the park? I mean to other people."

"Probably," I said.

"You, me, and the baby."

"The basic family unit," I said.

"This is the big day, you know."

"It is?"

"Absolutely."

I didn't know what she meant. I was watching the dark-haired girl in the blue skirt. She had moved away slowly and now stood on the curb, swinging her head this way and that, waiting for a break in the traffic. When it came she sprinted across the street, pausing at the center stripe, cars all around her. Then she sprinted again in a long athletic stride, arms extended as if she were thinking she

73

might fly, looking straight ahead; she didn't give a damn. The traffic jerked to a halt and I half rose, thinking she had been hit. But when I saw her next she was safe on the opposite sidewalk, hands on her hips, grinning like a candidate who had just won in a landslide. The sidewalk was crowded; people turned to look at her, smiling at her nerve.

"I don't know about married life," she said. "Do you have any fun, not being married?" She didn't wait for an answer. She said, "Let's get some ice cream." The Good Humor man was on the sidewalk, his bells tinkling.

I said, "I've got to get back to work."

"That's who you're married to," she said with a laugh. "Strange kind of wife, though. No time for a Good Humor. Sounds like a prison, your marriage. What is it today?"

"One of the western precincts," I said vaguely. "A new poll with some strange numbers. Needs a Toscanini. So I've got to go back and pick up my baton."

She said, "Who are the Democrats going to nominate?"

I thought a moment. "Kennedy."

She said, "Charles doesn't like him"

"Is Kennedy too liberal for Charles?"

"Too something," she said. "Maybe too rich."

"Too Catholic?"

"Too sexy," she said.

"Threatening," I said.

"Charles wouldn't put it that way."

"How would Charles put it then?"

She looked hard at me. "You love it, don't you? Your work." Then, "You love *knowing*." She leaned closer to me. "Why do you love it so?" She stared at me with such intensity, as if she expected a momentous answer. We did not know each other well; ours was only a casual neighborhood friendship. Once I had carried her groceries from the market and she had invited me in for a drink with her and Charles, Charles immediately suspicious and ill at ease. That, and a few times on the street and in the park was the extent of our knowledge of each other. Carole's Southern manners and English appearance were at odds with Chicago; she was as foreign in her way as Katrina Lauren had been in hers, yet up close no one could have looked more Midwestern. She had a cheerleader's dimpled freshness. At any moment I expected her to leap or somersault or produce a baton, all the while chewing on Wrigley's Spearmint; or slowly strip, demanding to know if I thought she was sexy. Now she was staring at me forwardly, waiting for the great secret. Her sincerity was transparent, so I told her about the big cats, and listening for the questions that would tell you what was happening actually, the reverence for an inside fact, the personality of the Man, and the ambience of the Hall and the Morrison. All this, in a few hurried moments.

She laughed. "There must be more to it than that."

I said, "There is. But I haven't got time." I stood up.

She said, "And it really matters."

"Yes," I said.

"That's what Charles says," she said.

I was surprised. "He does?"

"The money," she said. "It's where the money is. That's what he's interested in, money money money. He's about to become a partner. He's Mr. Mozart's protégé." She grinned provocatively. "Charles doesn't know what to make of *you*. He says you've got connections."

"It's Mozart who's got connections."

"He thinks you're a little bit slippery. And that I'm unreliable." She didn't wait for a reply but went on: "What is it that they do? What kind of law is it? Charles won't talk about his work."

"It's the kind of law where you don't have to open a law book, or even own one."

"Charles is a very good lawyer," she said loyally.

"So is Mozart," I said. "E. L. Mozart, La Salle Street's sexiest lawyer."

"Tell me about Mozart."

"Get Charles to tell you about Mozart." I looked into the carriage, where the baby was moving its arms like an uncoordinated orchestra conductor. "You've got a pretty mother," I said, and the baby burped.

"Do you think I'm pretty? I don't know," she said,

wrinkling her nose. "Sometimes I think the parts don't mesh. My eyes are too close together, like Modigliani's models."

"Unreliable eyes," I said.

"Sometimes," Carole said.

"And Charles doesn't like it."

"He doesn't trust the South," she said. "He thinks we're all off the wall. We talk to strangers in parks. We get strange haircuts. We talk all the time. We're never satisfied." With the tips of her fingers she gently moved the carriage back and forth, rocking it. She reached out to touch the baby, who began to bawl. Then she gave the carriage a push, sending it a few feet away. Carole leaned back on the park bench, her face to the sun; she eased her sandals off her feet, looking at me with a dry, candid smile. She said, "Isn't it sweet? Betsy just loves her father. I'm with her all day long but it's Charles she loves and any stranger. You. Betsy loves you. Like that gazelle dodging traffic a minute ago. She loved you, too, for those few minutes. Don't bother to deny it, that's the sort of thing Southern girls know very well. Better believe it." She turned to look at me, a weary expression now, without dimples. She ran her fingers through her fine, curly hair, the haircut obviously unfamiliar. She was pensive, drawn into herself. "Babies," she said. "She's only six months old but when she's with her father she's a flirt, just a little whore." Carole shrugged. "She's a demonstrative girl, she lets you know what she thinks. Nothing subtle about her. She leaves you in no doubt. I'm just a nuisance to her." There was nothing I could say to that, so we were silent a moment, listening to the baby fuss and the city's traffic beyond, Chicago's hum. I did not know very many married people. I knew my parents' generation. I had no understanding of the lives of young married people, what made them tick, how they fit. Nor had I any understanding of babies, but I had never heard one described as a little whore.

I looked at my watch; Carole looked at her fingers. "You're a happy man, happy in his work. How lucky. Good for you. Go ahead," she said. "You have to get back to work."

I looked around. The park was unusually crowded and noisy. There were people everywhere, many more than usual, even though the day was bright and warm. There were men in business suits standing on the curb. Suddenly the people began to move together, clustering along the wide boulevard dividing the park from the city. Behind us the lake glittered. There was an air of festivity and anticipation. Even the drunk rummaging through the trash can straightened up, alert. I watched the gathering crowd, puzzled.

"Isn't it great?" she said. "They've let people out of work."

"What is it?" I said.

She smiled up at me. "It's the big day, Jack. It's the Queen."

"Is it today?" I'd forgotten all about the Queen's visit.

She stood and we walked to curbside, where the people were. Carole picked up the baby so that she, too, could see the Queen of England. We heard a thin cheer, and applause. Presently motorcycle outriders appeared, their sirens on low. Then a flotilla of limousines containing politicians, sports figures, businessmen of the sort known as civic leaders, even Bayley; and in the car with Bayley, Elly Mozart. Then an open car, brilliantly black, the Queen and her husband in the rear seat. Phillip was supernaturally handsome, tall and slim as a prince should be. The Queen was smiling and waving. A great cheer rose as they swept past. Even the drunk was craning his neck; he looked like a fan watching a pop fly. I looked at Carole, her mouth set in a thin, hard line. She was holding her baby tightly, her face closed and apprehensive. In the distance I could hear the shooters at the Lincoln Park Gun Club. She whispered to me, *Isn't she pretty?* The cheers almost drowned her out. *She's a true Queen.* Carole turned away, openly weeping. Spectators glanced at her, and then at me; one of the men winked. A few men tossed their hats in the air, and young women turned to one another, commenting on the Queen's hair, her hat and her smile, and her gorgeous prince. How pretty she looked, she was a radiant Queen; how fortunate Chicago was. And the weather was so fine, sunny, balmy, a soft breeze off the lake. Carole cried out, then held her baby high over her head, the baby squirming, then whimpering, trying to escape her mother's grasp. I thought the limousines would come on forever.

7

WHEN my work was going well the numbers seemed to live, flowing from my Burroughs in a dense narrative. The numbers themselves were pure and neutral and did not lie; they were only inanimate numbers. When I rearranged them in my head and began to *tap-tap* on the calculator, they became something else, truths and half truths and errors, discoveries and misapprehensions. As in a half-finished novel, there was the character that wouldn't go away, the character the author didn't know what to do with; he was full of life, but a troublemaker. Every time this character entered the narrative the numbers began to fall apart; the symmetry of things was disturbed. He was the middle-class Jew who hated Nixon but was suspicious of Kennedy; his heart belonged to Hubert, Adlai's surrogate. Really, he wanted FDR but was too discouraged to say so. She was the young mother, white, comfortable, middle class in income, upper middle in outlook, an optimist by nature—but troubled. Nixon was crude, Kennedy slick. Kennedy's wife would be an ornament to the White House, however. Still, he was so young. Hard to believe Kennedy and Nixon were roughly the same age . . . Carole Nierendorf was this character's name. Win Carole Nierendorf and you've won the election.

My evenings followed a pattern. Around eight I made a martini and put music on the phonograph, Brahms or Schubert. I forced myself to sit still and listen, sitting as quietly as I could, looking out the window at the struggle between the daylight and the dusk, practicing repose. I watched, listened, drank the martini, and smoked a cigarette, the smoke curling as the numbers did when I was working the Burroughs, translating, the numbers moving from the data sheet to my brain to my fingers, *tap-tap*, in different form on the calculator's tape, no longer middle-class Jews or Carole Nierendorfs or black unemployed males or Italians over fifty or white Protestant males under thirty but the issues themselves, the issues with human faces, the experience issue and religion and personality and competence, the *image* of those things, and how the voters of a certain precinct understood them and what the issues meant to them. This was a novelist's brew, a fictitious population. But in moments the numbers I had been working on would begin to tumble in my head in time to the music, forming fresh patterns, replicating, multiplying, and mutating. Then I could begin to think creatively.

At nine I made another drink, put a steak on the broiler, and quartered a potato for fries. And sat alone in the kitchen, craning my neck to observe the little sliver of lake. The lights from the Outer Drive illuminated it. Often I pondered Carole Nierendorf and her married life, slight, sexy Carole, her tactless husband and demonstrative baby; lucky you, she'd said in her soft Southern accent, so suggestive, the corollary straining beneath the surface: unlucky me. She did not seem the sort of woman who would accept unlucky; she was one who made her own way, avid for life. If the Queen of England could have an ardent prince, so should she. I thought about married life, working the numbers. I wondered how often they slept together and how sex fit into their lives. I thought I knew how it fit into hers; I was less certain about him. Charles Nierendorf spent long hours at his office and was often away in Springfield. He would be the sort of man who needed marriage to give him stability, a trouble-free personal environment for his public career; unworried at home, he would be able to worry at the office. Marriage was a career requirement. A wife and a child and an apartment on the Mid North Side, later a move to the Near North or to Wilmette or Evanston, much later to Winnetka or Lake Forest. And Carole, what did she get out of it? Other than the thing itself, marriage; marriage as a kind of museum. She had looked at me slyly and said, You should have a girl friend. Then, She thought you belonged to me. That was what she wanted, someone to belong to her. And she would find one; if not Charles, then someone else. I thought about that, the way she looked at me, and the way I was drawn to her. No question, they were not suited. She would vote Kennedy for certain, the promise of romance, a hint of danger, even carelessness; and her husband would vote Nixon, if he bothered to vote at all. He would vote Nixon and lie about it because a partner at Estabrook, Mozart didn't vote Republican, even a junior partner; especially a junior partner. Butch Estabrook and Elly Mozart would want to avoid even the appearance of impropriety.

I finished my drink, staring out the window, across the street to their apartment. The lights were still on, a stripe of white between drawn curtains. Another house divided against itself, I thought. That was one of the curiosities my polling was beginning to show. The wives liked the cavalier, the husbands the roundhead. I had a few theories, nothing solid, nothing to go to Bayley with. Across the street the lights went out, *click*. The neighborhood was quiet, my glass dry in my hand. I sat in the darkness, smoking and listening to music, tossing my numbers. I suddenly remembered it was my father's birthday; he was fifty-six. I could not imagine being fifty-six. I rose to go to the telephone, then looked at my watch. It was too late; he and mother would be in bed; old people went to bed early. I sat down again in the dark, lonely, restless, thinking about Carole Nierendorf in the dark bedroom across the street.

A month after the Queen's visit, Carole started coming to my apartment. She warned me that she would, some afternoon when I wasn't expecting it; she was bored and she wanted company. She wanted to see what I did with my days, what it was that made me so content. What do you *do* all day long, Jack? And you must be lonely. I'm going to cheer you up. And I'm lonely and you can cheer me up. Isn't that a fair arrangement? What do you say we have some fun in Chicago?

She knew when I was home because she could see me at the window, working the Burroughs. She could hear the *tap-tap* in the street. She would call me on the phone, one ring only; and then she would arrive, having arranged for the neighbor next door to watch the baby for a few hours while she went shopping or to the doctor's office or the movies or lunch in the Loop with a friend. I watched the neighbor stand in the window watching Carole cross the street and enter my building, the neighbor frowning; when I told Carole, she flared. Nosy doll. Nothing to do all day long but watch television and spy. But what could you expect? People were naturally nosy. All Americans were nosy and the neighborhood was so impersonal, not like the cunnin' Tidewater town she grew up in, Blackford, Virginia, where everyone knew each other. Half the town was related, and some of the relationships were mighty obscure, unknown except to the parties involved. So if you wanted to tryst in Blackford you went to Richmond, and then you were safe for only about a minute and a half before the talk started. And what talk! People had long memories in Blackford and loved stories, the gamier the better, and there were so many stories they tended to cancel each other out. What was a town but its stories? People took each other seriously in Blackford, in the South generally. Not themselves. Each other.

Then she smiled, reassuring me. It didn't matter. You had your own life to live. You couldn't live someone else's. Charles was never at home. Charles worked all the time; he spent more time with Elly Mozart than he did with her. And when he was home he doted on the baby. Charles didn't give two hoots in hell what she did, and Charles would never know. In frozen Wisconsin, where he came from, you didn't inquire. It wasn't gracious to inquire; no stories to speak of in Du Cass, Wisconsin. But that wasn't the point, whether Charles inquired, or what Charles knew or thought. Charles wasn't involved. This is what *I* want to do, she said. *Me.* This is my idea, to cheer us both up. I'd like to be with you in the afternoons, Jack.

And don't worry about the nosy neighbor. She's probably just jealous.

August of 1959 was torrid in Chicago, one day after another of ninety degree heat, the sun thick and pale in the hazy sky. The days ended quickly, with none of the ambiguity of the early summer; one minute it was light, the next dark. At night it was eighty degrees, no breeze from the sullen lake or anywhere else. The asphalt on the streets softened and the cars made a *swish-swish* sound as they motored past. All anyone talked about was the weather and when it would break. I sat at my desk and watched the sweat roll down my chest, gathering in the waistband of my shorts. Matches wouldn't light. My fingers slid off the keys of the Burroughs, causing errors. The ink blurred on the tape. I had a fan but never used it because the breeze scattered my papers.

When Carole arrived the first time her face and arms were glistening with sweat from the effort of crossing the few feet from her apartment house to mine. She collapsed in my easy chair with an exhausted laugh, running her hand through her damp hair, grinning, hiking her skirt over her knees, kicking off her sandals. Her legs were slick with sweat; she leaned forward, massaging her ankles. She was sitting in a splash of yellow sunlight but did not seem to mind. We sat looking at each other, me at my desk and she in the chair, saying nothing at all. The torpor of the day reminded me somehow of my childhood, the insects whirring and buzzing outside, the stillness and heaviness of the air. I heard children in the street, their voices low and insistent. They were beginning to go to the beach.

I was surrounded by my work, the files and tapes, the questionnaires, the sheets of white paper with long columns of numbers. In the corner were my steel filing cabinets, and the headset telephone with the recording device. My books overflowed from the shelves behind the sofa. I was like a ship's captain imprisoned in his wheelhouse, ruled by the charts he navigated by. I had been working the Far North Side. That was where my mind was, on Sheridan Road north of the Edgewater Beach. She had arrived without knocking; the door flew open, and there she was in her coral-colored skirt and white shirt, grinning, kicking off her shoes. My fingers were still on the keys of the Burroughs, my mind filled with numbers, a skipper with his compass and sextant, navigating the treacherous waters of the Far North Side.

I did not immediately understand that she was in fact *there*, in my easy chair. I thought of her as a mirage; it was so unexpected.

She opened her arms and I came to her, squeezing into the chair beside her. My skin was as slick as hers. We stared at each other, my dark eyes into her light ones. She ran her fingernail up my shin, stopping at the white scar below my kneecap. We watched her red fingernail move through the damp hair of my leg, curving in a lazy 3. My leg twitched. The scar was sensitive, the result of a cut so deep the bone had been exposed.

Ax, I said. Years ago, when I was a kid.

A little boy, she said.

Yes, I said.

Is it tender?

Numb and tender, I said.

She took my kneecap in her hands and kissed the scar, a long kiss. She closed her eyes. I smelled her perfume, a light scent mixed with my own sweat, and hers. I touched her hair, moving my hand to the back of her neck. When she stopped kissing me, her lipstick remained, blood red on white. She shifted her hips so that she was facing me. We were jammed together in the chair. When she spoke I could feel her breath on my face. When I kissed her she began to tremble in her shoulders, her skin moving and fluttering. She was holding my knee in a vise, moving my leg left and right, her palms hot on my skin, then looking at the scar again, finally resting her cheek against it, rocking back and forth. Outside, the children were still whining. She smiled, raising her eyebrows; it was so incongruous. She was looking over my shoulder, taking in the room. I realized she had never been here, had seen only me at the window, and how strange it must seem. It was more office than apartment, except for the phonograph and the two-feet-high stack of records.

This is where you are all day long, she said. Her voice was almost a whisper.

Do you like it?

Love it, she said. Two people, alone in the afternoon.

I said, I didn't think you'd come.

I said I would, she said. Why wouldn't I?

I didn't think you would. It would've been easy not to. I wanted you to, but I didn't think you would.

I always keep my word, she said.

Always?

Almost always, when I give it. I don't give it often. She touched my cheek, looking at me closely. Let's, she said.

Right now, I said.

Now, she whispered.

She leaned back against the chair arm and took off her blouse, stretching. And when her arms came down they were around my neck, and she was whispering in my ear. The words came in a great rush, as if they had been detained and were now set free. It was so long since I had been with a woman. I ached for her. In the bedroom she glanced at Katrina's photograph in its silver frame on the bureau, Katrina at her most alluring. But Carole did not comment, and in fact didn't care and wasn't curious. At that focused moment, we were both beyond words.

She bought me things, a necktie, phonograph records, chocolates. She stepped into the apartment and put it down on the coffee table, shyly explaining where she had bought it and why she thought I'd like it, whatever it was. The present was always wrapped and she'd demand that I open it at once. She loved giving presents, something that people in the North never did. Presents were a sign of affection, and a custom in her family.

We never went out for lunch, never went out for dinner, never took a trip together, and she never spent the night. She arrived when she felt like it, always preceded by the one ring on the telephone. That gave me a moment to put aside my papers and take the phone off the hook, preparing my journey across the border. There seemed to be two countries, hers and mine, and little in common between them. I told her about Katrina and about my father and great-grandfather, Donald the Great, stock manipulator and friend to Harry Daugherty, collector of elephants and promises. She listened as if these were tales from Transylvania or the Transvaal. Weird, she said, so weird. She did not know what to make of Katrina because she had never known a foreigner, except for an exchange student from Spain, a prim and uncommunicative girl who struggled with English. No one got to know her well. World War II was so far away. Her father had served in the medical corps in Hawaii, but never spoke of it. She had never known anyone who had gone to prison; well, the boys occasionally spent a night in the lockup, too much beer and reckless driving. She came from a family of doctors, old-fashioned Southern GP's who had seen it all.

"It must have been hard on you when your father went—away."

"Prison," I said. "Yes. Me, my mother, him. Hard on everyone."

"And your brother," she said.

"Sam survived," I said.

"You don't like him."

"No," I said. "I don't like him."

"I have three brothers," she said.

"I'll bet you like them all," I said.

"I do," she said. "They're sweet. It's a Southern family, we're all real close."

I went to her country like any avid tourist, eager to discover the local customs and observe the scenery. She lived in a clapboard house on a dead-end street on the Hill, sycamore trees and lilac bushes, the good part of Blackford. Her brothers had a tree house out back. Her mother baked the most scrumptious muffins, and her father always came home for lunch. He loved delivering babies. Every time he delivered a baby he bought a cigar and smoked it after dinner. Her brothers were football players and she had been a cheerleader, just loved cheerleading and hanging around with the football players after practice or the game. Good thing her brothers were older than her, and not in school when she was.

There's something about the South, she said; the war, the defeat, the occupation. Adversity brings people together, but prosperity's more fun.

At the end of the holiday I returned to normal life. There seemed to be no consequences. There was never any question of living in her country. In time I learned the language and some of the customs, but that was about all I learned. I liked being with her and looking at her;

her past had no meaning for me, as Katrina's had. Berlin, so alluring and malignant, was alien. I could imagine Blackford all too well.

I could not believe my good fortune. I watched her hurry across the pavement in her long stride, a present under her arm. I heard the tap of her heels on the pavement and looked up to see her wink and wave. I counted to ten and she was at the door, breathless, then collapsing in the easy chair. I rose, waiting. The accountant put on his hat and left the office for the border, grinning. Swing street, indeed.

She loved to talk and had very many funny stories, most of them from her adolescence in Blackford. She did not speak often about Charles and their life together. I assumed they had no particular life beyond the baby and routine chores; whatever married people did together, polishing the silver, paying bills, watching television, cooking. Charles had his work, Carole had me. She was simply sexy, a whole-souled emotional appetite that could be abated but never satisfied. That was one of the many, many things she loved about it: sex was wide as the world itself, made for exploration. Some afternoons we scarcely talked at all, and when we had finished making love—the term is too demure for the disorder of those afternoons—we would drink beer together, one beer, sharing the can; and then she would leave. I watched her cross the street to her place, not hurrying now, often whistling softly. I had never met anyone remotely like her, entirely unself-conscious about our touseled afternoons in my apartment on that respectable North Side street, which somehow enhanced the romance of it.

You are so *ardent*, she said in her soft Southern voice, her sentences turned up at the end—half statement, half question—in the Southern way. She said she had never been "troubled" by sex, except of course for thinking about it all the time, and that was no trouble. She had never fretted about it. She talked about her old boy friends in Blackford, what good times they'd had and how uninhibited they'd been. Those wild boys were something *else*. I knew nothing about the South but had always thought of it as a closed society, buttoned-up and puritanical. She laughed when I told her that.

God, no. Where did you ever get that idea?

Well, I said lamely. It was that way in the North, anyway. In Chicago, the best you could hope for was groping in the front seat of an automobile. Girls took their virginity seriously. It was life's grand prize.

Really? I can't stand it.

It's true, I said.

I guess it is true, she said. That was Charles's point. Frustrated desire. But he approved. People ought to restrain themselves. He thought the South was loose, he was baffled by Blackford. She laughed and did a little pantomime of sexual frenzy. Of course she had not told him much, just enough. And if Chicago was bad, Wisconsin was worse. Charles loved Wisconsin. She described Du Cass, nothing but a wide place in the road through the northern woods, one small settlement in an enormous green forest, with small cold lakes. He called it God's Country, but she found it dour and vacant and charmless, somehow very German. Blackford was soft and crowded and conversational. Blackford was French. Was God dour, vacant, and charmless?

She said, "He's just a boy from a small town in Wisconsin who happened to go to the University of Virginia Law School on a scholarship."

"And you," I said. "Where do you fit in?"

She thought a moment before answering. We were lying in bed, an autumn rain banging at the windows; it had rained for two days. "I fit in anywhere," she said. "French or German or the in-between, as long as there's some fun in it." She looked at me. "Except Chicago. I don't fit in here. It isn't *free*, this city." She began to speak slowly, making certain that I got every word. She said that when she arrived in Chicago as a young bride she'd found it exciting, unlike anything she had ever known. It was so big and filled with commotion. Chicago did not welcome with a handshake; it crushed in a bear hug. So much the better if you were from the Old South or New England. It meant you had something to contribute. Chicago encouraged criticism, almost seemed to invite it. How do you like it here? In Richmond the question was a courtesy, in Los Angeles a joke, and in New York a taunt. In Chicago it was sincerely meant. How do you like it here really? Honestly now, tell me what you think. We're such hicks out here. What can we do together to change Chicago?

And when you told them what they could do, they'd nod their heads in agreement, Yes, yes, *God*. You're so right, Carole, so right, it takes someone from the outside to see it. But look, Carole, this is a tough town, a mill town, a four-sided monolith, the Babbitts, the Machine, the Syndicate, and the newspapers. It's a city for making money. That's what we do here, Carole. *We make money.*

"Can you *believe* that?" Carole said.

"Yes," I said.

"Where does the fun come in?"

"That's what it's supposed to be."

"What do you do with it when you have it, all the money?"

"You buy a house in the suburbs," I said.

"Great," she said. Then, "I always wanted out. And I still do."

"Out of Chicago?" I said.

"Why not?" She moved her shoulders irritably. "Who cares?"

"I do," I said.

"Do you really?"

"Yes," I said.

"What about you, then?"

"I'm here until the election."

"Yes," she said. "The election. What then?"

I shrugged. I hadn't thought about the future. The present was crowded enough. I said, "Mess around with politics, I guess. Here or somewhere else. That's what I do. Politics is my profession." I gestured at the door leading to the living room—my office, the filing cabinets, the Burroughs, and the rest of it. Talking about it with her made it sound solemn and—ludicrous, unimportant, without cutting edge. I untangled the sheets, freeing our feet; then I kissed her on the mouth.

She said after a moment, "That's what you'll do for the rest of your life, ask people questions? And then knock them down into categories and give the results to some character in a derby hat?"

"Most of them wear Stetsons," I said.

She looked at me sideways. "Come on, Jack. What's *next*?" She rolled over so that she was facing me. "You have to make it yourself. You have to create yourself. You have to *force* it."

"It's nice to think that," I said.

"It's *true*," she said.

"It's false," I said.

"You take what you want," she said.

"No," I said. "You don't."

"Scared to?"

I laughed. That wasn't it at all.

"I do," she said.

"And I wish you luck," I said. "But I'm scared of people who create themselves. Little *Führers* and *duces*, self-creations, imposters. They got what they wanted. And so did everyone else. Imposter's paradise." Head down on the hook, I thought but did not say.

She said, "You're such a pessimist."

"And when the time is right, I'll run for office."

"You will?" She rolled her eyes in astonishment.

"Yes," I said. "When the times are as pessimistic as I am."

"I can't see you hustling votes," she said. "It's hard for me to conceive of, even."

"It's just technique," I said.

"I don't think you want it badly enough."

"How do you know how badly I want it?"

She cocked her head, a dreamy look on her face. She said, "When I met Charles he was in law school. I had known all those boys in Blackford, funny boys, irresponsible, naughty boys. Charles was so serious. I met him at a party in Charlottesville. He was standing alone in a corner, wanting to join in but not being able to. I decided I was going to seduce him. I was going to get him into my bed that night." She laughed and kissed me.

"And did you?"

"Another girl was after him but I won. But I didn't seduce him that night or the next night. Eventually I did."

"And you fell in love with him."

"Later," she said. "Not right away. I fell in love with him after he fell in love with me." She looked at me, grinning. "Sound familiar?"

I said, "Here and there."

We were silent a moment, and then the doorbell rang. A look of dismay crossed Carole's face and she put her hand out; but I was already out of bed, pulling on my trousers. I told her to stay where she was, that I was expecting a messenger from Bayley's office, some figures he wanted me to look at.

But in the event it was not Bayley's messenger but Charles Nierendorf at the door.

8

HE rushed past me through the door into the living room
and stood there, swaying, his hands plunged in his raincoat pockets, looking around here and there in the room.
He nodded abruptly and said, "Where is she?"

Carole came to the bedroom door, standing very
straight in a posture unfamiliar to me. She was dressed
but disheveled; it was obvious we had just gotten out
of bed. Her shoes were beside the easy chair, where
she had left them. We all looked at the shoes and then
he bent over and picked them up, handing them to her,
first one and then the other. They looked at each other
without speaking, she straight and composed as a
dancer, he hunched or coiled, it was hard to tell which.
Charles Nierendorf was tall and very thin, with a
pinched Slavic face and a cleft chin, the sort of man
described as rangy. His skin was drawn tight over his
bones, his face closed. His hair was wet from the rain
and plastered to his skull, except for an absurd cowlick.
Without the raincoat and gray flannel suit he could have
been a Wisconsin farmer or merchant. He handed her
the shoes and flexed his fingers, looking at her all the
while.

I said, "Charles."

He said, "Shut up a minute, Jack."

Carole stepped away from the door, moving toward
him, but he put his hand up like a traffic cop at an inter-
section. She waited, and when he spoke it was in a low,
colorless monotone. He said he had come home early;
there had been some trouble at the office, trouble with
Estabrook and then with Mozart, an office matter. A con-

fidential legal matter, he said, looking at me. He had to get out of the office to think things over, so he came home. And she wasn't there. The baby was at the neighbor's. He knew that because she was crying and he'd know Betsy's cry anywhere, his own baby daughter. So he went next door and there she was, propped up in front of the television set. And when he walked in the neighbor was so flustered. She didn't know what to do or say. Couldn't say anything for a minute but kept looking out the fucking window. Said at last that you weren't there and she didn't know where you were, for sure. Maybe the doctor's. No, downtown with a friend. She looked at me the way you look at a sick person or a retard. So I understood, why I don't know. And I came here, just hoping to God that I was wrong. He looked at me directly for the first time. "Put your shoes on, Jack."

I didn't move. We were all rooted to our places, three points of a triangle.

"But I knew what I'd find," he said. "Not much doubt about that, but I was hoping anyway, on the theory that things aren't always what they seem. This has been some day for me, one of the all-time great days." Charles looked down at his feet, then across at Carole. "How long have you been fucking him?"

She moved her face as if she'd been slapped, and it took her a moment to reply. "Since the summer."

"The summer," he said. "August," he said.

"Late August," she said.

He said, "Do you love him?"

Her hands went to her mouth and I thought for a moment that she would burst into a great wave of laughter, her unmistakable raucous and high-pitched giggle that could fill a room. But she said instead, very quietly, "No, Charlie."

"You don't love him, is that it?"

"I told you. No."

"You're just fucking him then. Love doesn't come into it."

"Please don't use that word," she said.

"Oh?" He swayed, sighing, and I heard his bones creak. "Why not?"

93

"It's not like you, Charlie."

He looked at her, puzzled.

"You're never vulgar," she said. She spoke in the same faint voice but her words seemed to reach across the room, touching him; he looked at her through the words. He moved his hands and his raincoat opened. One of his shirttails was hanging out of his trousers. Looking at him, I realized he had walked from his office through the rain. He moved his shoulders, uncomfortable in his gray flannel jacket with its narrow lapels, a snug fit for his rangy body. He looked from her to me and back again, his eyes bleak. "Well, what is it, then, if it isn't love and it isn't fucking? Is it money?"

"A mistake," she said.

He nodded, a good lawyer recognizing a promising line of inquiry.

"Charlie?" she said, and made a move toward him; but he raised his hand in the same abrupt cop's gesture.

"What is it that you're doing? You're not fucking him and you don't love him. So what is it here? What's happening?" He looked at me, tapping his fists together. "Son of a bitch, I can *smell* it."

"Carole said it was a mistake," I said. I thought that was the way out. Everyone could recognize a mistake and salvage what was left. That would be the no man's land we could occupy, a kind of cease-fire zone. I talked reasonably for a moment, and when he turned, lunging, swinging hard, I caught his arm. We grappled for a moment but his heart wasn't in it and I easily trapped his arm. In a moment I had him in a bear hug, Carole's Chicago embrace. She had cried out, then tried to separate us. We were both breathing hard, but Charles had no resistance. He had all the advantage and no resistance. He was in the right, he had justice on his side; but that was not enough. He ceased to struggle, and I could hear him muttering under his breath; he was calling his wife a whore. I put my mouth close to his ear and spoke, trying to rescue us both, and Carole. I described a situation that had gotten out of control without anyone's foreseeing it or wanting it—

He said, "Shut up, you—"

Carole said suddenly, "It's me."

He seemed not to hear her. In any case, he did not reply nor ask her what she meant. He moved his shoulders again, twisting his neck as if his shirt collar were too tight. I let him go. The room was stifling and he was sweating, beads of perspiration on his forehead. He stood now with his arms at his side. The room was dark in midafternoon, the rain continuing to fall. He said, "I never thought about this. I never expected it. This is all new to me. This is outside my ken. I'm trying to take it in and figure out what to do about it."

"It's me," she said again.

"Well," he said in his colorless voice. "What difference does that make?"

She was silent, motionless in the bedroom doorway.

"You have any ideas, Carrie? I don't mind hearing your ideas. What I ought to do about this." He wrinkled his nose and turned away.

"I was so lonely, Charlie."

He looked at me, and then back at his wife.

"Every morning, every afternoon of every day. This cold, cold city. The nights alone with the baby and the television. This street. I don't recognize it. I have a dream every night that I'm back home, where it's warm and conversational and where people love each other every day and where there's *desire*, do you see? It's all balled up." She took a deep breath, her breasts rising; she was leaning back against the doorjamb, her hands behind her back, her eyes focused elsewhere, somewhere in the middle distance, not on her husband or on me. She had never looked more alluring or provocative, more winning; her throaty voice in the gathering darkness was soft and confidential, almost hypnotic. She said, "Charlie, don't cast me out. Don't do it. It's me, what I want. You know how badly I need it Charlie what I have to have Charlie how I can't be on the outside ever how I can't stand it. I've told you Charlie and you've seen it and there isn't anything I can't do, nothing I won't try." She paused, breathing. "You remember."

He looked at her, squinting.

"Charlottesville," she said in her Southern way, the last syllable turned up like a question; except it wasn't a question. She cocked her head, looking at him. She was seducing him in a kind of verbal striptease. "I love you, Charlie."

"I don't believe you," he said.

In the shocking silence she sighed and did not reply. She accepted the verdict with a little bow of her head. She had gone as far as she could go.

"People make mistakes," I said.

He turned to look at me.

"And you weren't around."

Carole said, "Be quiet, Jack. It's over."

He said, "Charlottesville was a long time ago."

"A very long time ago," she said. "Ages. Three years." And smiled, indicating the absurdity of it. She pushed off from the doorjamb and now stood in her dancer's pose, chin high.

"What did you think you were doing here?"

"We've been over that," she said.

He nodded acknowledgment. "You, then," he said, turning to me.

"I live here," I said.

"Never mind Jack," Carole said. "It's *me*, Charlie. *Me*."

"You," he said. He moved then, ponderously, retreating a little in the direction of the door. It was very dark now, but when he turned he saw the telephone off the hook, the receiver stuck under the sofa pillow. He replaced it with a fastidious gesture, and almost immediately it rang. No one moved to answer and after the fourth ring it was silent again. But for a moment the routine outside world intruded and that seemed to remind him of his other responsibilities, for he shook his head and said, "I'm leaving. I've got to see to the baby. The baby has a cold."

"Yes," Carole said.

"And call my office."

"All right," she said.

He said, "That stupid neighbor."

She said, "Very stupid. Dumb as a post. Let's go home, Charlie."

"What about him?" he said.

"What about him?" she said. "So what. It's over. I told you that."

"Yes, that's what you said."

She had moved toward him and was now only a foot away, looking up at him. He was a foot taller than she, standing with the brute angularity of a statue. He had a statue's rough exterior and poise; and we looked at him and saw something of ourselves, anger and bewilderment, and indecision. Suddenly he tore his fist out of his coat pocket, cocking it back and then violently forward; she flinched, bringing her hands up in front of her face, crying out—but he didn't hit her. He let his breath out. He stood looking at her, trembling, his fist in front of her face.

"Fuck it," he said.

She moved closer to him, unafraid now, looping her arm through his. He didn't seem to notice.

"We can try again, Charlie."

"Things won't ever be the same," he said.

"Yes," she said. "Yes, that's right. They can be better."

He gave a little snort and turned toward the door. She went with him, pulled by him.

She whispered to him, "Love me, Charlie."

He dropped her arm. "Let him love you," he said, and was gone.

And there we were, on the threshold of the modern world, where appeals to self-interest, common sense, good will, and universal understanding were ritual, a priest's commonplace remarks to the condemned. Carole stared at the door with—disbelief. In a few excruciating moments their world had gone to pieces. I found myself farther into someone else's life than I had any right to be; farther than I wanted to be; and there had been no warning. She continued to stare at the door, her hand outstretched; then she let it fall. Charles and I were not worldly men outside our public spheres. We knew how things were done downtown, and that was all we knew. But politics was only—politics, perhaps the structure of life, but not life itself. Charles's emotional reserve, a feature of his terrain no less than Wisconsin's cold flat lakes, was not equal to the great evil he saw in front of his eyes. I felt for him, identified with him, pulled for him; he seemed to me defenseless, as I would have been if the tables were turned. Carole had made her best offer; and had been turned down flat.

I imagined him walking from the Loop through the rain, arriving at their apartment, wet and frustrated by the argument at the office, a dispute with Estabrook or Mozart; they were always on the short side of things. I had no idea what he did at his firm, though I knew it was political law of some kind, building violations, tax cases, lobbying. He had hurried home to tell his wife, perhaps to ask her advice, perhaps to gain her sympathy, at any event to explain. Something's gone wrong, darling. I'm in a jam. This would be surprising; Charles was not the sort of man to take his office home, whining and complaining; he did his work alone, as a man does it. And finding the apartment empty, nobody home; this one time, when he needed her, she was not there. Then he heard the baby cry, at the neighbor's next door. But Carole was not there, either. When the neighbor, flustered and incompetent, had begun to stammer evasively, he was impatient, anxious for her to get to the point. Then, suddenly, he knew what had happened; he knew in his heart where his wife was and what she was doing there, and that he must go to her. He would have hesitated. Is it not better sometimes to leave it be, not to disturb the even surface of things? Probably he had expected it, anticipated it from the moment of their first meeting, had known that her soft South was different from his cold North, had known how passionate she was and how starved, and therefore how deprived; he had known her nature, and known his own, and this had frightened him, so he had done what people from the North do—ignored it, slipped the thought into a dark place in the manner of people who live precariously in a wilderness, the widening prairie

98

remote from, and forgotten by, the riotous coasts, where the unexpected was the norm. My God, my *wife*. That first awful moment, it would seem inconceivable; that was not the way people behaved. In the *afternoon*. Across the street with a *pal*, for that was the word Carole had used to describe me. *This is outside my ken*, he had said. But it wasn't, once he thought about it, not entirely.

"I love you, Charlie."

"I don't believe you."

A good lawyer took account of the evidence.

I didn't know this Charles who stood in my living room, solitary and without resistance, and of course and naturally without composure, until his final words, and his exit. I knew what had been explained to me; I had no firsthand knowledge. Carole's Charles, the Charles of Du Cass comma Wisconsin comma, the serious Charles, the Charles who was cold and unfeeling—that Charles was not the Charles in my apartment, standing in his wet raincoat and looking at his bed-rumpled wife, trying to disbelieve what was in front of his eyes and failing because it was in front of his eyes, a monstrous duplicity. I had thought of him as arrogant and self-absorbed, and no doubt that was true, one truth among many. I had shaken hands with him three times, had visited his apartment once, had waved from my window, had exchanged pleasantries. It was understood that we were not well met, would never be friends. I was his wife's pal. To him, I was the political operator with "connections." So he knew no more of me than I knew of him.

"Remember Charlottesville?"

I had no idea about that, either; some intimate event at the U.Va., Mr. Jefferson's place, a gentleman's university; but Charles Nierendorf was no gentleman, he was a boy from the Wisconsin woods. It could have been anything, a tender moment or a numb one, like my childhood scar. Worth remembering, however. Perhaps it was her seduction of him.

The baby had a cold and I hadn't known. Carole hadn't mentioned it. Why would she? She rarely talked about the baby, who was so demonstrative, who let you know what she thought, and who loved her father. Carole was with the baby all day long, when she wasn't with me. Theirs was a culture I knew only dimly, the way a traveler knows a country from a state-sponsored tour: the village from the window of a railway car, the seventeenth-century battlefield, the church in the capital city, the castle at the bend of the river; no mention here of the pogroms, the tyrant, the tyrant's heirs, the industrial slums. I did not yearn to know more because it was a country I would never visit. Carole and I had a specific afternoon life together, a life in aspic, as rigid in form as a sonnet. Her life across the street was suppressed, as though it were a subversive book; and of course the reverse was also true.

And when Charles looked at me, his eyes burning with humiliation and anger, what did he see? His wife's bachelor pal, a loner without family responsibilities (who was he anyway, and where did he come from?), some kind of political operator who worked at home, no office, no secretary, eager to take his wife to bed of an afternoon, no thought given to it at all, any time she wanted. Did she call, or did she arrive unannounced? When she walked in the door he took the phone off the hook. Did she say "I'm home!" She could not wait to get out of her shoes, had kicked them off and left them where they fell. And the smell. He could smell it. This was surely pleasant for Jack, an afternoon's lovemaking with no responsibilities and no consequences; and she wanted it so badly.

He knew that, too. He was in no doubt. She had been frank to say "It's *me*, Charlie. *Me*." And what a tremendous throw of the dice that was. At the moment she could do no less than tell the whole truth, her desire. *Me*, Charlie. *Me*. She wanted him to step back and look inside her, to see *her*, the way she was truly. She must have thought it a privilege, but she had asked too much.

A shadow had crossed his face. Was this truly happening? Standing in my unfamiliar living room—Carole's lover's living room, the darkness gathering in late afternoon—he could not respond. What could he say? Did she

100

want absolution? He could not see what she was offering, nothing less than her whole spirit. The truth was, this was too public for him, too abrupt, too naked, and too humiliating. So his attitude was ineluctable, alas; or perhaps not "alas" at all, for his own sense of himself, his own integrity and nerve were at stake. How was a man to act? If this had been Du Cass, Wisconsin—but it wasn't. He would tell himself that if this were Du Cass, Wisconsin, it would not have happened. However, this was Chicago, altogether more subtle; he did not know what the rules were. As she was obliged to falsify, so was he.

"I love you, Charlie."

"I don't believe you."

It was said of Tamerlane that he once had his prisoners cemented together to make a wall, a shrieking wall, that slowly trembled into silence and inertia. This was like that.

Carole and I stood looking at each other in the sudden silence. I moved to put my arm around her, but she shook her head. She stood with her arms wrapped tightly around her breasts, staring at the door as if it would open presently and Charles appear, his arms wide. I switched on the light and walked into the kitchen and poured stiff whiskies for us both. She took hers, looking at it, then sipping it thoughtfully. Her eyes were welling, but no tears fell.

"People don't *listen*," she said. "They won't do it. It'd make such a difference if they did." She looked at me bleakly. "Don't you think?"

"I suppose so," I said. The memory of him, his hands in his raincoat pockets swaying left and right, was still with me.

"You've cut your cheek," she said.

"It's nothing," I said.

"He drew blood," she said.

"A little," I said.

"You're strong," she said. "Stronger than I thought."

"Not very," I said. "He didn't have it in him. He was in shock."

"Yes," she said. "I suppose he was."

101

I said, "I'm sorry as hell about it, Carole."

"For him or for me, Jack?"

"You," I said. "Him. The baby. Your marriage."

"Don't worry about him," she said.

I said, "What are you going to do?"

She looked at me evenly. "I'm going back to my apartment, where I live."

"What can I do?" I said.

"There isn't anything you can do, Jack." She turned to look in the mirror, giving her hair a few swipes with the palm of her hand. She said, "I've liked it, being here. Did you like it?" She sipped whiskey, the light harsh on her face.

"Carole," I said. There was a rustle somewhere, a dissatisfied audience; cars in the street, I realized.

"You liked it well enough while it was happening."

"I sure did," I said. "And now I don't."

"What's the difference between then and now?"

"It isn't just us anymore."

She nodded at that, an obvious fact. "Do you feel anything for me?"

The speech had not been well received. The applause in the hall was tepid, and the audience restless. The awkward silence grew until I said, "Of course I do."

"You sound like you're ashamed."

"There's that," I said.

"You are," she said.

"Aren't you?"

"I'm sorry you're ashamed of it. I mean ashamed of me, because that's what you're saying." We looked at each other in the mirror, my stunned face over her right shoulder. When her tears began to spill she let them fall, then wiped them away roughly with the back of her hand.

"I'm not ashamed of you," I said. "I'm ashamed of me."

"We're here together, Jack. I don't see the difference. What's the difference?"

I understood then that she saw it as a matter of loyalties, my loyalty to her as opposed to "it," the situation, the thing itself. And that could not be judged alone. Whatever I believed about my own behavior must be as a result of our behavior together. Therefore, I would judge her as I judged myself.

"I'm speaking for me," I said.

"And me, too," she said. "That's the point. What's the difference between us here, please?"

"We made a mistake," I said.

"And I should be ashamed."

"I don't know you," I said. "I know me."

"And him," she said, her voice rising.

"Did you *see* him?" I said.

"I should've guessed that."

"That's the way it is," I said. "I felt for him."

"And me," she said. "Did you feel for me?"

"I felt for you," I said.

"Why didn't you throw him out, Jack? This is your place. I was here. He had no business here." She sipped her drink, holding the glass with both hands.

"Throw him out on his ass," I said.

"That's right."

"It never occurred to me," I said.

"It should've," she said. "I'm not his property. He doesn't *own* me. He doesn't have a bill of sale. These times, they were *ours*. He had no right. And you should have thrown him out. I was waiting for you to do it." She put down her drink and moved away to fetch her coat. It had stopped raining. She shrugged into her coat and stood a moment in the center of the living room, looking around at my gear, the filing cabinets and the Burroughs, the long sheets of paper with their columns of pregnant numbers. She was gathering herself to leave. "But it never occurred to you, you say."

"No," I said.

"To protect me," she said.

"I didn't think you needed it," I said.

"All our afternoons together, here, in there," she said, pointing at the bedroom door; we both looked at it, a frozen frame in the film. "And that's what it comes down to. The afternoons are *ours*. You care more about him than you do about me."

"No," I said. Yet she had a part of the truth; it would

103

have been more accurate to say I cared about their marriage.

"So why didn't you throw him out?"

"Teach him a lesson? Not to trespass? And to keep his dirty hands off his wife." I looked at her, suddenly angry. I never spoke roughly to her. I said, "We are not innocent."

"And he is," she said.

A cuckold is ridiculous; everyone knows that. The cuckold, ribald figure of fun in a thousand bedroom farces, many of them French. Baffled, injured, impaired, impotent cuckold—the last to know, always complicit in his own deception, living in a dream world of his own making, a cartoon figure. Yet Charles Nierendorf did not seem a cartoon figure to me; anything but. "Not innocent," I said. "But he didn't deserve to get thrown out, either."

"I expected more, Jack."

"I expected less," I said.

She said, "Sooner or later, one of these days, you're going to have to choose up sides."

"This isn't one of the days," I said.

"That's all we've got, each other," she said. "There isn't anything else to be loyal to." She opened the door and stood in the hall, facing me. "Your friends and your kin," she said. "That's what everything comes down to, loyalty. Don't they at least teach you that, downtown?" And then, with a cool smile and a little flutter of her hand, she turned and walked down the stairs. I sat at my desk by the window and watched her cross the street. She moved with the slow heel-and-toe step of a priest, never looking back. The light in their apartment was on and I could imagine the scene that awaited her . . .

And I tried briefly to conjure that up, and could not imagine it at all. Expectation was the enemy of prediction. Watching her disappear through the front door—she paused on the doormat to carefully wipe her feet—my eyes were drawn to my numbers, cold on the page. The phone rang. I reached for the receiver, then pulled back. My drink was warm, so I went for more ice. Looking at it, I poured it down the drain and made a new one. The rain had ceased and the moon was full, glittering on the surface of the lake. The phone continued to ring and at last I answered. Bayley was furious.

9

A year later the election was suddenly at hand and my conferences with Pat Bayley grew less frequent. He had other important business and my data were no longer surprising. The numbers tended to reinforce themselves, and the margin of error muddied everything. The election would be extremely close; everything depended on a heavy poll from the city to offset the downstate landslide. Bayley and his friends were very nervous. The Man wanted this badly and had made promises. My last conference with Bayley was scheduled for the Tuesday before the election. That was canceled and reset for Thursday. That, too, was canceled and we finally agreed on Saturday, the Morrison, one sharp.

Leaving my apartment, I carefully checked my numbers—how much to say, how far to go, remembering always the general's injunction to his intelligence officer: *What do you know that will help me right now?* Serious business, assessing your own strength and the enemy's strength; and it would all be decided in twelve hours of voting and eight hours of counting. In Chicago, the counting was more important than the voting. I slipped a single piece of paper into a manila envelope and set off across the park, rehearsing my presentation, boiling down paragraphs into sentences and sentences into phrases; Bayley liked things terse. There was always at least one unanticipated question, and that was the one they were most interested in. Talk to me about the ——th precinct. Tell me about middle-class Italians, Jack.

It was a warm autumn day, though you knew that winter was in the vicinity. Clouds boiled up over the lake, a cold front from Canada; a thin line of light separated the clouds from the water. From across the Outer Drive I could hear the shooters at the Lincoln Park Gun Club, the *pop-pop* of twelve-gauge shotguns competing with the hum of noonday traffic. The park was crowded with young mothers pushing baby carriages, and the occasional drunk picking through trash cans. The drunks were harmless, just old white men down on their luck. On Michigan Avenue I slowed up, watching married women in their smart suits and buttoned-up blouses heading off for lunch at the Drake or the Barclay Club or the Casino, a whiskey sour and the chef's salad, fuel for the serious chore of Saturday afternoon shopping on Michigan Avenue. What would induce such women to vote Democratic? For the young ones sex appeal, perhaps, so long as it was not aggressive; sex appeal in a cashmere sweater sailing a sloop in Nantucket Sound, and a glamorous wife who spoke French. Groups of women and groups of businessmen in felt hats, sports jackets, and golfer's tan, the groups maneuvering politely around one another. I thought about the businessmen at lunch, talking politics because the election was three days away, then moving effortlessly on—to business, a golf score, a child's success, a promotion, the new Ford line.

Past the Water Tower the buildings rose, rising thickly and handsomely. The city was best seen from the surface of the lake, the buildings rising then like the jeweled points of a fantastic crown atop a featureless watery face, lumpish as a potato; everything that you saw was man-made, low and tentative to the north, rising, thrusting as your eye swung south and then east at the extremity, petering out. The crown itself was the prize, dazzling in its promise, its gaunt instruction: Work and prosper. The wind picked up, scattering gutter paper; there were a few drops of rain. The governor's black limousine was parked in the no parking zone of Tribune Tower, its Gothic lines slim as a pencil, capitalism's Chartres. I had come to read newspapers in my own way. I always learned something new, but it was never the thing I wanted to know or needed to know; as information, it was usually beside the point. I thought of the press as the jeering bully in the grandstand, the boozy one with twenty-twenty hindsight and scant knowledge of the game and the players; all he knew were the obvious rules and some of the tricks to avoid them.

Deep into the Loop now, that circular city within a city, the buildings shabby and earthbound. They squatted in the autumn chill. The crowds lost their sleek, shark-like, suburban look. These were blowfish. Everyone was heavier, the women didn't carry handbags that matched their shoes, and the men had an unhealthy indoor look, white-faced or red-faced, depending on where they spent their time indoors. The heart of the Loop always put me in mind of a bazaar, though I had never seen a bazaar. Did they have bazaars in Hamburg or Lübeck? There was conversation, shouts, curses, and laughter. I watched a waitress run from a restaurant, pulling on her coat, jumping into a black convertible—the man not opening the door, not looking at her, silent behind the wheel as the convertible leaped forward and into the stream of traffic with a crescendo of horns. The energy of the Loop was stupendous and seemed to implode, the blue industrial haze evidence of things turning and churning, grinding and clanking, neither neat nor elegant, the neon ambience of progress—the working of a clever brute's mind.

A block from the Morrison I fell in behind two men. I recognized them as friends of Pat Bayley's. They were walking no faster than they needed to, and talking quietly, with economical hand gestures. To emphasize a point each would touch the other's sleeve or elbow. They wore huge rings on their fingers. One would shake his head, the other would laugh, with no sound at all, but the quiver of his shoulders suggesting dry amusement. Above them loomed one of Louis Sullivan's department stores, Sullivan's wide-eyed "fluency" as heavy and suggestive as the unheard conversation, as harmonious in these congested surroundings as a pyramid beside the crowded Nile. They were talking about an acquaintance, it was obvious, an acquaintance taken drunk or to the cleaners or under the weather or under indictment. A man in trouble. He had spoken out of turn. He had made a mistake, ignored protocol, neglected to answer a telephone call. And now he was in the deep shit, the poor son of a bitch.

Then I was inside the lobby and watching Pat Bayley talk to a sallow, sad-faced man. The man looked as if he were about to cry. He was listening to Pat and nodding his head vigorously. Yes, yes. They came to an agreement of some kind, Pat touched his arm, a deft disengagement, and walked over to me.

"Howareya Jack," he said formally.

"Pat," I said. We had become very friendly, almost friends.

He looked at me and shook his head. "You need a new suit."

"One of these days," I said.

He said, "Jesus, Jack."

"You're looking well," I said.

He said, "Shit. I'm so goddamned tired, can't stand up." He took my arm, steering me into the dining room. "You know Billy Cavanaugh?" He nodded at the sad-faced man, now lingering at the cigar counter, rolling a White Owl under his nose.

"The name," I said. "He's Oscar's nephew."

Pat was nodding left and right at acquaintances, moving swiftly so that we would not be intercepted. We sat at his regular table and he leaned back, yawning, smoothing the napkin over his belly.

"Brother-in-law," he said, smiling painfully. "Poor Billy. You know the kinda guy, Billy. Everyone knows one. Asleep at the switch. Nothing ever goes right for Billy. Billy goes out without a hat, it rains. Billy goes to Comiskey for the game, sits behind a post. Give a poll-watching job to Billy, he oversleeps. Send him on a little errand, say Springfield, he ends up in Champaign. His feet hurt alla time. Has trouble with his bowels." He stopped and looked up. I turned to see a priest lean over our table, one huge arm around Pat Bayley's shoulders; he whispered something into Pat's ear and stepped back, smiling. Pat smiled and thanked him and with a wink the priest was gone, threading his way through the tables to the lobby. Pat watched him retreat; he closed his eyes and muttered something that sounded like an oath. He said, "Where was I? Billy? Bowels. Has a bad back, goes out alla time. Rest of us humping like shit, Bill's absent without leave; hangover, flu, stuck in a subway, a death in the family. But he's married to Oscar's sister, you know? Faith, only weighs about four hundred pounds. And who's a ball buster and maybe that's why Billy's the way he is, maybe not. I haddim all set up, guy I know, doing some work around the office, making a call, maybe a delivery. And he screwed it up. Damned if I know how. With Billy, you listen to the explanation, your ear begins to hurt. Takes all day long, listening to Billy tell you it wasn't his fault. Oscar's a hell of a good friend of mine and's done me a turn or two so I don't like to let him down. *Won't* let him down if I can help it. So I got Billy a job driving for Judge Craxi, who's god damned near as dumb as Billy. Christ, and I'll give you any odds you want right this minute, the god damned car runs out of gas, first trip.''

He looked at me. ''What's so funny?''

''You're in rare form,'' I said.

Pat Bayley stared morosely at the cocktail the waiter had placed before him. He put his fingers around the stem of the glass and hefted it, smiling dryly, saluting me, swallowing, smiling again, running his tongue over his upper lip. ''So what do you have for me today, Jack? Be brief. Keep it simple. Because I've got a hell of a long day ahead of me.''

He listened distractedly during my five-minute presentation, glancing at my fact sheet, nodding approval; there was nothing new and I admitted as much. The election was in the hands of the gods and a few close friends, and if there was any last-minute shift I couldn't detect it. We both knew that the situation was insecure. Bayley looked up suddenly, smiling, and I saw how tired he was. His movements were slower than ever. I thought of Billy Cavanaugh, and how patiently Pat had spoken to him, solving the problem.

He raised his glass again. ''Luck.''

''Luck,'' I said, raising mine.

After a moment I asked him what the priest wanted.

''Giving me a preview,'' he said. ''Preview of the great sermon he intends to give, Sunday.''

''Can't hurt,'' I said.

''Probably not,'' he said. Bayley looked at his watch, then around the room, but warily, lest someone think he was trying to signal them and initiate a conversation. The room was in turmoil. The Saturday lunch hour began before noon and had gone on and on as if it were the eve of a holiday. Men were moving from table to table, exchanging information. The dining room was filled with men talking, a low excited rumble. They were talking across tables and among tables, a single topic, politics, shouted and whispered, frowns and then laughter—all this with their mouths full, drinks in their hands, and cigars and cigarettes smoldering in huge ashtrays—discussing the problems of downstate and Little Egypt, and the northern suburbs, fat-cat country beyond their control; and the news of other difficult regions, Ohio, Texas, California, and always New York. Democrats tore themselves to pieces in New York City; they didn't understand the importance of loyalty at election time so they impaled themselves, throwing themselves on swords left and right, Jesus, they had no sense at all. Michigan and Wisconsin looked to be secure, thank God for the UAW. Minnesota was all right. The men glanced at the door from time to time, hoping for the arrival of someone, anyone, with a fresh fact or set of facts: a poll from St. Louis, a newspaper endorsement in Indiana, a report of a conversation with a guy who knew Lawrence in Philadelphia, someone else who had seen one of Bobby's people, and what the handbooks were saying in Vegas. Perspiring waiters struggled around the tables, cursing, and when quitting time came each would hurry across the street to the tavern on the corner for one or two quick ones, telling the barkeep what he'd heard from his good friend Alderman Uh on the situation in Du Page County, where the Republicans were trying to steal the election. Bayley took all this in, his eyes patrolling the room, then turned back to me.

"We're very pleased with your work," he said. "I am personally and they are at the Hall. The Man is. So you've got a right to be proud of yourself. Your stuff's given us one or two insights we might not've had, otherwise." He saw the dismay on my face—only one or two? "Insights?" All that work, fourteen-hour days, the telephoning, the interviews, the collating—he shook his head, disappointed. "Jack, we're experts at this. This is what

111

we do for a living. You give the Man a new insight, it's like helping Michelangelo paint his chapel. His ceiling. See what I'm saying? Give us a break, Jack. Don't get the idea you've invented"—he glared at me—"the fucking electric light."

He looked away, slowly bringing the drink to his mouth.

"I take the point," I said.

"I hope to hell," he said, putting the drink down without tasting it. He listened to the roar in the room as any veteran seaman might listen to the crash of the waves and the howl of the wind during a squall, knowing that the ship was sturdy and the captain indomitable but that gales were unpredictable and only a fool ignored them and their potential; a gale was a great beast, likely to stampede. A gale was no more predictable than an animal, or the great mass of humanity. And every man in the ship's crew had to do his part. Bayley said, "Look at them. Listen to them. Ten pounds of shit in a five-pound bag."

"Politics is nine-tenths gossip," I said.

"No kidding," he said.

I said, "I appreciate what you said, Pat."

"Some of them didn't like it." He smiled. "Smart-assed college kid just in from the quadrangle, tries to tell them their business. They take pride in their work, just like you. Don't like to see it challenged. Not by a smart-assed college kid who's wet behind the ears. I say *was*. You've grown up a lot, Jack. It was worse for them when your stuff began to check out. Oscar thought you were full of shit, that time, you remember, until he went back to his people. Found out that you had it on the money and he didn't. So he adjusted. Oscar's no fool. But that's all in the past, or will be in three days."

"I thought that was Earl," I said.

"There was more than one time, Jack. Oscar let me know, not you. Get that kid out of here. But it checked out, so Oscar began to listen, because Oscar's the kind of guy, gets the job *done*."

"You want anything this weekend?"

"Anything you can give me. Anything at all. No specific instructions. Just any damned thing at all you think's valuable, give me a call. No need to worry about the

112

time. I'm here all day and all night except when I come down to the dining room to eat.''

"All right," I said.

"Any time at all. But it's our job now. Your job's done, really; and ours moves into high gear. We'll earn our money.''

"You let me know, anything I can do.''

"I've got a bad feeling," he said.

The waiter arrived with menus.

"You thought about what you're going to do, after the election?'' He was studying the menu, which was the size of a tabloid newspaper.

I shook my head. I had vague thoughts about moving on, but had no idea where. I hadn't thought beyond next Tuesday. I said, "I thought there might be something for me here.''

"Might be," he said. He did not look up from the menu.

"In the Hall," I said.

He was silent a moment and I watched him move inside himself, thinking. He put the menu aside and steepled his fingers, tapping them together. "Not the Hall," he said.

I said, "Where, then?''

"You're an elections man," he said.

"That's right.''

"What do you do between elections?''

"Plan for the next one," I said.

He looked up and smiled pleasantly at the perspiring waiter. "Mike, I'll have the strip steak medium rare, the baked potato with sour cream and chives, and the shrimp cocktail beforehand. Is the shrimp cocktail good?'' Mike nodded while he wrote. "And another martini for myself and my young friend. You're sure about the shrimp cocktail? Last time, the shrimp, mealy.''

"I'll see to it, Mr. Bayley.''

"Big ones," Bayley said. "Lots of cocktail sauce and some horseradish, and an extra lemon wedge.''

I said I'd have the roast beef medium well, and the waiter nodded and hurried off.

"We'll have our cocktails now," Bayley called after him. Then, to me: "Where were we?''

113

"Elections," I said.

"Problem there," he said. "There won't be anything here for four years and if we're lucky that'll be a walk-away, no problem, Christ, we'll just crown the little son of a bitch."

"I like it here," I said.

"Grant liked Galena," he said. "But the war was somewheres else."

"Grant hated Galena," I said.

"No shit," he said. "You're telling me he didn't like the general store, keeping inventory, sweeping up at night? I'll be god damned. I always thought he loved Galena, except for the fact that the war was somewheres else." He shook his head, then leaned across the table. "I've been talking to some people, not about you specifically, but about the general situation, you know, what's going to happen after and so forth and so on."

"Yes," I said.

"Might be a place for you, everything works out."

"Washington?"

"Our nation's capital," he said. " 'Course, if you'd rather sweep out the general store. Keep inventory. Shit, I can find you something. Maybe out near Cottage Grove."

"I never thought about Washington," I said.

The waiter came with our drinks and set them carefully on the table.

"Think about it," he said. "Let me know."

"I think I'd like it," I said.

"It all depends on Tuesday," he said.

I raised my glass in salute.

Bayley looked over at someone and winked. "You've done a fine job, Jack. We're appreciative." He reached into his jacket pocket and brought out an envelope, smoothing it, then handing it to me. Inside was a cashier's check for a thousand dollars. "This is a bonus, thanks from all of us. I wanted you to have it before Tuesday. It isn't tied to what happens Tuesday, unless of course we lose." This was a joke and he smiled.

I was astonished and said so.

"Our pleasure," he said.

"I'd like to come down, hang around on election night."

"Rather you didn't, Jack."

I looked at him, surprised.

"We'll be busy." He realized that wasn't enough, so he added, "It's family only, I'm afraid." There was a little silence while we drank and then he said, Oh shit. Had I seen the paper that morning? I replied that I hadn't seen a paper for days; papers came each morning and each afternoon but I hadn't had time to look at them.

"Phil Karcher died yesterday. I talked to him a week ago, he asked after you, and when I told him he seemed pleased, very pleased. Phil Karcher was a fine man."

"That's a terrible thing," I said.

"He was very sick," Bayley said.

I hadn't known that. I hadn't seen him in a year or more, and now I remembered him that day in his office when he told me of his connection with the Machine and that he had spoken to Bayley. I remembered how surprised I had been, and how startled at his denunciation of the university. Of course, remembering Karcher, I also thought about Katrina.

"Cancer," Bayley said. There was a hard edge to his voice. "So he committed suicide."

"He couldn't've committed suicide," I said.

"Got in his car, turned on the engine, closed the garage doors. Died of carbon monoxide poisoning." Bayley quickly crossed himself and changed the subject.

10

WE ate rapidly and emerged into a lobby filled with middle-aged men in groups; it looked like a convention. Bayley was intercepted by a friend who had news from downstate, that son of a bitch Elmer, Elmer this, Elmer that, what can we do about Elmer? Pat listened carefully, then introduced me.

Meet Elly Mozart, he said, and we shook hands.

Heard of you, Mozart said. Heard you did good work.

He did, Bayley said.

Very good work, Mozart said with an odd grin, which came and went in an instant. He stared at me with cold blue eyes implanted in a perfectly round rosy face. I stared back; it was inconceivable to me that he could have known about Carole Nierendorf and me, but that was the only explanation. Mozart said, You're lucky, son, working with Pat. Pat's the best in the business. Pat's a past master. And then he turned to Bayley, pointedly ignoring me, telling Pat again how Elmer was giving them fits and there wasn't a damned thing they could do about it. Elmer's security was as tight as the Pentagon's and in the last analysis they didn't have the *troops* and Elmer did. Pat nodded as Mozart spoke, then gave me a significant look: Adieu, Jack. I was reluctant to leave; the atmosphere in the lobby was electric, alive with rumor and conjecture. But I didn't belong there; it was a matter of youth and inexperience. In this hierarchy of professionals, I was still an amateur, or anyway a rookie. I stepped back, nodding at Mozart, shaking hands with Bayley, remembering that I had a thousand dollars in my wallet. I wondered what I was going to do with a thousand dollars.

116

I could buy a used car or take a trip somewhere. I hadn't had a vacation in years. I slipped away, to the cigar stand for a panatela, and then into the street. Bayley and Mozart were still deep in conversation, except that it was Pat doing the talking, his hand on Elly Mozart's elbow.

I paused for a moment, at a loss where to go. The weather was suddenly chilly and the sky gray, clouds crowding in from the west. I walked north, in the general direction of Lincoln Park and my apartment. I ignored the people and the traffic, feeling out of place. Without my manila envelope I felt naked. I did not know what to do with my hands, and I had no particular destination. I was self-conscious, face to face with my future, suddenly uncertain. I had not realized that my job was done. I thought it would go on and on, even after the election. The election had become a detail, a sort of undulation, one wave in a great ocean. The truth was, I could not imagine daily life without my data, my interviews on street corners and small West Side apartments and three-decker houses back of the yards and over the telephone, dialing with a pencil because after the first twenty calls my index finger hurt, the long hours putting the numbers into the Burroughs and then taking them out, making sense of them, and preparing my presentation to Bayley and his friends, identifying the trend lines. I was now an out-of-work surgeon, a surgeon in a healthy society where no one ever fell ill or died; except of course in Washington. In Washington they thought about the next election night and day. There was no time for rest in Washington.

Ahead of me, on the corner, a shabby old black man sawed away on a violin. He had a white beard like Uncle Remus. His violin case was open on the sidewalk, but there were only a few coins in it, nickels and dimes. He was playing Chopin. I listened to him a moment, pedestrians moving impatiently around me. I was filled with a sense of well-being, standing quietly and listening to the old man play Chopin. I dug into my pocket, found a quarter, and put it in the case. He nodded solemnly, looking up, and I saw suddenly that he was blind.

I hurried on, across the river, heading for Rush Street. The sky continued to darken and in a moment I felt the first few drops of rain. A police car hurtled through traffic, its siren shrieking. I was thinking about the violinist, unaccountably moved by his music. Then I understood: he had put a little blues into Chopin, some Storyville into Warsaw. I thought about my apartment and it seemed unbearably lonely, hostile in its loneliness, my desk and the irrelevant Burroughs, my phone books and directories and census tracks, the paraphernalia of election demographics. I wondered if it mattered who won. I wondered if it mattered to the violinist on the street corner and decided that it didn't. It mattered to me on behalf of the violinist, and to justify the many months of work I had put into analyzing the outcome.

The tavern was cool and smelled pleasantly of beer. There were only a few solitary drinkers distributed along the mahogany bar. The television set was on but the sound was turned low. I lit the panatela and made myself comfortable. In the wet darkness at the rear of the tavern someone was playing the pinball machine, *bing-bing*. Outside it began to rain in earnest. I ordered a draft beer and then a second and a third. Nothing so welcome as a neighborhood tavern at three on a wet Saturday afternoon; in an hour it would begin to fill up, but now it was quiet except for the *bing-bing*.

I had a thousand dollars but I had nothing to do with it. I had no place to spend it. I had an apartment but I didn't want to go to it. I couldn't keep control of my thoughts; they were banging in my head like the pinball. I thought about Professor Karcher, dead in his garage. We had lost touch, and I wondered what he would think of me now. I knew I was exhausted and wondered if soldiers were exhausted after a great battle, unable to control their thoughts. Of course they were, when the adrenaline ran out. I had no adrenaline left. I wondered why I had poured so much of myself into it, becoming an apparatchik; or a picador, goading the beast, weakening it, but not welcome at the kill. "Family only," Bayley had said. Was this the career that Phil Karcher had in mind? What would Katrina say if she sat down at the next stool? My father? Well, forget my father. I did not need Victor's sarcasm. I ordered another beer and tapped the panatela into the glass ashtray in front of me, staring at myself in the mirror back of the bar, my face blue in the light of the Hamm's beer sign. A face governed by reason, or by the environment, a face compatible with those observed on a prosperous street in Eastern Europe, perhaps Hungary.

I could take the thousand dollars and go north by train, to Milwaukee and north of Milwaukee, and when I found a quiet place I'd stop. It was too late for fishing, but the ducks would be flying. I would take a load of books, hole up in a cabin somewhere, and read. Shoot in the morning and read during the day, Karcher's list—Dreiser, Canetti, Conrad's *Youth*. It would be different, reading them for myself instead of for a class, for credit. He must have been sick, and in terrible pain, to take his own life. Gassed. I had never known a suicide. I would write to his widow: Dear Mrs. Karcher, I was so sorry to hear about Phil . . .

I had no idea what to say to her.

Outside, the rain turned to snow, hard little flakes that stung like pellets. I was unsteady on the slippery sidewalk. Rush Street, emptying, was dark in late afternoon. The streetlights winked on, a pale nineteenth-century glow. Hunched against the blowing wind, I walked toward the lake, then north again on my childhood street, a stolid celebration of the bourgeois life, a cozy village close, reclusive at dusk. My breath was pluming in the cold and I smelled stale beer. The brownstones were private and withdrawn, but the lights inside were cheerful with a kind of holiday festivity. Snow was beginning to gather in the cornices and parlor windows, the ledges black with city soot. Above the heavy doors were bas-reliefs, nineteenth-century hieroglyphics representing the lurid passions of the time, Freemasonry, free silver, the Grange, along with other, incomprehensible private enthusiasms, a snake coiled around a golf club, a black-suited businessman impaled on a bull's horns, a Turkish crescent above a Hebrew inscription. I thought I heard a symphony, then I realized I was humming to myself. Everything around me was familiar from another time. I was surrounded by the history of Chicago, indecipherable except for the spare log cabin carved into the stone above the bow window now at hand: Kinzie's dwelling,

Chicago's first, in the year 1820. The snow was softer now and I moved silently on the pavement. I was retracing the route I had taken as a schoolboy, wrapped in mufflers, books under my arm. At the park I looked left, up at our old apartment, half expecting to see my father at the window, a martini in his fist, waiting for the cardinal and his suite. But the lights were dark, the occupants not at home.

In Lincoln Park I followed a young woman in a sealskin coat and high-heeled shoes, the coat sleek and wet with snowflakes. She wore a red beret, a bright spot in the gray park. I was lost in my own thoughts, which now were of the future. The north woods were a bad idea. I touched the envelope containing Bayley's check and decided that when I returned to my place I would call somebody, anybody, and go out for dinner. The Drake or the Buttery, somewhere expensive and dressed-up. Then I was thinking about Washington, whether it was hospitable. After the election I would go to Washington to talk to Bayley's friends. My mother would be disappointed; there would be no one to hold the fort in Chicago. The woman in the sealskin coat turned suddenly, facing me. I had been following too closely and the park was empty. For a moment I thought she would cry out but then she smiled.

"My God," Carole Nierendorf said. "Jack, as I live and breathe."

I had not spoken to her since the afternoon in my apartment more than a year ago. I had seen her occasionally from my window, always walking swiftly, as if she were late for an appointment, never looking up. Once or twice I had seen her at a distance in the park, and she had seen me, but we did not speak. But the last time had been months ago, and I assumed that they had moved away, or perhaps had separated. Now, looking at her, I was glad to see her, but I did not know what to say.

"You were talking to yourself," she said, and gave a little shudder. "It scared me. I didn't know who it was, and there are so many weirdoes around."

"Really talking to myself?"

"Mumble, mumble," she said.

"I had a long lunch," I said.

She sniffed and smiled.

"I like your beret," I said. "And the coat."

"Thanks," she said. "A present from Charles."

"Very glamorous," I said. "What was the occasion?"

"Our anniversary," she said. "Married four years last Tuesday. He bought the coat himself, at Field's. They made him a partner last month, so he was able to buy me the coat. It was very expensive." She stepped back and looked at me critically. "Does wonders, a new hat and coat. You could use one."

I looked down at my raincoat, filthy and frayed around the edges. It had been so long since I had bought anything, for myself or anyone else, that I could not imagine what one cost. "I've been working," I said.

"Really, Jack. You look like a bum."

I laughed. "I suppose I do. So what?"

"You need a haircut. And what does working have to do with it?"

"No time," I said.

"Work," she said with a smile.

I looked at her coat again. "So Charles is a partner. And the law business is prospering?"

"Seems to be, Jack. And politics?"

"Fine," I said. "They gave me a thousand-dollar bonus today."

"My goodness," she said appreciatively. "But the election isn't until next Tuesday."

"Surprised me, too," I said.

"Is he going to win, your man?"

I started to describe the variables, in Chicago and downstate Illinois and elsewhere, watching her eyes slide away. I thought they were glazing, so I smiled, halting in midsentence. "I think he will," I said.

"So everything will've been worth it," she said.

"I learned a lot," I said.

"What did you learn, Jack?"

"I learned that there are people who are smarter than I am."

"Well," she said, smiling at me. "It's a beginning."

We began to walk together through the deserted park. The trees bare of leaves were bending to the wind rushing across the lake, the trees dark against the blowing

121

snow. Carole's red beret was the only spot of color anywhere. She had let her hair grow and in her new sealskin coat she looked like any young married woman from the North Side. The coat put her at a distance from me. I was thinking suddenly about money, deciding that I would need a new coat for Washington. And a suit. And of course a haircut.

I said, "Are things all right with you?"

"They're all right," she said. "We're moving."

"Out of town?"

"Evanston," she said. "Is that considered out of town?"

"Barely," I said.

"That's where we're going," she said. "Charles thought Evanston would be good for the baby. So many weirdoes in Chicago."

"Wait till you get to Evanston," I said.

"Since you asked," she said. "There were a few bad weeks. Bad all around."

"I'm sorry," I said. "I can imagine."

"I doubt it," she said. "I don't mean that unkindly. But you can't because for one thing you're not married, living with someone and sharing a bed." She hooked her arm through mine, firmly, so that I could feel the bone of her forearm. "He couldn't understand it, any of it. Still can't. And then I guess he decided he didn't have to, because one day we stopped talking about it. For weeks we talked of nothing else. Day after day of talking about *it*, why it happened and how and *who*, Jack. And then one day we didn't. And haven't since, though we will again sometime, have to. When it stopped it was a relief, to tell you the truth."

"Did you make any headway?"

"A little," she said.

"I'm glad," I said. "And I'm surprised."

"Charles isn't dumb," she said.

"I didn't mean that," I said. "I know he's not dumb. But I don't think it's a question of IQ. Maybe you ask too much."

"Too much?"

"He isn't going to *approve*, Carole. Why should he?"

122

"Don't be mean," she said. "And that isn't the point."

"If he forgives, that's all you can expect."

"We're so different," she said. "He doesn't *need*, the way I do. Men have a way of dividing themselves up, a piece here and a piece there." We walked along in silence a moment. She said, "And he had his job crisis."

"What was that about?"

"Some *deal*," she said. "He called it a sweet deal. They wanted him to do something and he didn't want to do it because he thought it wasn't right. It was on the edge, he said. Of what was legal." She laughed. "Charles said that in his firm he was the only lawyer. The only man in the firm who knew the law. The rest of them knew aldermen, judges, and county assessors. Policemen, sheriff's deputies. But he knew the law and he told them they'd end up in the clink."

"But they didn't," I said.

"No, it worked out fine. It worked out the way Mr. Mozart promised it would. They all made lots of money. And then Charles was made a partner."

"I met Mozart today," I said.

"Isn't he a sweetheart?" she said. "Isn't he a lamb?"

"Lamb?" I said. "No. Fox."

"Charles is Mr. Mozart's protégé," she said proudly.

I nodded. I could not imagine Elly Mozart and Charles Nierendorf together. "Mozart is the best political lawyer in Chicago."

"That's what Charles said. But I don't know what it means."

"It means you don't have to know any law, and you can spend your whole life . . ." I didn't finish the sentence. I said instead, "Charles is in good hands if it's political law he wants." We were approaching the southern end of the park. Apartment buildings came into view through the snow, accumulating now in shifting patterns on the sidewalk. My arm was warm where it touched her coat. I said, "How are you really?"

"I'm the same, Jack." She turned to look at me, brushing a lock of hair from her forehead, her eyes tearing in the cold. Her coat parted and I saw she was wearing a cashmere sweater and a short blue skirt and knee socks, and pearls; except for the pearls she looked like the old careless Carole. I imagined her body underneath the wrapping. She smiled a half smile, daring me. "The former Carole Harriss from Blackford, Virginia, Tidewater country. Homecoming queen, everyone's friend. Hot. I had the hots for everyone, and everyone had the hots for me." She laughed. "You know what they say about Virginia: Not much future but oh what a past. I'm just the same except I have a sealskin coat and a new apartment in Evanston. Not so far from Northwestern. On Saturday afternoons we can go watch the football game in Dyche Stadium, the Wildcats versus Wisconsin. What do you call them: The Badgers. Charles follows the Badgers. And the new apartment is much bigger, three bedrooms with a modern kitchen and a utility room with a Maytag. There's a nice small park around the corner where the coeds and their beaux come to flirt and play softball in the spring when the weather's warm. And the street is nicer than the one we're on now, and you're not around. That's how I am really, Jack. How are you?"

"I've missed you, too," I said.

"I didn't say that," she said.

I looked at her and she cocked her head, closing her coat.

"Well, we had fun."

"More than fun," I said.

"I've thought about it, too," she said.

"No more than me."

She rocked back and forth, shuddering, eyes down. I heard the creak of her shoes on the hard ground, icing now. "God, it's cold. Is it always this cold? It has been every since I've lived here; it seems like a century in this cold climate, the North." Snow stuck to her beret, white on red. She stuck out her tongue and caught a snowflake, and the sudden blithe animation of her mouth was so charming and unexpected that I laughed out loud. Her small face under the red beret was fresh, the face of a blond coed flirting. I moved to kiss her but she stepped away to the lee of an elm, out of the wind. This was the place where we had watched the Queen, smiling and waving from the back of a a black limousine, her handsome prince at her side. I leaned against the elm, happily falling in love with Carole. "Dear Jack," she whispered, smiling as if she possessed a great secret.

"You," I said.

"Me," she said, moving her shoulders and exhaling, her breath frosty.

"It'll be warmer in Evanston."

She smiled sardonically, sighing, looking at me, rocking back and forth. She put her arms around the tree, hugging it.

"Long-range forecast," I said. "Sunny and warm on Election Day, Machine weather."

"Is that what they say?"

"It's a promise," I said.

She was picking at the tree bark, concentrating on it as a child would. "I won't be here," she said.

"It'll be warm and sunny in Evanston, too," I said.

"I'll be in Blackford, Jack. I'm going to Blackford on Tuesday."

"On Election Day," I said.

"I lied to you a minute ago," she said. "I'm not moving to Evanston. I'm leaving him and taking Betsy. I'm going back home where I belong."

I said nothing for a moment, just stared at her. The park was hugely still, the wind dying, snowflakes suspended. Then she was in my arms and I was smelling her skin and light scent and the damp fur. She did not yield, remaining only a moment, her head light on my shoulder. She was so tiny. I could feel her backbone and the muscles of her back under the fur. Then she looked up at me with her Modigliani eyes, a level stare. "So that's that," she said. "I can't live the way I've been living. I can't do it and keep any part of myself alive, and that's my duty as I see it, leaving him. Going home."

Far away I heard the cry of a police siren.

I said, "Does he know?"

"He would if he *listened*, but he won't listen. They never do."

I said, "Who?"

"Men," she said. "That's one of the things you boys aren't good at, listening. And he doesn't want a wife, he wants something else. Maybe a housekeeper or an accountant. Maybe a sitter for the baby, a mom for the baby to love when he's not around. And he's not around much lately. He doesn't want a warm body, I know that.''

"Divorce,'' I said.

"Yes, of course.''

I looked over her shoulder. Across the park a derelict was rummaging through the trash can, looking for newspapers to fold under his clothes. He was wearing a torn tweed jacket a size too small and khaki chinos, a suburbanite's leaf-raking clothes. The old man paused, watching us incuriously.

She rocked back on her heels. "Old Jack, defender of family values. Come off it.'' She put both hands on my chest, pushing lightly. "What's the point? I could stay on another twenty or thirty years, even forty years, that's how long my parents've been married.'' She smiled. "I was a late child. I was an afterthought. How they loved each other, and still do. Papa comes home for lunch still. And then he takes a nap, he and Mama. Or that's what they say they're doing.'' She giggled into her hand. "They're going to hate this, just hate it. There's never been a divorce in my family except for my mother's brother and he's the black sheep, the family voluptuary.'' She cocked her head, thinking. "They never really took to Charles, though in the beginning that only made me more determined. They made jokes about him, and I used to invent the wildest stories, to make him seem attractive to them. They talked about him behind his back, 'the Badger.' They never got on; and of course he didn't care.'' Her hands were still on my chest. "So I could stay here, with him. He's going to make a lot of money, and it'll be a good life. Everyone wants that. We can move to one of the suburbs, have a house, join a country club. The schools are excellent in the suburbs, and the taxes low. There's no crime and no dirt. There's none of *that*.'' She pointed at the derelict stuffing newspapers under his tweed jacket. "And you and I could start up again.''

"Not likely,'' I said.

"No,'' she said, "not likely. Possible. Charles stays late to work, often. Mr. Mozart has become like a father to him. For a while I thought there was another woman and I'm still not sure there isn't. How do you tell? The other night there was a call, the person hung up when I answered. It's the third time that's happened." She looked at me. "It'd be easy to work out. All the women in the suburbs come into town to shop. I could come in to see you. Or I could find someone else. There are plenty of men around, though most of them are either married or frightened." She cocked her head, grinning. "Or ashamed. Some of them are ashamed." She gave another push with her hands but I didn't give, so she dropped her arms. "I don't blame you, Jack. I did then. I thought you'd become my enemy, worse even than Charles, because I expected it with Charles, and I didn't expect it with you. But I've thought it over and decided it was just one of those things, happens when you think no one's looking. Or even if they are, if it's one of the times when you feel you'll die if you don't live. It was exciting, wasn't it? We were so out of bounds. We were so naughty . . ."

She went on like that in her low voice. I remembered her in bed, rampant, stretching her neck, baring her teeth, eyes squeezed shut, tossing her curls, purring, looking down at me, her eyes suddenly wide open. That hot summer, we were slippery with sweat; hot all day long and hot at night, and when Indian summer came it was still hot. The summer wouldn't give up. I remembered everything, each detail, remembered it even as I was standing in Lincoln Park in the thickening snow, listening to her. I wondered what it was that she had told her parents to make Charles seem more attractive to them.

". . . but, as you say," she said, "not likely."

"I'll come visiting in Blackford."

She disengaged and walked off a few steps. "I'll write you when I get settled."

"My apartment's just a few blocks away," I said suddenly.

She lowered her voice and gave me a shy smile. "I know where your apartment is, Jack."

I returned the smile, but she had me.

"Just checking," she said. "Dat old black magic," she added, and laughed. "Write me," she said.

I said I would come to visit, because I would be living in Washington.

127

"You?" she said. "Leave Chicago?"

"Looks like it," I said. She burrowed her chin into the sealskin coat, only her eyes showing now. She was carnal with or without clothes. I took a step toward her. "I hope Blackford works out for you."

"It will. It always has."

"Always?"

"Almost always."

I said, "What's there, Carole? What is it about Blackford? What's in Blackford?" I believe she was retreating. People didn't smash things up only to go home, the place they started from.

She laughed gaily. "Naughty boys." Then, "I don't know, Jack. It's home, it's sweetness. It's people loving *you*. I don't know, really, but I'm hoping."

"Hoping," I said.

"What's wrong with that?"

"It doesn't seem enough," I said. "It's just a dream, it's black magic."

"Maybe," she said. She was walking away now, and then she turned one last time. "You were right, by the way."

"About what?"

"Mr. Mozart. We had a long conversation. He came to tea. This was a day or two after that day. We had tea, the two of us. He talked and I listened. He wanted to help me and Charles patch things up. He's very kind. He knows more than you'd expect him to know, man of his age. He even knows what he doesn't know, which was a surprise. It was nice. We had a good conversation. I thought he was sexy, just like you said."

"*Mozart?*" I wondered if she'd seduced him.

She smiled enigmatically. "Good luck, Jack."

And she walked away across the frigid park, her chin buried in her coat collar, her shoes scraping the frozen ground; her gait was unmistakable. She passed within a few feet of the derelict, who turned to say something to her. She paused, dug into her purse, handed him some money, and went on—throwing me a mischievous look over her shoulder. The derelict inclined his head, touching his forehead, an Old World gesture; then he drifted off in the opposite direction. In a moment all I could make out was her black sealskin coat and her red beret, now merging with the bare trees, now visible again, undulating in the cold. This was the prairie after all, I though. In 1820 there had been only Kinzie's log cabin on this landscape as bleak and unforgiving as anything in the Ukraine; and fifty years later there was a great city, a city built in a single lifetime; and then there was a fire, so they furiously built another, even greater. But it began with audacious Kinzie and a few Indians on the forked river, the prairie spreading west for a thousand miles, much farther than the eye could see or the imagination conceive.

The wind off the lake freshened, snow flurries whipping around me. I heard the drone of an airplane, low over the water, bound for Meigs. Lights winked on along the park's perimeter, the lights weak and indistinct. They did not point the way. Carole was there, moving through the trees, and then she wasn't. My own desire died. I was motionless, shivering in the cold, unable to move, reluctant to go home. Time itself was stuck. I shuddered, reminding myself: This was Chicago, election year 1960, and it was time to pull out.

PART TWO

'Seventies

1

HALF the wised-up population of the United States went to Washington that winter, willing filings attracted to the great magnet, adventurers drawn east as the restless and dreamy prospectors had been drawn west in 1849, infatuated with El Dorado, loving its spectacle, finding prosperity, staying on. A regnant culture was assembled, part clubhouse, part Park Avenue, with the dizzier aspects of Mayfair and Harvard Yard thrown in. In the winter of 1961 Washington was a kind of Forbidden City suddenly liberated, the Dowager Empress exiled to Gettysburg and the eunuchs to their corporate board rooms. Suddenly Marco Polo was in the Oval Office.

The lapses were still to come, follies of youth and inexperience, an understandable desire for action at all costs; and some of the costs were high. Much later, the capital settled into a Venetian intrigue, exhausted by its excesses and flamboyant development. The clamor and racket ceased, but the echoes were still in the ears of the population; many in the capital were ashamed and stricken, comforting each other as family members customarily do in times of great grief. It seemed that not everything was possible after all. The capital turned a sullen face to the country, stung by the accusation that it had failed and was unworthy of trust, that it had lost its nerve. That was the result of the flunked war and the squalid, inexplicable scandal, all of it so mercilessly public; Washington's cowardly underbelly had been exposed. The wounded city was like an animal blinded by the glare of a light. Frightened, mesmerized, it resolved to hold fast—consolidating, performing quotidian chores, exhibiting a new maturity. It was valuable to know that not everything was possible. Paris knew it and Bonn and London knew it. Now Washington knew it. The structure of things had broken down and the task now was to find a new structure, a new politics that would reflect the new caution. The era of impeccable compromise was over. That had always been Washington's great strength, compromise as both art and science, compromise unsoiled by ideology, compromise as secular religion, Washington's divine synthesis. It had proceeded from the capital's unshakable confidence in itself.

Besieged, we came to resemble the corporate world we had despised and derided. The city grew, the culture thickened, and the custodians multiplied, the government floating on a sea of debt; the world owed Washington a living. The film advanced, the reel accelerated—and in a minute I was in middle age, successful and conspicuous, a President's man. My minute: a congressman passed me along to a senator, an insider's insider so thoroughly a product of the Senate committee system that he was nicknamed "the Camel." I commenced an affair with the Camel's wife, a woman ten years younger than her husband, who understood the city's routine, and understood also the Camel's fierce enthusiasm for it. The Camel wanted to be a chairman, and that was all he wanted. Their married life had suffered, obviously. The Camel wanted one thing and she wanted something else, but that was often the case with two highly motivated people in a cautious, acquisitive city. She was a witty woman, filled with gaiety, and rich; her money had financed the Camel's political career. She was proud of that and proud of him. She was accustomed to having things her own way, and in that she was accommodated by her husband and the city's strange twilight mood. The affair flourished, and we talked of marriage; but she would not leave him, she had put so much into their marriage, and he needed her. And what are your prospects, Jack? We quarreled and the affair was brought to an end; this was about the time the Camel became chairman of his committee. It had been a wonderful affair, yet without consequence.

The Camel handed me off to a cabinet officer in political trouble, and at the end of that tour I was almost as controversial as the secretary. He survived, but it had been a hard win. We became very good friends. For most of a year we had been like an encircled army, though our morale never cracked, living as we were on adrenaline. During this time and later there were other love affairs, more often than not with married women. We attracted each other, drawn by the same appetite. I expected the affairs to lead somewhere but they never did. Arrangements were easily made and unmade, and I came to see married life from an unnatural angle of vision. I was an expert navigator who had interviewed all the best mariners but who had never been to sea, who knew about life topside and below decks, and heard the descriptions of the calms and the tempests but had never felt the deck below his own feet. This was not what I wanted but it was what I had, and I no longer thought of it as good fortune. A friend told me it was the life I needed. Obviously, she said; otherwise you'd make other arrangements, wouldn't you?

Administrations came and went. Interesting times, we thought, disappointing on so many different levels. My career was tidal, now up, now down, and always restless. It was that way generally in the capital, for women as well as men; there were many opportunities as the government grew, maturing. I thought of myself as a man with no fixed address in his private life, unable to find a comfortable domestic niche. My household was my office, and I was industrious. In time I had a place in the White House, my reward, a gift from the grateful secretary, the President's close friend.

One grew older and Washington ceased to be either adventurous or magnetic. It became a capital like any other, prosperous and generally kind to those who shared in the prosperity. It was comfortable living in Washington's neighborhoods, savoring the pretty parks and wide boulevards, and stately night life. We lived on Washington as insects lived on a tree. We were like functionaries everywhere, consolidating what we had and acquiring what we could. The direction of things was no longer so clear, but we adapted, learning, acknowledging that our faith had been uprooted. The winter of 1961, close

enough to touch, now seemed a part of the century before, a personal memory, now sharp, now dim. In its
shadows were fantastic shapes, which in time grew familiar. We looked up one day and discovered that we
were older than the President was that winter, remembering with a smile how young he seemed then; yet we
did not think of ourselves as young, anything but, wised-
up as we were; nobody knew the troubles we'd seen. And
the hilarious thing was, the generation behind us seemed
even older, a hand-me-down generation formidably focused. It was hard to discover what faith had been uprooted during our interesting times; faith seemed not
quite the word. Perhaps the word was rectitude. Whatever it was that had been uprooted, a nervous dissatisfaction had taken its place, and in that way we were an
example to the next generation. No doubt it had always
been there, unspoken and hence unrecognized; much had
remained unspoken. But we were devouring the tree.

In this minute one had oneself become gray and quar-
relsome, triumphantly at one with Washington's culture,
a willing accomplice. We struggled to regain coherence,
coherence a kind of mantra; and as the times blurred
even as they accelerated, people dropped out of the government. The action, as it was called, was elsewhere in
investment banking houses or public relations concerns
or law offices. I envied my married friends with their
children and their mortgages and their prosperous lives
in the private sector. In the old days no one wanted to
live in that sector, which was seen as a kind of peniten-
tiary. I yearned for the liberty of the bourgeois life, and
every time a married friend told me how lucky I was to
be in the arena still, single and without responsibilities,
I yearned for it more, and the creature comforts that went
with it. I owned a small house in Georgetown; how much
more agreeable if the house were larger, with a second
one in Maryland or Virginia. It was difficult to thrive on
a civil servant's salary in the new Washington. But opportunities were everywhere, most of them indistinguish-
able from the government itself; it was the same work,
the difference being that the money you got for it was
colossal, and growing. The city was rich and grew richer
as its political authority declined. The flow of easy money

became a flood, irresistible, saturating, and softening everything it touched.

Listen, there's just a hell of a good man over at the White House. Maybe he's bored, maybe not. I heard he is. Jack Gance, look him over. He's just smarter than a tree fulla owls, knows the Hill and the Triangle and I Street, gives good value, and's absolutely loyal and trustworthy, keeps his mouth shut. Not afraid to say No; more to the point, Jack's not afraid to say Yes. He's a Chicago boy, so you don't have to finish every god damned sentence you start. I'd guess forty, forty-two-five buys you Jack.

It was not all torpor and dissatisfaction. The surroundings were agreeable. I loved the milieu, the corridors of the Executive Office Building, wide, high-walled, marble underfoot. Your heels clicked as you walked. Angular, always in shadows, the corridors were reminiscent of an F. W. Murnau film set, Nosferatu just offstage. There were always odd characters lurking about in the shadows, people from the President's past; relatives, cronies, operators of one sort or another, lobbyists, lawyers, bankers, academics, cultural commissars, corporate bullies, and old soldiers from previous administrations. It was satisfying having an office in the EOB, recognized by the guards, greeted in the corridors, a hurried greeting, everyone busy busy busy. Only the name, and a nod.

"Jack."

"Susan."

"Jack."

"Henry."

Moving at speed around the corner, *click-click*, a near collision.

"Jack, sorry."

"Herman."

"Catch you later in the day?"

"After Bogsat."

The White House is a velvet mousetrap, a mousetrap by Hermès, closing with a Swiss precision, closing with a little furry rustle, closing with the tact of a dutiful lover, closing beautifully, yet closing as decisively as any simple hardware store mousetrap. The mouse doesn't know its back is broken, doesn't know it's wounded, until the day it looks up, tries to move, struggles, can't budge; but so what, the surroundings are so pleasant and secure and one fine day the Man will be defeated or retired or assassinated and then it'll be time, say bye-bye. Meanwhile, listen to the sedative Swiss *tick-tock*, listen to the rustle, enjoy the light touch of the dutiful lover.

A silver coffee service came with my office, the silver dating from FDR's first term. It's a beautiful thing, little pots for the cream and sugar, the urn curvy and chased, all of it supported by a heavy silver tray. The cups and saucers bear the presidential seal. No one knows I have this; my rank does not entitle me to it. I have coffee at eight each morning as my secretary, Marie, and I plan the day, sitting together on the couch under portraits of John Quincy Adams and John Jay, their Yankee faces not amused, clashing with my seductive German nudes, Schmidt-Rottluff's *Zwei Mädchen*, and one of Kirchner's Berlin streetwalkers, a Slavic face over a torso as slim as a railroad spike. The photograph of Katrina Lauren sits on the credenza back of my desk, the photo looking like a portrait from the nineteen thirties, a caustic study in light and shade; tilted, she is looking directly at potato-faced JQA, and every time I look at her I am consoled. Schmidt-Rottluff's nudes remind me of her, the tilt of their chins and their full breasts, two young women exchanging confidences; they are smiling, soon to dissolve into laughter.

This is always a quiet moment and I turn off the table lamps so that we can sit in plain daylight, refracted through the eight-foot windows. We are on the seventh floor of this elegant building, the Executive Office Building, formerly the War Department. I can see the White House lawn from my desk, its hedges and bushes and great elms. The atmosphere today is of a great country house, Lord and Lady Uh temporarily absent, up to London for the Chelsea Flower Show or Newmarket for the thoroughbred sales.

Marie is tidying up, preparing to put the silver out of sight. My predecessor in the previous administration was an old friend; when he learned I was to have his office he told me about the silver, its provenance, and the necessity for keeping it Top Secret, Nodis. Marie and I are talking quietly of this and that. There's nothing particular on the agenda this morning except for the regular Tuesday Bogsat.

"Look at your message sheet, Jack. Tap Gobelin called last night after you left."

"I see it," I said. "What did he want?"

She said, "I told him you were in a meeting."

Custom. In the White House, you must always be seen to be working at the public business, no time for rest. "You don't have to do that with Tap. He finds out, Christ, he'll print it and first damned thing you know we've got a cover-up and I'm out on my ass, Gancegate. And you'll be responsible. What did he want?"

"Wouldn't say. Very mysterious."

"Shit," I said.

"You don't think he knows about Willard?"

"Doubt it," I said. "Doubt it, but you never know." Willard was an assistant secretary at Commerce who was announcing his resignation, ill health, wants to spend more time with his family, et cetera, except that a grand jury in Pittsburgh would present an indictment Friday charging Willard with bribery, fraud, and extortion.

"I said you'd call him."

"After Bogsat, I will."

"He said you'd know what it was about."

I shrugged. I had no idea.

Marie giggled, moving her head in a way that reminded me of the two German girls. "It makes the boys so nervous when Tap calls."

"Who was in the office?"

"Herman," she said. "Sniffing around." I smiled. "He began to twitch and walk around my desk, trying to read the mail upside down. That god damned Gobelin, blah blah blah. Bolshevik. Jack shouldn't talk to him. Word gets around, he knows Gobelin, President won't like it. How often does Jack talk to Gobelin anyway? And what do they talk about?"

"The price of pussy and the time of day," I said.

"Watch your language, Jack."

"Herman's an idiot," I said. I looked at my watch, rising. "I'm off."

"Happy Bogsat," she said.

"I'll call Gobelin when I get back."

The meeting went longer than usual because the President was out of town and things were quiet. Five of us stood around drinking coffee and trading information. Not many items on the agenda but at the end of the meeting I had three assignments, two of them simple. The hard one had to do with a former law partner of the White House chief of staff. The lawyer wanted something and my assignment was to get it for him, no fuss and no broken crockery. Marie put her head in the door and said I had a telephone call. "Your brother; he said it was important." Sam and I had not spoken since Christmas.

I walked out of the conference room and hurried down the hall and through Marie's office to my own. All the buttons on the phone were lit, as usual. Marie said, "On five," so I punched the button and picked up.

Sam said without preamble, "Have you talked to Mother?"

I said No, suddenly tense. I was leafing through the pile of pink call slips and saw the note in Marie's neat hand: *Call your mother in Florida.*

He said, "Dad's had a stroke. Mother tried to get you earlier this morning, but you were unavailable."

I said, "How bad is it?"

"They're not sure. They think it's pretty bad."

"When did it happen?"

"Last night. He came home from bridge, wasn't feeling well."

"Christ," I said. "How's Mother?"

"Very upset, obviously."

I said, "Wait a minute." I put Sam on hold and buzzed Marie. I told her to cancel all appointments and make a reservation on the first available flight to Sarasota. I always kept an overnight bag with toilet articles and a fresh change of clothes in my office closet. I asked her to arrange for a car and to notify the airline to hold the plane if necessary. I said that my father was ill and she said that she was sorry, she'd get right on it.

"Yes," I said to Sam. I heard his irritated breathing over the telephone. "Which hospital?"

He told me, and gave me the room number.

"I'm leaving right away," I said.

"She was upset when she couldn't get through to you. She said it was hard getting through to your office."

"Yes," I said.

"And when she did, they said you were in a meeting."

"That's right, I was."

"So she left her name, she didn't want to disturb you."

"It was only the Tuesday Bogsat," I said.

"She speculated that you were in with the President."

"No, I wasn't in with the President." I turned to look out my office window at the old mansion across the way. Gardeners were at work raking leaves. The lovely old house looked almost deserted. A gray autumn rain had begun to fall and a bitter breeze scattered the leaves. It was Chicago weather. I watched a Secret Service man poke his head out the side door, look at the rain, and stifle an enormous yawn. "The President's in Europe, the summit. We're having a summit meeting with the Reds and he's in Geneva, along with about everyone else in the government."

"Well," Sam said. "Mother probably forgot about the summit meeting. What with this and that in Sarasota, I guess she forgot about the President in Europe. To tell the truth, I did too. So because she was unable to reach you she called me at the office. And my office reached me out here."

"Where are you?" I asked.

"Nantucket," Sam said. "I won't get away until tomorrow. And we're socked in with fog anyway, can't see your hand in front of your face."

"Pea soup, I'll bet."

"That's right, Jack. Nothing's flying. Tell me something. Couldn't they even get a message to you?"

"Yes," I said. "I just got it. The meeting ran late." The rain was driving hard against my office windows but the sky was strangely bright. I said, "Is he going to die?"

There was a shocked silence and then Sam sighed. "They haven't made a complete diagnosis," he said primly.

"Well, Sam. Since you've talked to Mother, and I haven't. What's your sense of it?"

"My sense of it is that Mother's very upset, and that he's very sick."

"All right," I said. "I'll see you there. When the fog lifts on Nantucket."

"I'll let Mother know," he said.

"No need," I said.

"She'll want to know," he said, "And if you're leaving right away, as you claim, you won't have time—"

I thought, What the hell. "I'll call her from the car, Sam."

There was a small irritated silence and I thought he had rung off, but then he said, "Just my curiosity. If it isn't a state secret. What's a Bogsat?"

I smiled. It was a common acronym around Washington, dating from the Kennedy administration. "Bogsat," I said. "Bunch of Guys Sitting Around a Table."

"Thanks, Jack. Thanks a lot."

"Always at your service," I said, and hung up.

In the event, there was no need for Brother Sam to leave socked-in Nantucket. Victor was out of the hospital in two days, his doctors revising their diagnosis from stroke to neurological "event," which might or might not recur. The doctors were frankly puzzled, and would say only that for a period of twelve hours the old man had apparently been incapacitated. Of course Victor did not help them much, being by turns silent and irascible. Is he always like this? one of the doctors asked me. Almost always, I said. The doctor's look invited further comment, but I refused to be drawn. I said that my father was a difficult man, to which the doctor raised his eyebrows in agreement.

Later in the afternoon on the day my father returned from the hospital we sat on their terrace in the damp heat, watching the boats in Sarasota Bay. We were drinking iced tea, saying very little. I had spent an hour in their bedroom on the telephone to Washington. My mother was fussing over Victor, until he gave her a sharp look and she stopped. I was eager to get back to my office and the thick of things. At seven o'clock I went inside to watch the news. According to the network, the summit was proving a qualified success, the talks were frank,

142

useful, and productive, though there were as yet few details. There was film of the President and the General Secretary, both of them looking dour, though the commentator's word was "businesslike." I tried to read between the lines but it was impossible, and I concluded that the words meant what they said until the details were released, if they ever were.

"You have anything to do with that?"

I turned. This was the first full sentence my father had spoken to me. He was standing behind me, watching the television over my shoulder. I laughed and shook my head.

"Jesus, he's an idiot."

"Who?" I said.

"The President. The person you work for. Your employer."

"No, he's not an idiot."

Victor looked me up and down, measuring, offering a sardonic smile. Then he went to the liquor cabinet and began to mix cocktails, measuring the gin into a silver shot glass and using tongs to fetch the ice. He was humming to himself, some long-ago show tune. When they moved to Florida, Victor's health had begun to improve almost immediately. He liked the syrupy weather. He gained weight and lost the dazed look he had taken with him from prison. His gray hair, so lank and lifeless then, was now white and bristly. It was almost a military sidewall. He was very tan, and with his erect carriage and brusque manner he had the demeanor of a retired marine colonel. I was conscious of my own indoor pallor and civilian fallibility. His smile seemed to say, Jack, when are you going to grow up?

He was arranging olives and lemon peel on a silver dish, working as carefully as a scientist in a laboratory. "What's he like?"

I thought a moment, and said I didn't know him really, which was true. I said, "I like his wife."

My father looked at me sourly. "I don't mean him. I mean the other one. The Red."

"I have no idea. How would I know?"

"I thought they made up personality profiles." He had poured the gin into a shaker and was stirring counterclock-

143

wise. "I read something about it in the paper. I thought that's what the spies did, over at that—installation. That billion-dollar palace they have. I thought they had computers that would analyze a personality."

"I don't know anything about it," I said.

"Well, don't they distribute that stuff in the White House? Where you work."

"Actually, I work in the Executive Office Building. But even if I were physically in the White House I would not be cleared for that sort of information. Even if there is such a thing as you describe, which I doubt." In fact, CIA did put together personality profiles. I had once tried to persuade a friend to gear up the computers on a senator who was giving us fits but he had looked at me and said, No no no no no no. That was something you could go to jail for, he said. And the "profiles" weren't worth a damn. I wasn't going to tell Victor any of that, however.

"That shows how much you know," he said.

I looked at him but he turned back to the cocktail tray. Without another word he picked it up and went out on the terrace. The news was over, so I switched off the television and followed him. He handed my mother a martini, straight up, olive and twist. He handed me mine on the rocks; he had splashed gin from the cocktail shaker, as if a martini on the rocks was beneath his attention. Then he poured his own, straight up from the silver shaker. He and my mother were drinking from traditional martini glasses, giving the terrace the look of a nineteen twenties verandah, Gibbsville or West Egg. My mother was idly flipping the pages of *Vogue*. Occasionally she'd stop turning pages and smile, looking at a young model in diamonds and a black evening gown, the model as pretty as she was once. She would smile and nod her head, turning the page, looking at it sideways.

Victor said, "They tried it on me, when I was in the clink." He stared at me over the rim of his glass, beading in the heat. He took a sip and gave a little satisfied grunt.

He had never spoken of his life in prison, had never referred to it in any way; and it took me a moment to understand the reference. I said, "A personality profile?"

"Yes," he said. "But it didn't work out for them. It didn't work out at all. I was smarter than the swami. I knew all about Rorschach tests. I imagine they're a good deal more subtle now, more refined in their deviltry. It was simple enough. Tit for tat, god damn it." He was speaking softly and I had to lean forward to hear. "After a while the swami caught on and asked what it would take to get my cooperation. I told him I wanted to play bridge, and named the three gents I wanted to play bridge with. There was a gent from East Saint Louis and another from Springfield and the one from Winnetka, good bridge player. I called him the Big Noise from Winnetka." Victor paused again, taking another sip from his glass, the glass small and fragile in his huge hand. "And the swami said all right, he'd arrange it. And he did. He thought I was an interesting case; he'd never come across anyone like *me*. He had a grant from somebody and was connected to the governor. The governor was his patron. So he got whatever he wanted. They didn't give a damn anyway."

"So you cooperated."

"Up to a point."

"What was it they wanted?"

"They were interested in a certain type of criminal."

I said, "You weren't a criminal."

He looked at me a long moment without speaking. My mother had stopped looking at *Vogue* and was now sitting quietly with her drink, listening. She blew a smoke ring, the ring perfect for a moment, sailing over the railing before it broke up. I wondered if she knew about Victor and the swami, the Rorschach tests, and the rest of it, "the Big Noise from Winnetka." If she did, she gave no sign. She was staring out over the bay, where the boats rocked gently at anchor, their lights cheerful and beckoning.

He said, "Jesus Christ, Jack."

My mother said, "Honey," a warning to me.

"Sorry," I said.

She said, "Look at the boats, Victor. They're so pretty, it reminds me of the time near Charlevoix." She blew another smoke ring in the heavy air.

Victor stared silently at me.

I turned to look at the bay. The apartment was on the fourth floor. A narrow park separated the building from the water but the boats looked close enough to touch. A few bars of popular music rose from the water; the yachtsmen were watching television; each boat had its point of blue fluorescence. I wanted my father to continue but the atmosphere on the terrace was charged, his anger a physical thing like Mother's smoke ring.

He said, "What did you think Stateville was, a reward for good citizenship?"

I said, "I have never thought of you as a criminal."

"It's a good thing you never had a personality profile done. You'd've flunked."

"Goodness, it's warm," my mother put in. Then, brightly: "How was the summit, honey?"

"He doesn't know anything about it," Victor said.

I said, "I guess it's going fine, Ma."

Victor rose and went inside and we heard him fussing with the ice bucket and the bottles. My mother and I looked at each other. She smiled vaguely and shook her head. Her look said, He's not himself. Victor came back to get the tray, and in a moment had returned with fresh drinks and a dish of peanuts. One of the yachts in the distance had slipped its mooring and was motoring out past the breakwater. Victor watched the boat go, leaning forward in his chair, his elbows on his knees and his fingers wrapped around the cocktail glass. It was his characteristic posture, as aggressive in its way as his scowl and his sarcasm. He looked like an animal waiting to spring, and, watching him, I felt a powerful tug back into my childhood, the apartment on the Near North Side, the cardinal's mansion and the gondola-shaped Cadillac, "Miss Otis Regrets" on the phonograph in the evenings, the Lincoln Park greensward, and the flat, placid lake beyond. All this went in and out of my mind in an instant, but the atmosphere was changed. He smiled suddenly, turning to my mother. "It isn't anything like Charlevoix."

"It's so damp here, I know. I was looking at the boats at anchor, so peaceful. And the fact that there's no breeze. Charlevoix was so cozy. This big harbor, it's more like Chicago, Belmont and the Columbia Yacht

Club." She reached out and touched his arm. "It's been a long time since Charlevoix."

"Since just after the war." He looked at me. "Do you remember Charlevoix?"

"Vaguely," I said.

"I think we took you once when you were a kid, the summer after we stopped going to Big Lake."

"That sounds right," I said.

"My father and I used to go to Charlevoix on the boat, fishing for walleye and muskies. Your mother and I went a few times after the old man died, before we sold the boat. Big damned thing, more trouble than a kid. Remember the name of the boat?"

"No," I said.

"El Baton," he said.

"Yes," I said. "I remember." My grandfather was a great music lover.

Victor smiled coldly. "It's 'notable' spelled backward."

I said, "What ever happened to Carl Fahr?"

"He's still there," my mother said.

"Same house, same everything," my father said.

"Practicing law?"

"Practice is right," Victor said. "Carl never played, only practiced. He practiced for the Mob, that's how he practiced."

"Victor," my mother said.

"And probably still is even though he's older'n Christ. He's older than I am."

"He didn't represent the Mob," I said.

"He sure as hell did," my father said.

"Some property things," my mother said.

"I always liked Carl," I said.

"Poor Carl," my mother said.

"Everyone liked Carl," my father said. "And Carl liked everyone. That was the god damned trouble."

I said, "Why 'poor Carl'?"

"I don't think he's had a very happy life," she said.

I said nothing to that.

"It's been happy enough," my father said. "He made a bundle off the Mob. But the hell with it. Who wants to talk about Carl Fahr?" He turned to Mother. "In Charlevoix there was the scent of pines, remember? There were pine forests all the way to the Arctic Circle. That was so many, many years ago.'' He sipped his drink, frowning, but when he spoke again his voice was almost cheerful. He described the resort towns of Michigan: Saugatuck and Holland and Mackinac Island, and Door County in Wisconsin. There were other towns but he'd forgotten their names. It was Prohibition then but there was plenty of bootleg in the Upper Peninsula.

"I wonder what it's like now?" my mother said.

I said, "It's like New Jersey."

Victor was silent a moment. Then, "Remember that time, Capone was in the slip next to ours. It must have been 'twenty-nine, 'thirty. We'd only been married a year and we didn't know who he was until the harbormaster filled us in. Capone had a chippie with him and they listened to opera all night on one of those windup phonographs.'' Victor leaned forward, peering into the darkness. "The locals came to pay their respects, was there anything they could do for Mr. Capone, make his stay more pleasant. Scarface Al didn't even invite them aboard. They stood on the dock and he sat on the fantail, listening to them and nodding. Smoking his damned cigar, the chippie in his lap. He couldn't have cared less. Quite a scene.''

My mother laughed quietly, remembering. "Goodness, she was so young. Scarcely more than a child.''

"Capone's cigar smothered the scent of pines.''

"We used to have a snapshot of him. I took it with the Kodak when he wasn't looking.''

Victor smiled. "The gent in the cell next to mine in Stateville used cologne. He was a nancy, that's how he got on. Everyone got on in some way, and that's how he got on. Not that he had much choice. He doused himself with cologne each night. It was sickly sweet stuff but there was something about the odor that reminded me of Charlevoix. Isn't that the damnedest thing? In the morning most of it would wear off, you know, evaporate. There'd be only this slight aroma, but it would be enough to remind me of Charlevoix, such a pretty place, so— chaste. The two of us on Dad's yacht, drinking real Scotch.''

"It's around here someplace. I had it in an album."

"That almost broke me, the nancy and his cologne."

I said, "How do you mean?" Victor shrugged and I went on, "Tell me about it, can you?"

He said, "No."

We three were quiet then. Mother blew another smoke ring but a breeze had come up and it scattered before it reached the railing. I wanted to find a way back into the conversation. My father had never spoken about Joliet, and of course I had never asked him. Ours was a conservative family of pauses and silences, privacy protected as other families protected an inheritance or a scandal. Rage was husbanded, it being too essential to broadcast indiscriminately; and it seemed all the more titanic for being buried so deep, though never so deep as to be inaccessible. This was the legacy of the frontier, and not uncommon in the Midwest: you did not interfere, and you did not want to be interfered with. You kept yourself in rein. Explanations were never "owed." They were given or not, depending. I grew up alert to nuance, a certain vocal pitch and tempo meaningless to outsiders but significant to me; it was the inaudible high-pitched whistle that animals hear and respond to. My father's life in Joliet had always been a mystery to me, except for the bridge games and, now, the Rorschach tests and the nancy's cologne. I suspected that this was all I was going to get, and in the context of my family it was something of a miracle that I got that much. As to how he almost broke—the details, the facts of the matter—I could only guess. I would continue to do what I had done all my life, listen for the meaning behind ordinary words and phrases. The truth was, my father had pulled himself together by main force of will. His life, his responsibility, his material. To understand oneself was after all the severest test of character; and there was no way back into the conversation.

After a moment, Victor rose and stepped to the railing, his hands in his pockets, his eyes narrowed in thought. He rocked back on his heels, looking at the stars in the thick Florida sky, then lowering his gaze to the bay, the park, and the palm trees at the edge of the beach and the boats beyond.

He said, "How do you like it?"

I almost asked him what he meant, but I knew what he meant. He meant the government, politics, and the White House. I said, "I like it most of the time. Sometimes I wonder where it leads to, except a heavier title, more power, and more money. I don't care for the form of it. I've been thinking," I said, but let the thought hang.

"What do you mean, 'the form of it'? What does that mean?"

I explained about the hierarchy, the long hours, taking care never to be far from the telephone—though the White House switchboard could find you wherever you were, and midnight and weekend calls were a sign of status. "The President wants you to . . ." And the siege mentality, similar to military units in wartime. You had tremendous loyalty to your particular unit. It was like being in love, and led to its own private language, a means of discouraging outsiders, keeping them in the dark at arm's length. GMT followed the Tuesday Bogsat. GMT, Greenwich Mean Time, named for the chief of staff, a lawyer from Connecticut. He got the junior staff out of the room so that he could speak candidly about what had to be done to whom. The Connecticut lawyer had a mean streak and a long memory and a list of enemies, and jargon from the board room and the Round Hill Club via Yale. Marie and I did not like him—he was ignorant of everything but the habit of command—but he was the President's man, and we had a loyalty to the President. So he would say, "The President wants you to . . ." and we would do it.

I looked at my mother, smiling an apology for her telephone call and my secretary's failure to interrupt the Tuesday Bogsat.

Victor said, "And what does he want you to do?"

This and that, I said. Make a phone call, cut a curb. When the call came, you dropped whatever you were doing and did what the President wanted or what the chief of staff or the special assistant wanted; it amounted to the same thing. When they stopped calling at inconvenient times, you knew you were in disfavor, probably

150

on the way out. It was a signal. White House doo-dah, White House stagecraft, White House naturalness.

"All the way from Chicago," he said.

I laughed. It wasn't as far as he thought.

"And Sam," Victor said. "All the way to Boston."

I looked at him warily. I didn't know what he was getting at.

"Sam fixes up people's estates, you know. They have a little problem with taxes or a prodigal son or a half-assed daughter, he figures out a way to shelter the money and cut them out of it. He camouflages things. That's what he does and he's very well paid for it. Very well paid, he's at the top of his profession in Boston, one of the top ten, wouldn't you say?" He turned to my mother but she didn't reply, wasn't even looking at him at that moment. She was lighting another cigarette, and I could see her fingers trembling. "I always knew that Sam would be a tremendous success in the legal profession; he's got the eye for it, and the self-confidence. Sam was always very good with money. Sometimes he wasn't so good with people, but for a lawyer it's an eye for the fine print that counts, a man who can look at a thicket of language and find a path through it, like Daniel Boone or Kit Carson. He's a kind of scout, a paleface scout. He knows how to screw people eight ways from Sunday, my Sam. He's just like me."

My mother threw down her cigarette. "He isn't just like you." Her voice was hard as iron. "He isn't like anyone. And he isn't your Sam. Or mine either. He isn't like any member of this family, so never say that again, Victor. He's a little prick. I always thought that was a good name for a man, prick. Prick," she said it again, louder. She wasn't looking at Victor or at me but at the water below. She was sending her words over the railing, where they dropped, falling, heavy as they were. "You bring them into this world and you love them, but that doesn't mean you have to *like* them, and I don't. And that's as it should be, Victor, because he doesn't like me, he doesn't like you, and he doesn't like Jack. He probably doesn't like his wife or his children, either, but I wouldn't know about that. And I don't like him, the prick. He's a weasel. He measures

151

people by the depth of their bank accounts, and their respectability. He knows nothing of life the way it *is*. He doesn't have anything to do with this family. He can't find the time for us, because we don't fit in. So don't say that again, Victor."

"All right," my father said.

"He's a stranger to us," she said.

"Yes," my father said.

She had hardly moved during this extraordinary declaration; I had never heard anything like it from her. She was a woman who preferred to paper things over, and I had often thought of her emotions as a series of beautifully wallpapered rooms, floral patterns, scenes of the English countryside. My father and I were silent, abashed, waiting for her to continue—but she had said what she had to say. Now she turned, dipping her head, and said to me, "You've had a fine career, Jack. You should be proud of yourself."

I mumbled thanks and said something to the effect that it was all right, nothing special.

"Yes, it is," she said. "It's very special."

Victor raised his eyebrows. "The White House is nothing special?"

I said, "There are a lot of people in the White House, or attached to the White House. Hundreds. Political people, money people, legal people, academics, military. It's not like Lincoln's time, two secretaries and one of them had to be on the payroll of the Commerce Department because Congress wouldn't approve his salary."

"Isn't that interesting," my mother said.

I was only warming up. "Honest Abe's bloated bureaucracy . . ."

Victor was nodding slowly and I knew he wasn't listening. I thought he was thinking about Sam, prick and weasel. His jaw muscles were working and he was gripping the terrace railing, his knuckles white with the effort. "I couldn't be bothered," he said. He looked down at his shoetops, his head dangling between his forearms; it looked as if his neck were made of rubber. "There was a period in Chicago, four, five years, maybe it was longer, I've forgotten. It was a long time." He looked away, pursing his lips, deep within himself; this had nothing to do with Brother Sam, and I leaned closer to him, not wanting to miss a word. "I was sick of everything, sick to death of the hustle, sick of the grab. Sick of my business, tired of everything. I was sick of you. I was tired of signing my name to things. I was no longer self-reliant." He looked up and smiled as if he had made a joke. "That was what I did all day long, *sign my name to things.* Deeds, mortgage contracts, leases. Whatever it was, I felt that every time I signed my name I was signing away my life." He made a little erratic motion with his fingers, a flourish of a signature. "I felt. I felt I was surrounded by the city, and I couldn't fight my way out of it. I had gotten lost in the city. And after a while I didn't do the things I'd agreed to do, what you had to do in order to get on in Chicago. They warned me, but I said: The hell with you. Get me if you can." He looked at me accusingly. "I didn't do this and that. I didn't cut the curbs."

My mother said, "Victor," in a soft voice.

"It's all right," he said. The telephone rang suddenly, its bell sharp in the still night. No one moved to answer it and after five rings the caller gave up. Only once before could I remember not answering a ringing telephone, but I knew that if I answered this one my father would stop talking, and I would never know the this and that which he didn't do, the curb that wasn't cut.

He said, "One winter I didn't leave the apartment for six weeks. It was that damned cold winter, the lake froze, god damn near to Holland. Did all my business from the apartment that winter. Business went to hell. God, I hated them." He turned heavily and I could see his tongue darting like a serpent's between his lips. "One day I looked up, the tax men were at the door. The bankers followed the tax men and the lawyers followed the bankers. The police followed the lawyers, or maybe it was the other way around. Someone tipped them. Never found out who, and oh how I tried. That period, there were a hell of a lot of blue suits talking at me. Every time I looked up there was another blue suit, handing me a piece of paper that required a sig-

153

nature. The police took me out of the apartment in handcuffs, quite a scene in the elevator. And then I was sitting in a cell in Stateville playing bridge in the afternoons and smelling Charlevoix's pines in the morning, except it wasn't pines, it was a nancy's cologne. I closed my eyes and remembered the harbor, the boats; and when the swami gave me the Rorschach tests I'd look at the inkblots and say, sloop yawl ketch cruiser catboat *elephant*. That backed him up. It made his whole god damned day." He stopped talking and turned away.

"Who tipped them?" I asked.

"I don't know," he said. "It doesn't matter now."

I agreed with that; and suddenly I didn't care. I wanted him to go on, to remember what it was about Charlevoix, the old houses, the water flat and cold, broiled perch and real Scotch in the evenings; I wondered if he and my mother lay head to head on the deck of the boat, looking at the stars. I wanted him to remember it all and give voice to the memory so that I could see him again as a young man, a newlywed with his pretty young bride, lying on the deck of his boat listening to a windup phonograph.

He spoke directly to me: "And seeing that fat slob with his chippie in his lap, blowing smoke at the sky, on the fantail of his yacht, receiving the powers that be. *Christ*." He shook his head, straightening, still looking at me. I did not avoid his eyes and I remembered the judge's words and my father's reaction to them, and his cold stare as they led him from the courtroom. I remembered my own dull confusion, my mother and I sitting stiff as statues, watched by everyone; and what I was thinking, what I was unwilling to admit then and later, was this: How could you do it to *us*?

He said, "All those years, I remember every detail. He wore black shoes with black socks; black socks with red clocks. He had rings on his fingers and two scars on his left cheek, the fat slob. Every time I thought of Charlevoix I thought of him, too. That boat was a cathouse."

"Dad," I began.

"They got him two years later."

"Yes," I said, knowing what was coming.

"Income tax evasion. They couldn't nail him for murder or extortion or prostitution or bootlegging, so they nailed him for income tax evasion. He got eleven years, although he didn't serve eleven years. And when he died, it was just after the war, in which he did not serve either, aldermen offered to be pallbearers. Congressmen, judges. They had to restrict access to the funeral, the whole damned city of Chicago would've showed up." I laughed out loud; he had his witty side. "And then you went to work for them."

"Victor, please," my mother said.

"I didn't go to work for the Mob," I said.

"I guess you thought it would be secure, the good life. I guess you thought they couldn't get you, the way they got me. But they will, Jack."

"I didn't go to work for the Mob," I said again.

"Same god damned thing," he said.

"No, it isn't."

"What's the difference? They're all grafters and con men."

"They're not all grafters," I said, cutting him off. I was furious. Who did he think he was? "And it isn't nineteen thirty. And Capone's dead. Charlevoix isn't Charlevoix anymore. The yacht's gone. And you didn't pay your taxes so you went to jail." I was trembling with anger. "And we took the consequences."

"Stop it, Jack!" My mother looked at me fiercely.

"Tell him to stop it. He started it."

"He's trying to tell you something," she said.

"He's telling me I'm a criminal."

Victor smiled broadly. "You making any money, working for them?"

That was unexpected. I shrugged. "Getting by."

"President's staff, all got raises. I read about it. Can't attract good people to the government if you don't pay them well. Mortgages, children in private schools. That was the argument, so you all got raises."

"That's right," I said. "We all got raises."

"I was trying to save my business, back then. I thought I could do it with numbers, move them around. Eddie

Snethan was a wizard with figures, a sleight-of-hand man. He thought they could be made to understand, at the trial. He wanted to tell them everything about my business and how I felt about it, just spread the dirty linen everywhere. It would've made me look like a fool. So I stopped Eddie. I wonder what ever happened to him?'' Victor paused, staring into the middle distance. ''I liked the idea of building things in Chicago, buildings, office buildings, apartment buildings. The land and the architect and the contractor, you fit them together like a jigsaw and at the end of it you had something. People lived in it or worked in it, made things in it or sold things from it. Loved that little business, and then they stuck it to me.'' He looked away and the silence thickened, broken only by the scratch of flint and the hiss of butane, my mother lighting her cigarette, looking at me through the smoke. ''You've got to put it together properly and that's where Eddie Snethan came in.'' Victor paused again, thinking. ''They don't allow you any mistakes and you'd better have your conversation with the right party to make sure you don't. In Chicago, everyone's in for a slice. Sweet little business, though. I managed it out of my hat. Probably that was the trouble. Remember that apartment building, the one on Wrightman? Hell of a nice building, pretty fenestration. That dopey widow's walk on the roof. All those city permits.'' Victor turned to look at my mother and then seemed to decide something, for he sighed heavily. His life went into the sigh, a kind of last will and testament. He sipped his drink and then looked over at me and said mildly, ''Do you go to Chicago much?''

''Hardly ever,'' I said.

''I thought Chicago'd be important to you.''

''It is, but it isn't my assignment.''

''Just as well,'' he said. ''It's finished, you know.''

''Chicago's finished?''

''It'll go belly-up.''

I smiled. ''Don't tell that to City Hall.''

''We used to get along without a City Hall. Hell, it was there but it didn't mean anything. White House didn't mean anything either except as a kind of monument, like

Lincoln's Memorial. Something for the tourists to look at. There was just enough government to keep the peace. Barely. Sometimes.''

I leaned forward, listening. It was like hearing the voice of the frontier, the real one.

He said, ''We got taken over. It was a successful take-over bid.''

I said, ''The government took over the country?''

He said, ''They wanted it and they got it. Only god damned thing the government's good for is to start a war. That's what happened in 'forty-one. War got us out of the Depression. It was a hell of a high price to pay.''

''Well,'' I said.

''My business did well,'' he said.

''Because of the war.''

''And it'll happen again.''

''No,'' I said.

''Who's going to stop it? That idiot you work for? That idiot and his summit? Don't give me that. Believe that and you'll believe anything.'' He looked away, and then with an effort pulled back. ''My beautiful little business,'' he said. ''You don't remember the way things were.'' Then, ''Oh, Christ, Jack. You're such an innocent.''

''Me?'' I said, stung. That was one thing I wasn't.

''You,'' he said, as if that settled everything. He extended his hand to my mother, and she rose, un-winding. She carefully extinguished her cigarette in the ashtray. He said, ''Lose your self-confidence, you lose everything. You must be self-reliant.'' They stood together in the darkness, then began to move into the interior of the apartment. For the first time I noticed the elephants, arrayed now on a low coffee table in the corner of the room, and the letter from Mary Lincoln to Iva Jackeson over the upright piano. My mother switched on a light. She had her arm around his waist, supporting him. I heard their footsteps, muffled on the carpet. At the door to their bedroom he turned, having one last thing to say. ''I hated it when you joined them. I thought you'd forgotten where you came from, and the principles of this family. And I think you have. Don't expect that they'll protect you. Don't

157

expect that you'll be safe. Don't expect them to be kind. Don't *expect*.'' And then the door closed and I was left alone in the silence. It seemed to me that the silence spread to the limits of the known world. Even the stars faded, dim and undistinguished in my blurred vision.

2

I took a handful of peanuts from the dish and made myself another drink. When that was finished I went into the kitchen for more ice. I drank another martini and a third, sitting on the balcony and thinking about my father and the life he had led and the lessons it had taught him, he who was nine-tenths below the surface; as I was; as we all are. They were hard lessons, and they were not my lessons, but I could not find much to contradict, either. I had never expected utopia, and I did not believe in happy endings. I had expected some protection and had received it, for whatever it was worth. My father was the other side of Professor Karcher, not that that explained very much. One came from an old frontier, the other from a very old frontier; both were far in the past.

I was watching the yachts, the points of blue fluorescence winking off one by one. I had been thinking about my early days in Chicago, the university and what came later, Katrina and Katrina's accident, and my withdrawal. It was as if these events had happened to someone else, a dear friend or relative—the seminar, the nights in my apartment and hers, comedy at the Proletariat, her account of Berlin in the war, and spring break in Fort Lauderdale. And then Karcher and all Karcher had meant to me, and Bayley and Bayley's friends, and the summer of 1959. I still had the Burroughs, tucked away now in a closet; and every time I looked at it I thought of Carole Nierendorf. Somehow I had lost touch with all that, the first skirmishes in a long campaign before the objectives had been defined and the tactics tested under battlefield conditions. It was a campaign that had brought me to an office with eight-foot-high windows and a silver coffee service, a Bogsat on Tuesdays and an occasional hand-written note from the chief executive himself, not to mention Greenwich Mean Time and the photographs, hundreds now, taken by the White House photographer at official ceremonies and inside the Oval Office and in the Rose Garden. The President always called me "John" or "our young friend from Chicago," and when he heard that Marie and I were seeing each other he arranged for her to be included on the various lists for lunch and dinner, official functions. He thought it odd that I had never married.

Katrina's stories rarely came to me anymore, yet from time to time one would surface and I would hear her low voice, its special timbre, her particular vocabulary and diction, and remember where we were, the time of night, the look of the apartment, and her voice concentrating in the distance. I could hear her speak, at my elbow. It was not a matter of mere recollection, Katrina's stories being more vivid and immediate than recollection. I could listen to Katrina Lauren the way you listened to a symphony, alive in your skull; it just didn't happen very often anymore.

It was convenient to believe that Katrina had spoiled me for other women, perhaps in the way that growing up under FDR had spoiled you for other Presidents. President Roosevelt; that sounded correct, and none of the others did, *President* Eisenhower, *President* Kennedy. President *Nixon*? Katrina Gance sounded right, if what you look for in a woman is a history, a narrative that's hers alone but that can be shared and, when shared, lives in a new way. When shared with you, it lives; with anyone else, it's just another story. And of course your own history comes alive, is animated; one is at last able to speak the truth, and be believed. You held on to that, and then you began to let go. After a certain period, the prisoner ceased to think of escape, ceased to *believe*, although the days were still carefully marked on the walls, as the weeks became months and the months years.

I said the hell with it and made another drink, filling the glass to the top with ice, sloshing gin over the ice, adding an olive and a lemon peel, looking at myself in the mirror, lifting the glass in a sardonic salute. A martini was a cheerful drink, as dapper as a gent in a tuxedo, easy to prepare, pretty to look at, good to hold, a confidence builder. And the consequences were as certain as death and taxes.

The night was calm and quiet except for a yacht's motor somewhere in the harbor. From a radio far away I heard music, a popular song; someone else was up, looking at the harbor as I was, trying to tell the time, too edgy to go to bed or to think clearly. I thought that the music was the sort of music a lonely woman would listen to, midnight music, music with soft horns and a ready melody, the piano carrying the melody, and a baritone voice with perfect phrasing singing a song with a private history. Perhaps this woman was drinking gin, standing alone on her small balcony, disheveled, wondering what the point of it was. She would be leaning forward with her small hands gripping the railing, leaning out into the humid night, noticing the veins in her hands, the watch on her wrist, admiring her slender fingers, humming the melody. Then she would look up, over the water to the black velvet sky. She would brush a lock of hair from her eyes; take a last hopeful drag on her cigarette, letting the smoke out slowly; and pitch the cigarette over the railing, watching it arch, tumbling, until it disappeared in the darkness below. The night was calm and quiet. The stars were out of reach and the harbor was dark; the palm trees were motionless. I decided that Florida would be a terrible place to be lonely in. It was too humid, too Latin, too loose and impermanent, too unreliable, its nights furtive and its days glaring.

Jack?

I stood still, listening.

Come on, Jack. What's *next*?

I wheeled, hearing Carole Nierendorf's Southern voice at my elbow, hearing it as clearly as I heard my own breathing, feeling her presence, seeing her shadow. But I was alone on the terrace, and the living room was dark. I looked left and right into the shadows. Everyone was asleep. There was no Carole, or anybody. I turned back to the harbor, listening for the popular song; but it too had vanished, along with Carole.

161

Around midnight, the peanuts gone and the gin watery, I got the idea that I would call her. We had not spoken in years. She had taken her daughter and gone home to Blackford on Election Day, 1960. We had corresponded for a while and then the correspondence stopped. I had a sudden urge to know what had happened to her, if Blackford had worked out. I got her number from Information and dialed at once, knowing that if I thought about it I'd wait until morning, and in the morning, sober, I wouldn't call.

She answered on the fourth ring, her voice groggy, thick with sleep. It took her a moment to locate me. Jack Gance, from Chicago? Jack, is that really you? What are you doing at this hour? Where are you?

I told her, and then she began to talk; her voice was as I remembered it, low-pitched and smiling. She was living with her folks, the house she'd grown up in. Betsy was at the university, a little wild but doing well. Not too wild, she said; not as wild as I was. As for her, she had been engaged once but had broken it off; just one of those things. It would never've worked out, he was older and they came from different worlds; and she knew what that meant. She knew chapter and verse of the book of different worlds. I couldn't go through another breakup, she said. Now she was a bachelor lady and likely to remain one, although she was going out with a man from the newspaper and—who knew?—that might lead to something. Or not. It didn't matter. Not a bad life, all things considered; not bad at all. We were feeling our way back into the past, our own history. She said she had a job in a newspaper office, the library. I'm in charge of the morgue, she said, laughing. I'm the office mortician. And I know you work in the White House, I saw your name in the newspaper. So I started a file.

The White House, she said. I'm proud of you, Jack. You always wanted to get there, and now you are.

Come up to Washington sometime, I said. I'll give you a guided tour.

All right, she said. All rrrrriiiiight.

Did she ever see Charles?

After a little silence she said No, she never did. Charles sent Betsy a birthday present, always very expensive, and remembered her at Christmas with a check and a telephone call, but did not visit. And never would.

Is he still in Chicago?

New York, Carole said.

Practicing law?

I guess so. I don't know, Jack.

Sorry, I said.

I don't mind, she said. It's just that we don't speak, ever. I think he has something to do with investments. He said something to Betsy that indicated that. He left Chicago not long after I did, but I thought you knew that. I was surprised that he went to New York. I thought he'd go back to Wisconsin.

No bright lights in Wisconsin, I said.

I guess not, she said. Though Charles was never one for the bright lights. That wasn't his thing.

I said, We ought to get together, the two of us.

That would be nice, she said. I'd like that.

I said, I bet you haven't changed. I meant that; she was the sort of woman who wouldn't age dramatically. I tired to picture her, adding a pound here and there, some gray in her blond hair, wrinkles.

She laughed her familiar laugh. And you? Have you changed? Describe yourself, Jack.

I had a mustache but I shaved it off.

And your beaked nose, she said.

No changes there. The mustache didn't hide it.

And the scar, she said.

Scar's where it always was.

And I suppose you're married, Jack. Tell me about your wife?

Not married, I said.

It's hard to believe, she said.

How about tomorrow? I said. I'll stop off in Richmond on my way back to Washington.

Darn, she said. Oh, what a shame. She was leaving tomorrow for Europe, just her and an old friend from school, her oldest friend, a widow. They were going to Paris to shoot the works, the first time for both of them. Jack? When we get home—

Yes, I said. When you get home I'll drive down and we'll have dinner. I wondered if Blackford had changed much; she had described it as French, so I had always thought of it as lush and slow-moving, a pastel sort of place.

As long as we don't talk about the old days, she said.

I said, Fine.

I want to hear all about the White House, she said.

And you can tell me about you, I said.

Honest. There isn't much to tell.

Really?

Really, she said. You'll drive down then?

Sure, I said.

Okay, she said, and gave a light little laugh. She knew I never would. This was it. It was now or never. Go to bed, she said. Get some sleep.

Yes, I said.

It's real good hearing your voice, Jack. Real good.

You, too, I said.

Wasn't that—wasn't that just an *awful* time we had in Chicago.

Yes, I agreed. Awful.

So humiliating, she said. Stupid.

Well, I said. *We* had fun for a while.

'Deed we did, she said.

Chicago's finished, I said. I pressed the receiver tight against my ear, wanting to hear every last syllable. Listening to her, I heard Chicago's electricity and heat and industrial rumble. I thought I could recapture 1959 by force of will.

Really? she said.

That's what they say, I said. I heard it all slipping away, film soundtrack's fadeout.

Good, she said. I hope so.

To hell with it, I said.

Jack? You're really not married?

No, I said. Never got close.

Never even close? I'm surprised. That surprises me a lot.

Maybe a little close once.

What happened?

We came from different worlds, I said.

So you live alone, she said.

Most of the time, I said.

164

I used to think it was unhealthy, living alone. That was when I was married. I wondered how you managed it. Then I found out that you managed quite well, thank you, with a little help from your friend.

A memory stirred and I didn't listen for a moment. Then, Tell me something. Remember that time in the park, a couple of days before you left for Blackford. You were wearing your sealskin coat. You told me that Mozart called.

Yes, she said.

And that you'd had a long talk and that he knew more than you expected him to know. Sexy Mozart, you called him.

Well, she said, and I imagined her smiling in her bedroom, remembering. She began to speak aimlessly, collecting her thoughts, thinking she could tell the story in two minutes and be done with it. But she kept recalling details and her voice quickened as the memory blossomed, her mind's eye sharp and alert. In telling her story she seemed to recognize its value for the first time, not just any story but her story, and Mozart's.

It was the day after Charles had charged into my apartment. She was feeding the baby and wondering what to do about dinner when the doorbell rang. She had not met Mr. Mozart before but knew right away who he was, standing shyly in the doorway—a portly man in a blue suit, a gold watch chain across his belly, on his pink head a wiry crown of white hair, cut short like a soldier's. His blue eyes twinkled and his voice was pastel-soft. He hoped he wasn't disturbing her; but he was in the neighborhood, and. She asked him if he wanted a drink and he said No, but if she had tea; tea would be nice. He often took a cup of tea in his office, late in the afternoon. So she made a pot of her best tea, and put cookies on a plate, and they sat in the living room and had a kind of high tea. She brought out her best china and the silver spoons from her grandmother's service. She was happy that she'd cleaned the apartment, but she needn't have worried. Such a charming man, he had exquisite manners. She was immediately at ease. He was so sweet with the baby, calling her by name. I was putting her to bed. Here Betsy, he said, and reaching into his pocket had brought out a stuffed animal, a bear, and handed it to her.

Children love bears, he said.

Do you have children, Mr. Mozart?

Two, he said. Boy, girl. They are superb, both of them at Northwestern.

It's a very good school, she said.

Yes, he said. Richly endowed.

She said, You weren't just "in the neighborhood."

No, he said.

Charles asked you to come, she said.

Oh, no, he said. No indeed. It was my own idea, absolutely my own, and if I'm intruding—

No, she said. And she spoke the truth. She found it was pleasant talking to him; somehow he was a reassuring presence, someone from Charles's world, the world that was so mysterious to her.

I've wanted to meet you, he said.

She said, Charles talks about you all the time.

He did not tell me you were so pretty.

Charles loves working for you. He thinks you're the best lawyer he's ever seen, and that if he ever got into trouble he'd want you on his side.

The lawyer sipped his tea thoughtfully and did not reply. He indicated by his manner that while he knew there was a crisis of some kind he knew also that there was a solution to it. All crises had solutions, and perhaps he could be helpful in some subtle and undetermined way.

You know about Charles and me, she said.

He said, Not exactly.

What did Charles tell you? she asked.

And he smiled; it was a smile between them, a smile that seemed to put them on an equal footing, two worldly people who could discuss an intimate matter in a graceful, mature way, the way an experienced woman and an experienced man deliberated, and, conversely, perhaps Charles was . . . overwrought.

So she told him, and it surprised her that she told him so readily. She was circumspect, even delicate, but no one could have missed the facts; certainly E. L. Mozart did not miss them.

Do you love him? he asked.

166

She experienced a moment of panic, not knowing whether he meant her husband or her lover; and of course Mozart noticed this and nodded, a complicit, sympathetic nod, while interpreting her silence as No both ways. She perceived this at once.

I love my husband, she said at last, thinking that perhaps it was true.

Now the lawyer sighed; it was neither a weary nor a sarcastic sigh, merely a sigh of understanding. She fancied this was his usual response to clients—and that was how, suddenly, amazingly, she thought of herself now, as his client—who did not always know their own minds.

Goodness, he said.

It's a mess, she agreed.

He made no sign that he heard her at all, folding his hands in his lap, twiddling his thumbs, his eyes focused on the middle distance. He began to speak, and his words appeared at first to have nothing to do with the matter at hand. He described the work of his firm, and she found herself fascinated, listening to Mozart describe the cases that came to them, how the work was divided, who dealt with what; and the stakes. The firm was often, and wrongly, known as a political firm. How could anyone get that idea? All law was political. Who made the laws? Men. Men in legislatures, men in courthouses, men in jury rooms. Moses was a man, a political man if there ever was one. He named a firm, a jumble of Anglo-Saxon names that meant nothing to her. This was a firm that tried to set itself apart, claiming clean hands while every other hand in La Salle Street was filthy, yet those firms had their Jews and Irish and Italians, ambassadors to Springfield . . . His voice had risen and now he halted, smiling wryly.

I apologize, he said.

What for? she said.

I hate it when things are misinterpreted.

Oh, she said. So do I!

But we have to live with it, he said.

Yes, she agreed.

It's the price of success. Envy, he said. The lawyer reached for his cup and took a tiny sip. He said gravely, There has been some pressure lately. We've been very busy at the office. Your Charles has worked long, long hours. As you have occasion to know. Late nights, weekends, he's been a trooper, really. But he's overworked. It's worried us, his diligence. My partners and I, we know how to husband our strength—the word came out "strent," and for a moment she thought he'd said "strain," strenuous Chicago. He said, We know how to pace ourselves. The younger men, he said with a sigh. Then he looked up and clucked, *tut-tut*. The folly of youth, he said. They don't know when to quit. The trouble with young men is that they just go flat-out, and become exhausted.

And neglect their wives, she said. She was immediately sorry she'd said it, subject as it was to misinterpretation. She poured more tea and there was a long moment of silence. She could almost see his mind working, though she had no idea what he was thinking. A varicose vein pulsed in his forehead. Suddenly she thought to herself, Why is he here? Obviously he had come to tell her something, and just as obviously he would not be hurried.

He said, There was a little problem at the office, but that's all fixed up now. He leaned toward her, lowering his voice. It was understood that what he was saying now was confidential, between the two of them; the lawyer-client privilege went both ways. It was a business matter, nothing to worry about. Still. It had been a worry. Perhaps Charles mentioned it.

She looked at him, and the word was out of her mouth before she knew it. She spoke from instinct, without thinking, one of the few unforced lies she had ever told: No.

He smiled.

I knew there was an argument, she said.

Yes? he said.

But I don't know what it was about.

He sipped his tea and asked her if she liked Chicago. He heard the South in her voice. Virginia, wasn't it? The heartland must be quite a change for her; and, in its own way, for Charles too. Illinois would be different from Tidewater Virginia, as Chicago itself would be different from the Wisconsin woods. The weather, for one thing, so raw, the wind off the lake and the prairie. And the people were raw, too, brusque, sometimes tougher than they needed to be. Some of it was an act, naturally, though the city had changed over the years, becoming more sophisticated and forgiving. Still, it was a particular style, suited to an inland region. For himself, he liked the pace of life in the South, altogether more subtle and—*dense*, a complicated society, where honor counted for something and you never forgot a friend. Of course he knew very little about it, only that hotel with the golf course and riding trails—

The Greenbriar, she said.

Yes, that was the one. It was what he imagined the plantation South to be, civilized, the Negroes so polite and helpful, the speech so soft. The soft speech often concealed active, witty brains. In the South it was customary to relax and take stock of things, and consider alternatives. There would be nuance, and historical perspectives. You could ask yourself: What would have happened if Gettysburg had gone the other way? If Pickett had succeeded! In the civilized South you could wind the clock back and make believe. In the South you could pretend. That was hard to do in Chicago, the hurly-burly, the newness of everything. In Chicago—he chuckled at his joke—it was almost against the law!

She watched him carefully, alert now. He was looking directly into her eyes while he spoke, his expression one of understanding and sympathy. His voice was soft and furry as velvet. He was concealing something, but she did not know what it was.

Sometimes people got off base, he said.

She nodded. That was certainly true. It was true even in the subtle South.

He continued, And with the particular pressures—

Yes, she said. She watched his rueful smile and his eloquent shrug. She poured more tea. He asked whether she minded if he smoked and she said No, and in fact she would join him. He offered her a Chesterfield from a silver case.

He said, Chicago and its pressures, its insistence on success, on *doing*. Its insistence that things be done thoroughly. Chicago made people unpredictable, do some things they wouldn't ordinarily do. Sometimes Chicago backed you into a corner. For example, home life.

She heard something feral in his voice now, the velvet bristling. Something was moving behind it, and she was instantly on guard. Yet his varicose vein was still, and his manner serene. She realized they were sitting in near darkness. His cigarette flared when he pulled on it. She had drawn the shades against the bright afternoon sun. But she did not move to turn on the lights, unwilling to break the spell. Home life? she asked.

It's the first thing to suffer, he said.

The weekends are difficult, she agreed.

And the late hours, he said. All the late hours in the office.

She remained silent, alert, listening for the meaning behind the words.

He said, It's lonely work, law.

Yes, she said.

Hard on the emotions, he said.

She had it now, but she waited for him to say it.

Charles needs our support, Mrs. Nierendorf. Carole. May I call you Carole? Charles has been doing important work for my firm, work that means a very great deal to all of us, difficult work, work requiring concentration . . .

Mozart continued to talk but she didn't listen. It was something about money, enough to go around for everyone, and after a moment she tuned in. She felt like a child listening to an Arthurian legend or a bedtime ghost story; and still there was the thing unsaid. She listened now with all her might. He was saying that he could not afford a Charles who was distracted and depressed. Now he reached up and turned on the lamp and in the sudden glare she observed his powerful arms and shoulders, the thick cords in his neck, and his very blue, shrewd eyes.

No, he said, it would not do; for the sake of the firm, for the sake of the future, Charles's future, for this very complicated business arrangement was unorthodox in its legalities, irregular . . . His voice had softened into an almost Southern cadence, and its effect was hypnotic in its mnemonic associations, moving her into her own past, oblique Southern discourse on a hot summer afternoon on the verandah; her father took such pleasure in conversation. However, she was not so beguiled that she did not understand, to the last syllable, what he was proposing, and what was coming next.

So you have to give up Mr. Gance, he said.

Jack?

Charles has to know that, and know that you mean it. I know it is what you want to do anyway.

But what if it isn't? she said.

Not for good, he said. Not forever. But for the moment.

He reached across the table to take her hand. His own hand was rough but his grip was gentle. She was aware again how strong he was. She felt he could snap her fingers like matchsticks. She noticed perspiration on his temples and his shirt collar was damp; the lawyer was sweating, and smelling pleasantly of talcum powder.

For Charles's peace of mind? she asked.

Jack Gance is a turd, he said.

She began to smile—careful to display no trace of mockery or of sarcasm. What an extraordinary exchange this was! She felt she was deep inside a secret world; Jack had called it "downtown." It couldn't be that Mozart's concern was solely the success of a business "deal," illegal from the sound of it.

He said, How much do you know about him? His background.

She stared at him, then shook her head slowly, and something in that combination warned him off. Expert negotiator that he was, he took care to read the opposition and never go farther than he needed to. He never wanted to force; he wanted to convince. She had given him an invitation to proceed, but he declined to do so, moving instead to the heart of the matter.

Will you do this?

I don't know, she said. That was a lie, though a forced lie. She wanted to know what came next; she wanted him to open the full bag of tricks.

I must insist, he said, his tone of voice pleasantly businesslike, the voice of a man picking up the check at dinner. He said, You see, people could get hurt. Charles could. We're dealing with hard, difficult people, Carole, who concentrate on one thing at a time, who commit

171

themselves wholly and completely and expect their partners to do the same; it's business.

It was the first time he had spoken her name since he had asked permission to do so, and the effect was to draw her closer to him. Charles hurt? How?

It's Charles's idea, he said. Charles set it up, put it together, and it was brilliantly done, superb, he's such a bright young man . . . She tuned out again as the lawyer explained, or appeared to explain, the facts, something about land, and the financing of the land, "nominees," a holding company, and a particular piece of legislation now before the legislature.

Oh, she said, bringing herself back to the present moment.

It's very complicated, he said.

She nodded, not having understood a word.

The point is this. The next two weeks are critical to us. And Charles has to be on the ball. This is the World Series and he has to be alert. This is business, and nothing must be allowed to interfere. We almost lost Charles yesterday, a dispute over a trivial legal question. We settled that this morning; and that was when I learned there was trouble at home. This is a valuable lesson that Charles has learned, that he must stand up, that when a deal's done it can't be undone and that when you give your word you keep it. And then I learned about this and knew that I must come to see you, to see if we could work it out. You understand the importance now?

His hand was in his coat pocket. He seemed about to continue, then didn't. He produced an envelope; it materialized like a rabbit from a hat. His varicose vein was pulsing again. He pushed the envelope across the table, smiling shyly. His eyes moved here and there in the room. She could hear the baby tossing in her crib, beginning to whimper. He said, My partners and I wanted you and Charles to have this, diffidently nodding at the envelope, surely an inadequate token of a firm's appreciation. Two air tickets to Nassau, the room's all arranged . . .

Yes, she said. Then, Does he know you're here?

He said at last, Yes.

Then it's done, she said.

Thank you, he said.

172

You're welcome, she said. She moved the envelope with her fingernail; it was equidistant between them on the coffee table.

And you'll do your best, he said.

My best what? she asked.

He sighed, looking at her; he touched her hand, a caress.

Good-bye, Mr. Mozart, she said.

And when the door closed behind him she discovered she was exhausted. The baby began to cry but she did not move. A seductive man was E. L. Mozart. She could see how Charles had been seduced. He possessed authority. He seemed beyond doubt and beyond fear; men would follow him the way they followed a military leader. The way they had followed Jackson. Stonewall Jackson always obeyed orders, and his men always obeyed Jackson. He would be attractive to men, offering them certitude, and control over their own destinies, or the illusion of control. Really, he offered them power. And he would be attractive to women, too; perhaps a little less attractive to women than to men. Women would see him as a rival. He would be very attractive to a certain kind of woman, a woman who had no ambition to enter a man's sphere, because that was a contest that Mozart would win every time; and when he lost he would call the winner a coward. Men followed other men and so much the better if the women were watching as when men went to war. That was what it meant to be a man, to put yourself on an equal footing with other men, and not disgrace yourself in their eyes. Like any great struggle, it was an affair of pride. Except there would always be the Jacksons a rung above. That was the way of the world; she saw it clearly now. Men wanted heroes and women needed lovers.

She heard the downstairs door open and close, and Charles's familiar step. The baby was crying in earnest now, and she pushed off from the wall. She stood in the center of the room, disoriented like an animal caught in the headlights of a car. She stood a moment looking across the room, through the window into the darkness. The baby was crying. Somewhere she heard the wail of

173

an ambulance. Charles's key turned in the lock. She would have to feed the baby.

It was quite a séance, she said to me.

I never knew, I said.

Of course not. Why would you?

So you stayed, I said.

For a year, she said. I didn't have anywhere else to go, or thought I didn't.

The deal they were putting together, I said. I know what it was.

I don't care, she said. It's ancient history.

That deal made history, I said.

Sure, Jack. Go to bed. Get some sleep.

And what Mozart said was true, Charles had put it together, a sale and lease-back, the land bought at auction, sealed bids, ha-ha, first time it had ever been done, with the land annexed by the city so there'd be fire and police protection, lowered the insurance rates. They annexed the land the way Hitler annexed the Low Countries. And at the end of it they had a shopping center, and everyone got rich.

Ancient *history*, she said sharply. It's nothing to do with *me*.

Damnedest thing, I said.

She said, Go to bed, Jack. You'll feel better in the morning.

I laughed at that. No, I won't.

And I've got to get up at six, she said.

I was standing at the French doors leading to the balcony, my hands in my pockets, phone jammed between my shoulder and my ear. She was talking but I wasn't listening. I was imagining Carole and Mozart alone in her living room, their extraordinary exchange, and what Carole made of it. I reached for the gin, raised the bottle, and took a long pull. Her voice grated on my ear, a fingernail across a blackboard. I was watching a yacht creep into the harbor, its spotlight swinging from port to starboard searching for a mooring. The salon was brightly lit and I could see a man at the wheel; a girl was on deck shading her eyes from the glare. Suddenly she pointed, turning, and the yacht maneuvered to the buoy. The spotlight froze, a brilliant white light. I saw that she had a beer in her hand and she was topless; she put down the beer and picked up the buoy hook. The light swung again, and she was lost to view.

I said suddenly, I've had a lousy day. My father had a stroke.

Oh, dear, she said. Is he all right?

I don't think he is, I said.

I'm sorry, she said.

Poor old bastard, I said. The man had come out on deck to help the girl with the buoy chain. She stood back out of the light and picked up her beer. She was gorgeous in profile.

It's time to go, Jack.

I told her to have a great trip, see all the sights, every sight there was. I gave her the names of two restaurants, spelling their names. A good friend was deputy to the commercial attaché and I gave her his name, and the number at the embassy. I told her about Fouquet's château, Vaux-le-Visconte near Melun, and the forest at Compiègne, must-see places, and there was an auberge at the edge of the forest that was particularly good news and I gave her that name, spelling it out. She shouldn't miss Rodin's museum, with its wonderful nudes and dough-faced Mrs. Potter Palmer. She wanted sexy, Rodin was sexy. The mighty bronze of an imperious Balzac in his dressing gown included the great writer's morning erection. I asked her where she was staying and she said she'd forgotten, so I gave her the names of two hotels on the Left Bank and one on the Right, moderate-priced hotels where the staff was cheerful. One of the hotels didn't have a dining room but I couldn't remember which one. The lights of the yacht suddenly went out; it looked like a ghost ship.

Well, she said.

Bon voyage, I said.

Thank you, Jack.

It's a great city. I've been there four, five times. I like Europe.

Do you still think about her, Jack?

Not as much as I used to, I said.

What was her name?

175

Katrina, I said.

And me. Do you think about me?

I thought about you tonight. And sometimes in the morning.

Yeah, Jack.

It seems like a long time ago.

It was, she said.

No so long, I said. Nineteen fifty-nine's just the other day. They have different concepts of time in Europe.

They do?

I'm thinking about you now, I said. I was assembling her in my reeling brain, her curly blond hair, her cheerleader's smile, the sweat on her skin that summer when it was so hot. She had the smallest hands I had ever seen. I wish you weren't going to France, I said.

It's my first time, she said, and yawned.

Do you think . . . I began.

She laughed softly, smothering the yawn, pausing before she replied. I doubt it, Jack. We were suited in only one way, just *that* way, not any other way that I could see. But I don't know. How would I know?

Hard to know, I agreed.

I'm going to bed, she said.

Yes, I said. It's time.

She wished me a good flight back, and good luck generally. She said she'd light a candle for my father in Notre-Dame. That touched me and I told her so. We promised each other to get together when she returned from Europe.

Sorry to bore you with Mozart, she said.

I wasn't bored, I said. And then I rang off.

I went back into the living room and made another drink, a real one, with ice. That finished the bottle and I reflected that I was too old to drink a bottle of gin at one sitting; tomorrow would be a nightmare, death and taxes. I remembered that I hadn't had any dinner. When I put my drink on the coffee table it slipped and slid into the elephants, scattering them. They made an awful clatter but I picked them up one by one, ivory elephants, porcelain elephants, silver, china, jade, all slipping in gin. I was sitting in darkness, arranging the elephants.

Then I returned to the balcony. I looked at the dark

waters of the harbor, and the boats swinging at anchor, and remembered my father's caustic words. We would be forever out of touch; I had repudiated him. I was out of touch generally, had been for years. Yet I did not want to believe that what he said was true. I saw my mother's hand reach toward him. I noticed him sway a little, like a man uncertain of his footing aboard ship. And then he began to smile; it seemed almost a grimace, as if he were in physical pain.

Mozart had said, How much do you know about him? His background.

This much, Elly:

I observed him stoop as he took her hand. She was grinning, light on her feet as she ground her cigarette into the ashtray. She whispered something in his ear. They looked as they did when I was a child, so gay, the handsomest couple in the park, he so tall and broad-shouldered, she so fine. I saw her thin arms go around his waist, squeezing, her radiant smile for him alone, my one and only—and then I knew, with a sudden cold certainty, that he was dying.

3

THE aircraft heaved, banking, and we followed the Potomac River into National, CIA on the right side, and then on the left Georgetown, the Kennedy Center, the Washington Monument, the Capitol, the Court, and the White House, with its great trees and lawns. Your eye was drawn to the symmetry of the Ellipse, the mansion and the needle facing each other. Through my narrow window I stared at the White House and the Executive Office Building, craning my neck as they slid from view, aft. All in all a shapely city, trees and lawns giving it a suburban look, a place where people lived as well as worked. *As You Like It* was playing at the Kennedy Center. Official Washington was tightly packed: it would fit into the Loop with only a little spillover. My father called the capital a company town, a Potemkin village erected by the state to deceive and infatuate the voters; everyone knew that the real business of the country went on elsewhere, until lately.

The plane heaved sickeningly, dipping to starboard now, and the monuments were lost to view. I watched the gray river rise to meet us, Arlington's neat graves and the Pentagon sliding by. Joggers were everywhere, flashes of red and blue here and there against autumn's drab backdrop and the white grave markers. Beyond Washington's boundaries were the rolling hills of Virginia and Maryland, killing grounds in the Civil War, Bull Run, Chancellorsville, Antietam, and the others; they said that all modern war began with the butchery at Antietam. All the European generals studied Antietam, the better to organize Sedan in 1870 and Verdun in 1916 and Bastogne in 1944. At Antietam iron and bone still leeched to the surface, as they did at Verdun. Washington's parks and boulevards hinted at none of this, however. I thought of Chicago and its monotonous southern and western suburbs, reaching into the level and pacific prairie, no battlegrounds, no monuments, no single thing of historical interest in the waving fields of grain until you got to Lincoln's Springfield and, farther south, the Mississippi. In Illinois there were only Indian burial mounds, and the individual histories of the homesteaders.

National was full and we had to wait for a gate. I recognized a congressman and the under secretary of labor, deep in conversation two seats forward. I always saw someone I knew on planes at National Airport. At last the aircraft began to move, creeping, the oxygen hissing; men were already crowding the aisles despite the stewardess's warnings. I did not rise and as a consequence was the last passenger off the plane. The stewardess smiled sympathetically.

The terminal was crowded, everyone in a hurry. I was light-headed, apprehensive, moving slowly. The terminal was as claustrophobic as the airplane. I stopped to buy a newspaper, feeling suddenly disoriented; a group of soldiers next to me were thumbing a copy of *Penthouse* and guffawing. I had been in National Airport a hundred times but now it seemed foreign to me, as if by mistake I had landed at Omaha or Phoenix. I looked at page one of the newspaper; everything above the fold concerned the summit. I stood against the wall near a bank of telephones, staring at the newspaper. There was a photograph of the General Secretary and the President and their aides, everyone solemn. They were standing coatless in a garden, everyone looking chilled. I was thinking about my father, and my eyes filled with tears.

"Hi, Jack."

I looked up blindly, smiling; someone touched my arm and was gone. I couldn't remember his name; he worked somewhere on the Hill, one of the subcommittees. I watched his back, moving away. His name was Howard Something, a protégé of the senior senator from Pennsylvania or Maryland, one of those two.

I thought I would call my office and then decided not

179

to. Yet that was what I always did, arriving at National, call my office and ask what was up. I tried to remember my assignments from the Tuesday Bogsat, who wanted what and why. Well, the why was unimportant. I tucked the paper under my arm and pushed off, sliding a little on the polished floor, an elephant slipping in gin. My emotions were so close to the surface that anything could make them spill. I was breathing hard and perspiring, my shirt soaked through. I had the fantastic idea that I was having a nervous breakdown. I was moving rapidly now, a busy magnifico in a hurry, eyes cast down. I looked left and saw the stewardess, striding along beside me, trim in her blue uniform.

"Cheer up!" she said. "You look like you've lost your best friend."

I smiled but it was not much of a smile, because her eyes widened and she hurried on without another word. With difficulty I made my way across the lobby and through the heavy doors to the street. Outside, I took a deep breath of the chilly air and immediately felt better, except for the throbbing inside my skull. I realized I was trembling, the sweat drying now on my forehead; I thought I could smell gin. I stood a moment to let things settle, feeling bad about the stewardess, who was only trying to be friendly and cheerful.

I joined the taxi queue. Across the circle passengers were stepping into the Dulles shuttle bus. I watched them idly, then started as Carole Nierendorf turned and looked directly at me, adjusting her eyeglasses; there was no recognition at all. She looked straight through me, another face in the crowd. I stood very still, observing her, confounded at the coincidence; but life itself was coincidental, and my nerves were stretched tight as piano wire. I would never have recognized her were it not for the telephone conversation; she would not have been on my mind, and I would have passed over her as one does any anonymous face. She was plumper and her hair was streaked with gray, an attractive middle-aged woman. She was climbing on to the bus now, giving a careless toss of her head, smiling and saying something to the woman in front of her. Two Southern ladies bound for Paris, France. Two Southern ladies taking French leave. Suddenly she laughed and even from that distance I could recognize it, a deep, throaty, womanly laugh; I remembered it from the old days. Perhaps she was reprising the telephone call, describing it to her friend. Woke me up in the middle of the night, man I hadn't seen in just ages, lonely, wanted to talk, we must've talked for an hour, I have the addresses of hotels, restaurants, he *did* go on and on, and so did I, about something that happened when Charles and I were breaking up, an event in which old Jack played a supporting role . . . Then she was gone, the doors shut, and the bus accelerating, moving into the stream of traffic leaving National.

It began to snow, huge fat flakes so widely spaced you could count them. A November surprise, everything suddenly gray. A moment later I was in a cab bound for the Executive Office Building. A convoy of limousines overtook us, little flags flying from their front bumpers, a head of state or an ambassador down from the UN. Impassive black faces in the rear seats; it ceased snowing. The Dulles bus was ahead of us. When we passed it I did not look up. I was deep into the newspaper, reading about the summit, a political plus for the President, everyone agreed. No other news that day in our one-issue capital. The lines of type blurred in my vision and I found myself saying a prayer, for my father and for Carole Nierendorf. I wanted my father to live and I wanted Carole to have a wonderful holiday, a holiday as lusty as her laugh. Perhaps she would find romance in Paris. Many did and led happy and productive lives without remorse. I asked for several good things for myself as well. The cab driver was looking at me suspiciously, his eyes narrowing in the rearview mirror. I realized I had been talking out loud, saying my prayers. I glared at the cab driver and his eyes shifted, though he could not suppress an angry shake of his head. Everyone knew that Washington was filled with dangerous crazies, people who held grudges and were often armed. He banged the heel of his hand on the steering wheel, stepped on the accelerator, and the cab shot forward.

She had looked right at me but did not recognize me. No wonder. I was not myself.

* * *

I do not remember the rest of that day or night. I went to the office and, I suppose, did what I normally did, attended meetings and talked on the telephone to try to fix what was broken; and when the day was done, I went home and slept. I awoke very early and made a pot of strong coffee and sat in my living room, listening to music and watching the street develop in the dawn. In my part of Georgetown you cannot see the sun until it is well risen. I stared at the street through a pane of window glass with a whorl at its center, an imperfection as familiar to me as my own eyesight. The newspapers thumped against the door. At seven the neighborhood began to stir, people leaving for work, school buses collecting children. I could hear the high-pitched voices of the children in the street. People and things undulated in the window, distorted as a desert mirage.

A government sedan pulled up to the house opposite mine, a young man with a briefcase alighting and ringing the doorbell, nervous, looking at his wristwatch, straightening his tie; he bumped his briefcase against his knee while he waited. The weather was chilly and I could see his breath. Presently the secretary appeared, sober in a dark suit with a vest and a gold chain. He shook hands with the young man, then leaned close to him, talking, a fatherly hand on his shoulder. The secretary was very tall and broad, a fixture in Washington, a prince of our realm, a favorite after hours, a great raconteur; a lawyer in civilian life, he was a master bureaucrat. They stood talking a moment, the young man nodding vigorously: Yes, yes, *at once*, Mr. Secretary. Then they disappeared inside the house, only to emerge a moment later and vanish into the sedan, the young man first, lunging to the far side of the rear seat, making room for the burly secretary, who followed; he was undulating in the whorl of window glass, the newspaper folded under his arm, its contents surely deconstructed at the breakfast table. The working day had begun. The secretary's sedan slid away from the curb like a cruiser leaving its slip for maneuvers on the high seas. And from an upstairs window a curtain moved, someone waving good-bye.

I was trying to remember what I had done the day before, wondering if I had been successful at it, whatever

182

it was. I listened, hearing the little furry rustle some-where in my overheated imagination. Failing to recollect the specific, I thought about the generic, the working life, the effort and the reward. Mine was not a life of great drama, like an athlete's or a soldier's during war-time, or even an ordinary doctor's office hours. I moved a piece of paper from one part of a building to another, made a phone call, got a letter signed, arranged an ap-pointment or prevented one. My work was rarely impor-tant. Sometimes it was conspicuous, owing to the surroundings in which it was conducted, and the public-ity. My life and my work were inseparable—in Washing-ton, inevitable. That was the bargain I had made with myself long before, choosing politics for the protection it afforded; and it seemed great, great as history, conse-quential, as exuberant as a jazz band and as organized as a barracks. In the beginning the work was the reward, and you needed no other. When it ceased being the re-ward—or reward enough—your culture became corrupt, and commenced its decline, and you were in a knot of your own making. You had to slip the knot to discover a new reward, something of value that would last from to-day to tomorrow; otherwise you were a failure. Your grasp was greater than your reach, your jazz band off-key, your barracks a whorehouse. You lived in a bland temperate zone, Indian summer, neither this nor that, without fire and without ice. It was not difficult to begin again but discouraging, because the results of men who had tried were everywhere to be seen. They recreated themselves because they wanted their youth back, not the youth they had had but the youth they believed they were entitled to. They believed they had been robbed of it. They had been under duress and had neglected their brightest, freshest years, the American birthright accord-ing to the American novelist. But it wasn't youth; youth had nothing to do with it. It was courage they wanted, though this was vulgar to admit. It was hard being your own man, because you did not know who that was, after so many years in the crowd; or you thought you knew all too well.

The postman materialized in the window and I heard the letters slip into the box; and then he was gone and I knew that if I closed my eyes I could summon my old apartment on the Mid North Side of Chicago, a Burroughs calculator and a telephone with a headset, a sexy woman in the apartment across the street, the Man inscrutable downtown, and my wonderful numbers alive at my fingertips; and the Queen of England approaching.

But I did not close my eyes. I poured another cup of coffee and went upstairs. I took my time showering and shaving; and then I read the newspaper. I walked into my office at eleven.

Marie and I talked about the summit for a moment. The President and the senior staff were due shortly and we were all expected to be in the Rose Garden to greet him.

"And Gobelin arrives in fifteen minutes," she said.

"Here?"

"Of course. I told you yesterday. You looked a little out of it, Jack, yesterday."

"Was," I said. "I need a vacation."

"We can go to Camp David this weekend. We're on the list and the President and Mrs. will be in New York. It'll be quiet and easy, not too many people around."

I grunted No. I thought of the wives and children, shop talk and word games at night, commissary food and Napa Valley Burgundy. It was tactless to bring your own wine to Camp David. "You want to take two weeks and go to Europe?"

She said, "Yes, but it isn't going to happen. Too much on our plate here."

But I was already in France, on a crowded corner of the Ste.-Germain-des-Prés. We were deciding about dinner, fish or flesh; everyone was laughing in fine anticipation of the meal to come, and the raucous conversation. I was wearing my beret. And then someone remembered that place near the Invalides, oysters and cassoulet, very reasonable. And then we were off, striding down the great boulevard in the cold of November . . .

Marie was looking at me strangely.

"I was thinking about Paris," I said.

"I'm thinking about your buddy Gobelin, due in fifteen minutes. Shall I arrange for the marine band?"

"Very funny," I said. "What does he want?"

"Wouldn't say."

"That's right."

"Remember?"

"Very mysterious."

"That's him."

"What do you say we quit, Marie?"

"Quit what?"

"Quit this."

"You're full of surprises."

"Think about it."

"I'll do that."

My telephone buzzed. Marie took the call, listened, said, "He's here early," and asked sweetly if she should lock up the silver.

"Forget the silver," I said.

"I'll think about it, Jack."

"We could go into business together."

"Here," she said.

"Chicago," I said.

"What do we do in Chicago?"

"I'll figure something out."

"You do that, Jack," she said. She looked out the window. "Aren't you going to miss this?"

"Yes," I said.

"Me, too," she said. "Tah *dah*," she said, opening the door to the outer office. She stood there at attention as Gobelin marched through. I half expected him to be flying a little flag, like the limousines cruising out of National. He executed a deft bow to Marie and shook hands with me. He was dressed in his working clothes, a tweed jacket and a black turtleneck sweater, corduroys, and beautifully polished brogans. And behind him, standing quietly to one side, was a girl young enough to be his daughter or mine.

"Meet Camilla, my assistant," he said, and we all shook hands, Marie departing with a lascivious look at me. Tap said, "It'd be good if Camilla could sit in, Jack, if that's all right."

"Sure," I said.

"They decided I need help," he said with a grin.

"It's the legs go first, right?"

"No," he said, and tapped his skull. "The memory. So they got me an assistant. Camilla's from Chicago."

I looked at her. "So am I."

"I know," she said.

"Northwestern," Tap said.

"I'll be damned," I said. "I thought you had to go to Harvard to write journalism."

"Jack," he said reproachfully. "Camilla's got a double major, economics and politics, with a minor in psychology."

"Stress," she said, "I did my paper on the effects of stress, Vietnam and the Holocaust. On the survivors." Her voice was clipped, almost curt; she would have to learn the Pennsylvania Avenue bedside manner. And I had no doubt that she would. I looked at Tap to see if he was putting me on, but his expression disclosed nothing. "And now you're in Washington," I said pleasantly.

"Where else?" she said.

"I'm sorry about your father, Jack."

"It wasn't as bad as we thought," I said. "Dad's gotten old." I would have gone on except for Camilla. I had met Tap's parents and often we talked about our families. But she was too young to understand. Her parents would not be ill; her parents would be worried about their parents, her grandparents; her parents were probably younger than I was. I wondered if they knew about Gobelin and, if they knew, what they thought. "Thanks for asking," I said.

"Glad it wasn't serious," he said. He and Camilla took out notebooks. "Do you know why we're here?"

I looked from him to Camilla and back again. "Not at all. Am I supposed to be under stress?"

"No joking?"

"No joking," I said. I was mystified.

"So you haven't heard, the grapevine."

"I guess I haven't."

"There's some unpleasantness in your old home town." And then, in his professorial manner, he took out a pipe, tamped it, lit it, and sat watching the smoke rise; that was a change, the last time I'd seen Tap Gobelin he was a chain smoker, like me. I suspected that stress-expert Camilla had something to do with it, and when he glanced at her and smiled, my nasty suspicion was confirmed. Then I noticed that despite his country gentleman duds he was looking seedy, hair unkempt and uncut, his full belly straining at the cashmere turtleneck, he who had always been so careful about his weight. I knew then that her hooks were into him, that she had told him that she loved him for himself alone, his *mind*, and he was so cute in the morning, rough and shaggy like an old grizzly bear, so *sexy* . . .

"Municipal corruption," Tap said. That was the story now, his story, the great theme of the decade. Let the wimps dick around with nuclear or the Reds, the future of America was her great cities, and that was his assignment for the year. He would begin with Chicago because, hell, they'd invented corruption in Chicago and because, as it happened, he had been "furnished" with a document from the Justice Department Strike Force, he'd never read anything like it, the Windy City's in a class by itself. He laughed suddenly. "You know what Marx said about Prussia. Not a state with an army but an army with a state. That's the Chicago Machine."

I said, "It wasn't Marx; it was Mirabeau."

"Whatever," he said.

I said, "What does this have to do with the White House?"

"Nothing," he said. "The White House is not involved."

"That's a relief," I said.

"They've caught their first fish," he said. "A guy you know. That's why we're here, to talk to you about him. I figured you'd've heard."

"Who is it?" I said.

"Patrick Bayley, Esquire. Bribery of a federal judge."

"Shit," I said.

"The judge was wired and they had cameras and tape recorders. The thing's on film, open and shut. The envelope goes across the desk, camera's in on it nice and tight. The judge opens it, counts it on camera. Damn near gives Bayley a receipt for it. Jesus, he's dumb, Bayley."

"No, he isn't," I said.

"Could've fooled me," Tap said.

"You worked for him," Camilla said.

I nodded.

"You were his protégé."

"I was his boy," I said.

"What was he like?"

That was the floater; the harder stuff was coming. "Pat Bayley is a good man," I said, emphasizing the present tense. When I saw Camilla begin to write, I opened my mouth to put the remark off the record. She noticed and raised her pen a fraction, looking at me with a condescending smile. "A hell of a good man," I said. "And when I knew him, Pat wasn't into bribing federal judges or anyone else."

"What was he 'into,' then," Camilla said.

Score one for the cupcake. "Elections," I said. When Tap laughed, I added, "We had them, even in Chicago."

"Yes," he said, "What did Patrick Bayley, Esquire, do, exactly, at election time?"

"He got out the vote."

"And what did you do, Jack?"

"I was polling. That's how I started in this business, asking questions on street corners."

"And you reported to him."

"And a few of his very close friends."

Gobelin was silent a moment. "My frog at the Justice Department tells me that everybody, but everybody who was anybody, was on Pat Bayley's payroll."

I said, "I was. I don't know who else was." We stared at each other a moment.

"He was a bagman, Bayley. He had a payroll as long as your arm."

Camilla said, "Is that how you got to Washington, Pat Bayley's patronage?"

"Absolutely," I said.

"Who was his contact in the administration?"

I named a man, now dead, who had known President Kennedy.

"So Bayley had Washington connections also, even as far back as that."

I glanced at Gobelin, who said, "Most people in the

political business do, Milly." Then, to me, "He doesn't seem like your sort of man, Jack."

"But he is," I said. "A quality man."

"You see much of him now?"

"I haven't seen him in years and years."

"That would answer my next question."

"Yes, it would," I said.

"That you're not on his payroll now."

"Pat Bayley never gave a crap about Washington."

"Funny case," he said. "Didn't involve much money."

"What was it about? What was he allegedly bribing the judge to do?"

"Not allegedly," Tap said. "And not *to do*. It had already been done. Justice had the judge cold and promised leniency in return for cooperation when Bayley arrived with the money. They knew His Honor'd been reached; they just didn't know who'd reached him. It was a tax case, corporate bankruptcy. Didn't involve more'n a hundred thousand dollars, best you can judge, because the accounting's a little complicated. Anyhow, no big deal in the city that works. Bayley's the tip of the iceberg, but an interesting tip."

"What did the company *do*, Tap?"

"It was a company with city contracts, 'goods and services,' though what those goods and services were is a little obscure."

I said, "You got the names of the corporate officers?"

"They won't mean anything to you."

"Try me," I said, and when he began reading from his notebook I realized he was correct; none of the names was familiar.

"Nominees," he said.

"Ghosts," I said, and smiled.

"Pissant operation," he said.

"As opposed to what," I said. "Watergate?"

"Tacky," he said.

"Teapot Dome?" I turned away, unsuccessfully swallowing a laugh. I was defending Chicago as a major league center of corruption. Our crooks are greater than your crooks! When he said "tacky" it was as if he were criticizing the city's look, its dress; dowdy, frumpy Chicago, where even the criminals were mediocre.

"Poor Chicago," I said.

"What do you mean by that?" Camilla said. "And what's so funny?"

"What do you two want from me anyway? You want to use me as a character reference for Pat, feel free." The phone buzzed and I took the call, walking to the window. It was Marie wanting to know if I needed anything. Meaning: Did I want to be interrupted with a fictitious urgent message. I said, Keep talking. Very slowly she read the list of people who had called. Among the names was Patrick Bayley. I made a cryptic comment from time to time, listening to her and looking out the big window at the White House lawn. The weather had turned again and it was warm, balmy as June. The gardeners were hurrying about, making the grounds tidy for the President's arrival. I watched a White House car pull into the driveway and stop, the driver alighting and then polishing the chrome with a cloth. Protesters were marching on Pennsylvania Avenue, but I could not read their signs through the iron fence. They were orderly, middle-aged protesters. I watched them and thought about what Gobelin had told me. Bribery of a federal judge, a pissant operation, tacky. I had not seen Pat Bayley since leaving Chicago, though we had talked a few times on the telephone; and it looked as if we would talk again, though I could not imagine what he thought I could do for him. No doubt he was frightened; there would be messages on desks all over Washington. Give me a hearing, I need help, can you do anything for me, I'm in a hell of a jam. It would have been difficult for him, placing that call. I was young enough to be his son, and in Chicago age and experience still counted for something. The affair depressed me. The Bayley I had known was a hard case but no bagman. Of course administrations had changed, in the Hall as in Washington; and perhaps Pat Bayley had changed with them. I hated to think of him with his back to the wall, without protection; if he had any real protection, he would not have called me. I focused again on the White House lawn. There were people everywhere and in the distance helicopters arriving from Andrews, the President and his suite; no emperor or pope ever arrived with greater punctuality, or suddenness. The helicopters were aloft, and then they were down. The White House clocks, ignored for five days, would begin to tick again. There was a pretty blanket of leaves on the White House lawn, a Wyeth composition, meticulous and unquiet; it was a somber view from my window, and I was going to miss it. I said something into the telephone and hung up.

"Anything you can tell us," Tap said, "because it's Bayley we're profiling first. You know, what he did and how he did it, way back then, and the sort of fellow he was. We want to flesh him out."

"I haven't seen him for many years," I said.

"Yes," Tap said. "You mentioned that."

"Very able, very bright," I said. "Intelligent is the word."

"How did you meet him?"

"A friend of mine at the university."

"Name?" Camilla said.

"He's dead," I said.

"You said intelligent," Tap said.

"Very," I said. "And loyal."

"To the Machine."

"You betcha," I said.

Tap closed his notebook and looked at me over steepled fingers.

Camilla said, "I presume you want this off the record, Mr. Gance."

"No," I said.

"Well, well," she said.

"Jack's a stand-up guy," Tap said. "We go way back, Milly. We've had a drink together, chased around together." He grinned at me. "Remember Chicago, 1968? The Hilton, that night. The night you got your head busted, that kid from the Iron Range. Remember him?" He winked at Camilla, who had been doodling in her notebook. "Jack's tough, when he wants to be or needs to be. How long's it been, we've known each other? Many, many years, from the time we were a couple of yeomen at Camelot, that's how long. I was working on the Hill and so were you. We couldn't find our ass with both hands, back then. All those old farts talking at us, we couldn't make out what they were saying half the time, mumbling and using that short-hand, that Capitol Hill code. Remember the Camel? He could go for a week without water, that one. You always liked him, I could never figure out why; mean as a camel, though his effectiveness was never in doubt. The Camel taught us a thing or two, about keeping your head down and going for a week without water. Couple of amateurs in the United States Congress, that was us, trying to learn how to get along. But we traded information and helped each other learn what makes this town go, who succeeds and who doesn't. And we sort of followed each other up the ladder.'' He turned to Camilla, who was listening hard now; he was speaking half to her and half to me. ''And here you are in the White House and here I am with my column and I suppose we're the old farts and no one understands what we're saying. Except us. We understand each other and we're friends and so forth and so on because we've grown up together. We've always tried to look out for each other, we've offered counsel even when it wasn't asked for or welcome. So I'm surprised at what you've said and the way you've said it, and I have this little bit of advice. You ought to keep this conversation off the record. I'm willing.''

That was the pot of gold at the end of Tap Gobelin's wordy rainbow. When young Camilla looked at him in astonishment, he raised a warning finger.

''Let the man speak, Milly.''

I said, ''Pat Bayley was like a father to me when I needed one.''

When the reporters left I sat a moment, thinking. I was suddenly back in Chicago, trying to imagine the place as it was now, the Hall and the Morrison, Bayley and Bayley's friends, all of them years older. I could imagine Pat Bayley hiring a bagman. Election time was a general payday and you had to distribute the money somehow. But it wouldn't be to a federal judge and it wouldn't be across the table in a white envelope, return

192

receipt requested. Yet I admitted to myself that I didn't know very much about that side of things in Chicago, and of course anything was possible. That was one of the things that you learned, the longer you stayed in the business. Stupidity and greed had no limits, as the rules changed.

I turned on the television set, the President live from the Rose Garden. I asked the switchboard to get me Patrick Bayley, Chicago lawyer, and stood at the window with the telephone. I could see the reflected glare of the television lights, harsh in the outdoors, and then, turning to the screen, could see the Rose Garden itself with its dais and microphones. Members of the White House staff were clapping and waving, and the President and his wife were smiling and waving back; a commentator described the action, such as it was. The camera suddenly panned high over the White House and for an instant I saw my own window with me in it, a man with a telephone, coatless, smoking a cigarette, a row of identical windows that dissolved back to the Rose Garden, live. Then Bayley was on the line.

He sounded exhausted and out of it. I could hear a television set in the background; he too was watching the President, live. He said he was home, making calls; and having a drink, if I wanted to know the truth, though it was not yet noon and he never drank before noon, except on special occasions. He said it was good to hear my voice but it was a different voice than he'd known though that was to be expected, I'd been out of the area for so long. He meant I'd lost my Chicago accent; and that was not a compliment. I said it was good to hear his voice, too, and that I knew he was in a jam. I said he needed to be careful. The newspaper gumshoes were tracking him and they had documents. I thought that if the Justice Department could leak Bayley to Gobelin, I could leak Gobelin to Bayley.

He listened in silence, except for a tiny *tsst* sound and the rattle of ice cubes. He chuckled wearily and said he was in a fix, all right, and had called me to find out if I'd heard anything. That was his way in.

"Only from the reporters," I said. Ruh-porters.

"Jesus," he said. "How did they find out?"

"In this town," I said, "they're the first to know."
Firs ta no.

He sighed heavily, and I could hear the rattle of ice cubes again as he switched the phone from one ear to the other. He said, "It's complicated." He paused and I listened. "More complicated than it appears," he said, his voice dropping.

I said nothing to that.

He said, "Grand jury'll indict any day now and I don't know if I'm coming or going. It was quite a surprise, the whole thing, and it's only just beginning."

I said, "I'm sorry as hell, Pat."

"I guess it comes with the territory. I never thought it did, but I guess it does."

I said, "Are you all right?"

"I'm worried about my wife," he said. I put my hand on my forehead, listening to him. I knew he had a wife, in the way that I knew he had a mother and father; but I had never heard him mention her. We shared business together, and that was all.

After a moment I asked him if he needed any money. He paused before answering, very formally, No, thank you. I thought I had insulted him until I heard him cough, and sigh.

"That part of it'll be taken care of," he said. "Supposedly. But I'm going to take a fall and there isn't anything you or anybody else can do about it. That's the way it's been set up. That's what happens." He coughed again and I could hear his breathing; the ice cubes rattled. "And my health is lousy."

I said, "Stateville's a bad place for a guy in bad health."

"You think the judge'll buy that?"

"No," I said.

"I don't, either," he said gruffly. Then, after a pause: "I'm watching the President on the tube. Why aren't you in the Rose Garden along with the rest of them? The vice-president and the secretary of state are there. Their wives. Goodness, that's a young staff. Some of those boys and girls are wet behind the ears, still. The President's making a speech. It's quite a show."

"Because I'm talking to you," I said. I turned from

the window and watched the President a moment. I had watched him speak so many times I could almost read his lips. He was buoyant and elated, but the cameras tended to do that; adrenaline was an addictive drug.

Pat said, "I guess it's quite a success, the summit."

"What do they think about it in Chicago?"

"Christ, I don't know," he said. "We've had a cold snap, almost a record yesterday. People're talking about the weather, and how the Bears are doing. Except me. I'm talking about two to ten at Stateville."

"Pat," I said.

"I don't like the Commies," he said.

"Nobody does," I said.

"Is that a fact. How come we do so much business with them?"

I was staring at my Germans, listening to Pat Bayley lecture me on the Communist Menace, worse every year. Kirchner and Schmidt-Rottluff were two of Hitler's leading degenerate artists, dangerous subversives. The *Mädchen* were subversives also. The President was still talking and I made out the words "historic" and "confident." His eyes were glittering and he was talking faster than he needed to.

Pat said, "Are you still there?"

"Who's your lawyer?" I said.

"Elly Mozart," he said without enthusiasm. "You remember Elly, never did much trial work. Elly hasn't opened a law book in a hundred years, but this is different. They told me to get Elly, so I got Elly. Elly's on the case, for whatever that's worth. He's supposed to know his way around. And what Elly wants to do is plead."

I grunted negatively.

"Tell me about it," he said.

I said, "You want a character witness, tell Mozart to call me. He might not want to do it, but tell him anyway."

"You serious, Jack?"

"Yes," I said.

"It's a mistake," he said.

"No," I said.

"You don't want to get involved. They're going to hang me out to dry," he said. "I appreciate it, your offer. And the money, I appreciate that, too. I didn't expect it. I didn't call for that reason."

I said, "Good luck to you, Pat."

"Why wouldn't Elly want to do it?"

"Elly and I go way back," I said.

"That Nierendorf business," he asked.

"Yes," I said, surprised. "How did you know about that?"

"Who do you think kept you out of the deep shit? They were going to break your kneecaps." He hesitated and the ice cubes moved. "Not literally. But they were triple-pissed and they came to see me, ask me to straighten you out before they did. They wanted their young lawyer happy and alert, happy at home and alert at the office. I told them to work it out among themselves, that you were on my payroll and protected." He laughed shortly. "That was when I had a payroll and could actually protect someone. So I said you were off-limits. You belonged to me."

"I didn't know that," I said. "That Mozart had called—"

"Lot you didn't know in those days, Jack. You were younger than springtime. You were as young as those kids in the Rose Garden. You're probably up to date now, though. So you'd know what the situation here is, not anything like it used to be. We had a hell of a nice town then, everybody liked Boss City, good working-man's town. But it's not the same. I suppose you know that."

"Nothing's the same, Pat."

"Some things are. Death and taxes, for example. Revenge is always in style. Not loyalty, except maybe in your town. Where I am, there isn't any control anymore. There used to be. There isn't any power anymore, there's just the electric box. Power used to make you money. Now money makes you power. Politics in this town. There never was as much money in it as people thought, though the scale was different then. Money wasn't as important as control. You had to have the money because you had to live, so the money followed the control, but it *followed*. It didn't lead. Hell, we're old, worn out, out of it, run to fat. We're an old heavyweight, the Brown Bomber. Even the wiseguys aren't worth a damn. No power and no money, except over at La Salle Street. Who needs politics? It used to be a family business, but the kids didn't care. My two moved away, one of them to Milwaukee, for Christ's sake. Bratwurst and cuckoo clocks. So the business passed into new hands, as it was bound to do but, Jesus, didn't it happen in a hurry? Maybe it all started to go to hell in 'sixty-eight, that mess of a convention. You think that was it, Jack?''

"No," I said. The camera panned back, and the President and his wife waved; those in the Rose Garden burst into applause, even the roses seemed to quiver in the lights. I saw myself in the window of my office, my back, the telephone to my ear. I was leaning against the sill. Then the screen went blank to ignite a moment later with an anchorman looking grave but friendly; or perhaps the reverse.

"There he goes," Pat said. "Bye-bye, Prez, you wimp."

"That was me in the window," I said.

"No kidding. Which one?"

"Seventh floor. Me talking to you on nationwide television."

"You better hope they don't have a wire."

"I don't care about that," I said. "And they don't."

"I thought that place was wired for sound."

"Not anymore," I said.

"That god damned tube. Can't even identify your friends."

"I was pretty high up," I said. "Hard to see."

He laughed at that. "Boy, Jack."

"Let me know about Mozart," I said.

"Okey-doke."

"He can call me here."

"All right."

"Let me know what's happening."

"You can read all about it, looks like."

"I'd rather hear it from you," I said.

"It's quite a story," he said. "I'll call."

197

I said, "Okay, Pat." He didn't want to leave the telephone, except that his drink was probably finished.

He said, "I've got to find some way, tell my son in Milwaukee. He's a good kid, works for one of the breweries. I've got the one boy in Milwaukee and the other in Saint Louis, still in school. I've got to tell him, too. No one stayed home except me."

"Good luck to you, Pat."

"Jack? Thanks, more than I can say. I didn't expect it, what you offered, and I won't hold you to it. But I appreciate it. Elly will, too, probably." He seemed about to say something more, then thought better of it and hung up instead. I was left with a dead line and a friend who was frightened to death and bewildered, drinking to calm his nerves. In the old days, Pat Bayley had never been bewildered. He had a payroll and people he protected, "family only." Professor Karcher and Patrick Bayley, my introductions to the modern world, along with Victor; and now this. It sounded to me like a sting, but perhaps not. It didn't matter anyhow. Bribing a federal judge was no small thing; there was much iniquity in the world and on that scale Pat Bayley did not weigh heavily. There were innocent men in prisons all over America, not to mention the rest of the world. Pat had made a mistake, got caught, and would pay. He was not innocent. I did not know what had brought him to it, and would never know. There would be testimony and the subtext of the testimony, and gossip in the Hall and the Morrison and probably on Pennsylvania Avenue, the Justice Department. There would be plenty of speculation, most of it having to do with motive. But that would be words, tailored for the company; they would look good on the person who spoke them; one more small-time grafter trying to bend the rules and traduce the state, blundered, got caught. Wouldn't be the last, wasn't the first. But the whole story would never be known, not that there was tremendous interest, because the world went on. There was something new every day. Even Pat himself would not be able to give the whole story because no man was omniscient, least of all with his own life.

* * *

That was the day I went home early. I did not go to work the next day or the day after. I got bronchitis and the flu, which developed into pneumonia. I was in the hospital for a week, so sick I was hallucinating. Pat Bayley was in and out of my hallucinations, a gallant if irascible commentator. I imagined various futures, believing that if I could observe them I could navigate my way through them or find a place in them, a safe haven to drop anchor for keeps. The futures were there to be seen, acts already written and cast; there seemed to be a variety of authors. I was lost and desperate to find my own role, something distinguished, risky, apt, and consequential. My fantastic hallucinations multiplied and when at last the fever broke I looked up to see my Marie, lovable, sarcastic Marie—as distraught now as I had ever seen her. I imagined her caught in a herd of elephants, dodging and sidestepping, the elephants clumsy and frightened, crashing into one another, a family ready to stampede.

I said, How about a cigarette?

She laughed, and burst into tears.

We talked self-consciously of this and that. She did most of the talking, watching me carefully. Then she sat, drawing her chair close to the bed. She said she had bad news. Victor had died the day I went into the hospital. There had been a funeral service and she had gone. It was very sudden, a stroke; he suffered no pain. Your mother was with him. The White House sent flowers. Your mother was so pleased. We didn't know how long you were going to be laid up, she said. God, you were so sick. And your mother wanted to get it over with. So we went ahead.

Good, I said.

Tell your mother that. She was worried.

I said, She's all right?

Yes, Marie said. Exhausted, though. Otherwise she'd be here.

I said, Was Sam there?

Yes, she said.

Good, I said. The old man would've liked that.

Sam was in and out in a day, she said. Dressed fit to kill. On the telephone a lot. On the telephone to Los

Angeles, in fact, where his wife was and where he had business.

As long as he was there at all, I said. Good. I wish it'd been me, though, to wish the old man a bon voyage.

I gather you had a complicated relationship.

He thought I was a gangster, I said.

She began to laugh. A gangster, our Jack? I laughed, too, until I started to cough. I could feel the fever move behind my eyes, shut now, conjuring up Victor, Victor as a young man, he and my mother on the deck of the yacht at Charlevoix, watching Capone and his chippie, listening to music and drinking real Scotch, the boat rocking gently, the smell of pines, the look of the weathered clapboard houses along the shore, men in white trousers and blue blazers and women in wide-brimmed hats. Then I was asleep and when I woke Marie was still there, dozing in the chair by the window. I had lost track of time and wondered whether I had dreamed Victor's death or whether it was real; perhaps both were true. I slept again and when I woke Marie was up drinking coffee, leaving only when I picked up the telephone to call my mother in Sarasota. Her "hello" was uncertain, distant, and unfamiliar, but my own voice was so choked I could scarcely speak.

When I left the hospital I went immediately to Florida. I stayed ten days, so weak I was no help to anyone. I slept in the mornings, and in the afternoons and evenings I sat on the balcony and watched the boats in the harbor, big, heavy-prowed yachts made of fiber glass and steel; ephemeral Florida, balmy, humid, indolent, unreliable. At night my mother and I had drinks on the balcony and talked of the past, Chicago in the old days, the look of the Near North Side in winter, the icy lake breeze, automobile tires crunching on hard-packed snow. Chicago was so remote from Sarasota, hard to believe they belonged to the same country. Yet as we talked of it we could almost touch it, smell the coal dust, feel the wind. It was an inheritance. She related old family stories, so well-worn, like cards from a wallet. They were ironic stories and a little malicious, but indisputably ours. We could do with them what we wanted, believe or not.

I asked if she wanted to go back home and she said No. Her home now was Florida, for better or worse. She couldn't bear another move, the turmoil, the packing and unpacking, the hassle. She nodded at the coffee table as a for-instance. The damned elephants; and they were the least of it. And all her friends had moved away, out of the city to the North Shore, or to Scottsdale; those who were still alive. She hated looking at the obituary page, it read like an old dance card. There came a time when it was better to stay put.

So many widows, she said. She lived in a nation of widows.

The men, I said.

They're worn out, she said. It's a tragedy for a man to retire. Six months sitting around the house, they look like capons; and then they get sick. I couldn't look after another sick man. Victor was different. Victor was mine. Another one wouldn't be mine, he'd be someone else's. We'd have each other on loan. I don't look forward to going to Big Lake alone, though.

Why Big Lake? I asked.

Because your father wanted it. He wanted his ashes scattered at Big Lake. His last inconvenient instruction.

Big *Lake*? I couldn't believe it.

Oh yes, she said.

I'll come with you, I said.

No, honey, she said. That's *out*. I'm going alone.

Why Big Lake? I asked again.

And she replied that she didn't know for sure. Victor's request surprised her, too. The vacations at Big Lake had been her idea, not his. He always complained about the drive, and you and your brother fought so in the car. Bicker, bicker, bicker. It drove him nuts. But maybe he remembered looking at the stars, and sitting on the dock in the evenings; and the war news on the radio. And Carl Fahr was his oldest friend, though we haven't seen him in years and years. I don't know. But the day before he died he mentioned it, casually but definitely. So she would take him back to Big Lake as she'd promised she would.

My last morning in Florida I woke early, though the sun was already high behind closed curtains, and hot; the air conditioning never concealed the heat. I had been dreaming about Washington, a nonspecific dream. It had no plot that I could remember. The old magnet had lost its force. Washington was more burned out than I was.

At breakfast my mother said, What about you, Jack? What are you going to do? That nice girl who came down for the funeral, Marie, said you were talking about quitting the White House. She couldn't believe it. And I can't believe it either, it's such a fine position, and so responsible. Isn't it shortsighted, just to quit?

I said, No.

She said, You young people move around so much.

I've been in Washington for a very long time, I said.

You know what I mean, she replied.

It's time to go home to Chicago, I said.

That's a bad idea, she said. Your father believed that Chicago was finished.

He was wrong, I said.

Victor? She said. *Wrong?* And gave a great whoop of laughter.

I flew home to Washington that night and a week later quit the White House, pleading burnout. This was a convenient explanation and not entirely false, though no one believed it. The President's wife was particularly suspicious but listened when I told her I had come to the end of the line in their administration. I was stale and needed a change. I felt like a picture on my own wall.

Take care, she said. Let me know if there's anything I can do to help, later on.

I thanked her and said I would; and later on, I did.

I went private, against the best advice of worldly friends who said the time was not right, that I would lose my shirt and be stranded in the cold with no protection. Washington dealt harshly with those who had no institutional support. Marie agreed. I pleaded with her to join me but she refused; they had offered her my old job, and she could not resist. A silver coffee service all her own! So I opened an office on I Street. And the

202

worldly friends were wrong: the time was exactly right and the rewards unbelievable. My network of friendships was larger than I expected, and the loyalties were strong. Politics had become a business, and demand was strong.

That was how it came to be that I was drawn back into Chicago's hurly-burly. It seemed that everyone I knew was running for something or working for someone who was; and not only Chicago, the entire region. I gradually shifted my operations west, and at last bought an apartment on the Near North Side, not far from the building I had grown up in. The news was good, then not so good, then terrible. Abruptly, a great stillness settled over the region. No one now stood on the plains of the upper Midwest and reached for Boss City, the ticket out. Newspapers failed; a great bank went into receivership, its vaults stuffed with bad paper from Tulsa, Rio, Mexico City, Des Moines. Even the mighty Syndicate aged, the dons exhausted. The wiseguys took their orders from younger men in smaller cities. The Machine creaked and groaned and, leaderless, failed to deliver. People laughed at it.

Marie left Washington for Cambridge and the government in exile; there was no action in Chicago, she said.

Pat Bayley died a week before the sentencing.

Things were breaking down all over the Midwest, and it came with such suddenness, like the summer squalls on Lake Michigan, except there was no turbulence, only a sullen inland torpor. The old foundryman went out and bought a new suit of clothes, said he would be a serviceman, dapper in a striped tie and an English suit. But the clothes didn't fit; he was accustomed to overalls and steel-toed boots and a side-of-the-mouth manner that did not go well with his new wares.

I settled in for the duration. And I realized, with a rush of gratitude, how much affection I had for the city, how well I understood it, and how much I owed it. In decline, the city had grown querulous—but is it reasonable to expect confidence from one who is frightened to death? Pat Bayley had mentioned the year 1968, and that had startled me; no one spoke of it now, that ancient summer. It might as well have been 1868. Yet

I remembered so well standing with Tap Gobelin and a girl on the fringes of the crowd in Grant Park, red flags and American flags, hair and obscenities and slogans. A boy emerged from the crowd, big and raw-boned, with a shock of yellow hair and a wide flat forehead, a Minnesota boy down from Hibbing on the Iron Range, grandson of an old Red. How the Minnesota radicals hated Hubert! Hated him worse even than Nixon, hated him with a cold peasant hatred. He began to speak to the police, not loudly but with such a concentration of feeling that those in the immediate vicinity fell silent. I was over thirty and his opinions were not mine but he expressed them with a fine edge of conviction, what the Irish call a fresh mouth, taunting the men in blue. He could have been on the barricades in Paris in 1848 or Moscow in 1917 or East Berlin in 1953, Budapest in 1956 or Prague a few months before that very night. Then the police surged and the crowd of young fell back, all but the yellow-haired boy, who did not move, who waited for the enemy with stoic patience as any young martyr is supposed to do. They knocked him down and beat him with billy clubs and all he did was put his arms over his head. When I reached his side they beat me, too, working with a mirthless enthusiasm. But they concentrated on him because he was younger and because he had taunted them; and perhaps they saw something of themselves in him, the anarchic something that had suppressed itself in service to the state. Blood was everywhere on the boy's face and in his hair. When Tap showed him his press badge he talked through broken teeth; and that was how we found out about his grandfather. The boy gave me a hand, helping me to my feet; we were suddenly comrades. The girl we were with said I was bleeding, too, from a cut on the forehead; but she was looking at the Minnesota boy, who was paying no attention. Staring then at Tap's badge, he gave a snort. Capitalist press! Pig newspaperman! He staggered off to join his comrades, turning at the last moment to run a finger down his chest and wipe the blood on Tap's press badge, a grisly reminder, a souvenir of the siege of

Chicago. That was my memory of 1968; and I still had the scar.

Now, so many years later, I wondered about the next act. I wondered how frightened they really were, Chicago's old men, with the money running out and the basics unattended to. America's heartland was calling itself the Rust Belt and pleading for federal intervention. The region had lost its nerve. I began to hope that there was one more step I could take, to settle my debt and perhaps collect one.

PART THREE

'Eighties

1

THE old senator had been talking for ten minutes, reprising his last campaign, how ungrateful his constituents, how merciless the media, and how expensive it all was. Gracious, the high cost of losing! I was looking over his shoulder, out the window. The warm autumn wind scattered dust in the empty street; we may as well have been in Duluth. The air above was bright and clear because cold smokestacks do not foul the atmosphere. Across the street a drunk slowly made his way along the curb. He stopped to lean against a boarded-up storefront. The faded lettering above the door said HABERD SHER. The drunk leaned there a moment to get his bearings, a man without resources, infinitely depleted and harmless. The burly parker who had taken my car was suspiciously watching the drunk. When the parker moved, I could see the snub-nosed revolver tucked into his belt, not quite concealed by his jacket. The parker made a threatening motion with his hand, but the drunk looked at him without comprehension. The parker's lips moved and the drunk smiled foolishly, an ingratiating smile. The empty street separated them. Finally the parker turned away in disgust, shooting his cuffs, reflexively touching the weapon with the fingers of his left hand, tidying up.

A dangerous neighborhood, but it was where the senator wanted to meet, not because it was dangerous but because it was out of the way. A quiet lunch, Jack. Just us two, and we can chat a bit and get the measure of things, the current situation, and discover where we've been and where we're headed and so forth and so on. We were sitting in the dining room of a once-fashionable restaurant. In the old days, before the neighborhood went to hell, it had been popular with professional athletes and politicians. And a few of them still turned up, Elly Mozart for example, seated at the quiet table in the far corner, away from the bar and the dining room. His companion had his back to us, and they were deep in conversation. The senator had not seen Mozart. I noticed him only because my father and I had sat at that table, almost forty years ago; he had taken me to lunch on my birthday.

The senator patted his mouth with his napkin and cleared his throat. We had finished our lunch, the small talk was over, and he was ready for business. I leaned forward, thinking about the lunch with my father, my father then much younger than I was now. George Halas was lunching with Red Grange and I had gone over to get Grange's autograph.

The waiter said, "Gentlemen?"

I said, "Nothing for me. Senator?"

"Coffee," the senator said. Caaaaawwwwwwffffeeeee, a sonorous six-syllable word, spoken with the portentousness of a declaration of war. The senator looked at the waiter and smiled his hundred-watt smile, his ruddy face twinkling and crinkling. He was very tan, having just returned from Palm Springs. The waiter flushed with pleasure. He did not know the identity of his customer, but he knew he was famous, noticed immediately the little ripple that went around the room when the old man entered and strolled to the table, fifteen minutes late. A character actor perhaps, or a former big-league manager. "And I think a cognac. Jack, have a cognac." He said, "Two cognacs, son. Courvoisier, thank you very much." The waiter nodded and withdrew.

"Senator," I began.

"So you're going to go, is that it?"

"Yes," I said.

"That is your own decision," he said. He raised his hand and fluttered it at someone nearby. "I wouldn't attempt to influence it. I'm out of the game now. I'm just an old retired politician." I looked at him, thinking about my father. Victor Gance would never have allowed himself to be patronized. This was the moment when Victor would have sighed, brushed a speck of lint from his blazer, fixed the old senator with a surly stare, and said, *You are a fool*. And departed immediately for the Chicago Athletic Club and an afternoon of reckless bridge. His advice to me would have been quite different, however. *What's the matter? Do you think you're too good to listen to a United States senator?* Consistency was never Victor's long suit. I listened to the senator tell me how old he was, and how out of it. A clean bill of health from his doctors, though, and he had worked his handicap down to fifteen. He said, "I assume you've done your homework, that you've polled and spoken to the people you must speak to. And, first and foremost, that there's money available." He looked at me without expression, knowing that money was a problem. "That you have a reasonable chance of success. You'll certainly have my support"—and here he smiled, fifty watts this time—"after the primary. You understand that, of course."

I said, "Of course." His endorsement was not worthless, but it was not very important, either. I wondered if he knew that.

He said, "I wish we knew each other better. I was always so busy with the committee, the meetings on the Hill and downtown. When Jerry was in the White House." He sighed. "Last one who understood how things worked, so I saw quite a lot of him, informally. A little drink in the evening, just us two. He was a hell of a nice guy, and a patriot." He looked sharply at me to see if I agreed; as a matter of fact, I did agree, so I nodded. "You rarely had a matter before the committee, so we didn't see as much of each other as we should've. Your interests were always . . ." He paused, seeking a neutral word.

"Domestic, Senator."

"Yes, I daresay. And political." He shook his head. "My wife says that if I'd had you on my team we wouldn't've gotten licked. She still talks about it, talked about it only last night. She called me a stubborn fool, not to understand the threat that son of a bitch posed." He looked up, smiling formally. "She says you would've found a way, discredit the son of a bitch. Is that right? Would you have found a way?" He leaned forward, angry, waiting for the answer; and then he relaxed, smiling again, leaning back as the waiter arrived with the cognacs.

I said, "Probably not."

"She disagrees."

"Your wife flatters me. But it wasn't your year, and you had bad luck."

"Luck?"

"You need luck in politics."

"That's true, of course," he said. "Luck and timing, we were talking about that, too, the other night. It surprised her, surprised both of us, to learn that you were going in. You've been an inside man, behind the scenes for so long, hard to imagine you out in the sunlight. The pit. That's what Dick Nixon called it, 'the pit.' So she asked me to ask you. Why? You're so successful back in the woodwork, why go out front? You know what happened to the great and terrible Oz, ha-ha. The curtain parted and it was just an old fart cranking a Wurlitzer. You, so many years in the shadows, speech writer, idea man, advance man, pollster, advertising man, ah, ah, alter ego. Mr. Fixit, Jack Gance. So if it isn't a secret, why? Why now, if you don't mind my asking."

"There's an opportunity," I said.

He said, "This region, there's always an opportunity, though I agree that this year's a special case. Goodness, the other side has screwed up. God, they've made a mess of things. Not entirely their fault, but who cares about fault. So you're correct, there's an opportunity. But it's no day at the beach, out there in the pit. So there must be another reason." He lifted the glass of cognac. "Your very good health, Jack."

"Look out there," I said suddenly. I nodded at the window, over the senator's shoulder. He turned, curious. The drunk had fallen and was on his knees, like a fighter taking the count. The wind had picked up and bits of paper and refuse were mixed with the dust, everything vivid in the yellow sunlight. The senator was looking into the street, but then I remembered that he was near-sighted and too vain to wear glasses and too old for contact lenses. I gave him a quick history of the neighborhood, which I knew well; I had used it as a

212

laboratory thirty years before, when I was a student at the university. Thirty years ago it seemed as secure and stable as Switzerland, but now it resembled Beirut, chaotic and violent, without industry, and still a way to go before it hit bottom. As I talked I watched the drunk. He was tall and sandy-haired and I wondered if he was one of the refugees from downstate, a busted farmer come to try his luck in the Emerald City. I hated it, what had happened to the region; in the old days, there had been money to burn. I went on like that a minute until the senator began to fidget.

"Your opponent—" he began.

"Doesn't understand the problem," I said.

"You helped her, last time out."

I nodded; that was true enough. She won easily.

"Word is, you designed her campaign."

"Not entirely," I said. I pointed again at the drunk. "For example, I was more interested in his right to life than the right to life of the unborn."

"Yes," he said. "But she won, and she went to the House. And now, after only one term, she wants to be a United States senator. Don't they move quickly? Gracious, they move like lightning, one thing to another. They're rolling stones." He leaned forward, speaking softly now. "My wife thinks you hung the moon, she thinks you're just the smartest thing, a nonpareil. And we can't figure it out, Jack. Why are you doing this?"

I nodded at the window. "I want to do something about that. I intend to do it."

He was silent a moment. "I see what you're saying. It's cause for grief. Our region has been left behind, and Springfield's been unresponsive." He talked for a moment about Springfield's responsibilities, a history of legislative failure. While he talked he tipped his glass this way and that, watching the legs the cognac made. "You've looked at all the angles?"

"The ones I can see," I said.

"Jack," he said. "She called me the other day, wanted to have a little chat. Listen to an old head, as she put it. So we played the back nine out at Oak Knoll, just the

213

two of us, with a cart. Goodness gracious, she's an aggressive young woman."

I said, "I think she wants to be President."

He said, "It would be a historic candidacy."

I said, "What did she say, during your little chat in the golf cart?"

"She's thorough," he said.

"She's mean as a snake," I said.

He said, "She's got the book on your father."

I laughed. So that was it. "Ancient history, Senator. All you've got to do to get the book on my old man is to call up the morgue at the *Trib*, one clipping after another. And he's been dead a long time."

"She'll do whatever she has to do."

"Senator," I said. What he didn't know about the modern world would fill an encyclopedia. I said, "See this?" I held up my cigarette, then stubbed it out. "According to my polls, this costs me votes, my opponent wants to make an issue of it, and she will. And the TV cameraman shows me lighting up or, worse, blowing smoke in some child's face. It's worse than about anything, except possibly AIDS. And at least with AIDS you get some sympathy. So last month I gave them up. I need every vote I can get, and giving up cigarettes, two packs a day, doesn't cost any money. I don't have to buy TV time to get the votes, I only have to give up smoking, which I did. And in that month I got the shakes, I gained twenty pounds, I was drinking half a bottle of vodka a day, and I was impotent. So I considered the cost, an obese drunken capon with the DT's and said the hell with it and went back to the smokes." I looked at him, hoping to win a smile so that we could wind up the meal and get back to work. He could say he'd delivered his message. But he was as grave as ever; perhaps he hadn't heard me. So I spelled it out for him. "She wants to make my late father a campaign issue, that's fine. I invite her to do it. I reckon a sympathy vote more than enough to equal my cigarette addiction. There probably is a way to make it an issue but she isn't smart enough to find it."

"Jack," he said. "We don't want to tear ourselves to pieces." He took out his glasses and put them on, slowly

214

surveying the room. "And it's a mistake to underestimate your opponent. She's a little weak off the tee, but she's superb around the green. Her short irons. She kills with her short irons. Isn't that Elly Mozart in the corner?" He fluttered his hand at Mozart, who smiled, nodding. "Who do you suppose that is, with Elly?" Mozart and his companion rose and moved toward us, threading their way around the empty tables. Mozart and the senator shook hands, and when Mozart turned to present his companion the man smiled and said, "I know Jack. Jack and I go way back." He saw the bewildered expression on my face, for he smiled more broadly and added, "It's been a long, long time, hasn't it, Jack? Charles Nierendorf."

I had not seen him since that day in my apartment in 1959, but there was nothing about him now that reminded me of him then. He was older, naturally; but a man's mannerisms do not change after the age of twenty-five, his way of walking or standing, his look in repose, his voice. This Nierendorf was larger and thicker than the one I remembered. He wore a neatly trimmed mustache, and moved more slowly. He was expensively dressed, a blue suit and vest, and a heavy gold watch. The Nierendorf I had known was lithe and rangy, in constant motion, filled with energy. This one was composed and static, almost ponderous, though he gave the impression of physical strength. I looked at him in astonishment, seeing the resemblance at last. Mine was the reaction one has when shown an unfamiliar painting and asked to guess the artist. Picasso, one is told, and then one sees—of course it's Picasso, it couldn't be anyone else, yet when the painting was first shown, it did not look like Picasso, or anybody.

They sat down and the senator signaled for another round. Nierendorf and Mozart declined; they would take coffee. The senator removed his glasses and put them in his breast pocket, and immediately turned to talk to Mozart, sotto voce. Charles Nierendorf and I stared at each other.

Without waiting for me to ask, he said that he lived now in New York. He had gone to the West Coast "when I broke up with the woman I was married to" but the

West Coast didn't suit him so he moved east. He had lived in New York for twenty years, married again. Happily, he said. He was an investment banker, but when he named the firm I didn't recognize it. It's very small, he explained, only a few partners, a private firm. And quiet; they didn't go in for publicity. His tone suggested the man who says he has a little place in the country, which turns out to be fifteen rooms with a swimming pool and two tennis courts and a hundred acres for the Black Angus, out near Middleburg or Barrington. He said, "The law didn't agree with me so I gave it up for banking." This was his first visit to Chicago in, oh, fifteen years, and the city had certainly changed, except for the Loop. The Loop and the Gold Coast were booming, so there was still business to be done and money to be made. And they loved to deal, in the Loop and the Gold Coast. Most of his business was in the East but Elly had invited him out for a walk around and some conversation, and lunch. We're partners again, after all these years. Isn't he amazing? Charles said, nodding at Mozart.

He certainly was, I agreed. Amazing was the word. The old lawyer was eighty at least, and from the look in his eyes had lost none of his cunning.

Charles said, "I hear you're running for the Senate." This was a statement, not a question. He continued, "And from what they tell me, you're in for quite a battle."

No need to ask who had supplied that information. I lit a cigarette and said that all primary campaigns were battles, fundamentally unpredictable.

He said, "I don't know anything about it." Then he leaned forward and spoke softly. Who was the gentleman talking to Elly? Elly had told him but he had forgotten the name and didn't catch it when they were introduced. I told him and Charles sat back, nodding; yes, the name rang a bell.

Charles said, "He's with you, in your campaign?"

"Not yet," I said.

He said, "I'm interested. What will it cost you, the primary campaign? And if you win the primary, what will it cost to win the general election? Round numbers," he said to show he wasn't asking for confidential information.

I gave him two figures, both low, and he nodded sardonically, cocking his head to show he didn't believe me.

"Jack," Elly Mozart said. "Jack, Jack. More, I think. Much more. I think you're out of date." He turned to the others. "Jack's spent so much time in the barn, maybe he's out of touch with conditions in the field." He looked at the senator for confirmation, and then began to speak in his slow precise way. The senator was examining his fingers, and nodding. I thought that I must be losing my wits not to see what was coming from the moment I walked into the restaurant and saw Mozart sitting where Victor and I had sat a hundred years ago. This was not Mozart territory and never had been.

"Listen to Elly, Jack."

Mozart was being patient, talking about money, so much for staff, so much for travel, so much, so very, very much for media. Television, devilish, an infernal deity, but so vital. If a political campaign were a war, television would be the air force. You needed it to break their morale. You bombed their civilians. And if somehow their defenses were superb, you simply bought more bombs and more aircraft, and you let them know, always, that there was more where that came from, that there were no limits, that whatever it took, you had. Why even in Naperville—and he recited the rate card from memory—so much for thirty-second and one-minute spots, prime time and regular time. So much for direct mail and phone banks, so much for billboards, so much for radio. On the whole, dollar for dollar, radio was an excellent investment, just excellent. But you had to have television, too, the heavy high-flying bombers, essential in a contested primary (not to mention the grisly general election itself). And you had to have the right people behind you, and that was costly. "You'd know that, Jack, you who've done it for others. Who's one of the best in the business, who knows the value of things. You know what we say in the legal profession. A lawyer who represents himself has a fool for a client. And where's the money to come from?"

Charles Nierendorf put his hand to his mouth, stifling a belch.

"You must want her very badly, Elly."

"Jack," he said, disappointed.

"What's she got, Elly?"

"She's an excellent fund raiser," Mozart said.

"And trustworthy," the senator said.

"I'll bet she is. How much will she have, round numbers?"

"I'm told," Mozart said. He hesitated, thinking. "I'm told she'll have as much as she needs."

I looked at both of them.

"And she's tough. She's a scrapper."

"Short irons," I said.

"That's it exactly," the senator said.

Charles said, "She's a good-looking woman. Alert."

I said, "You know her?"

"Elly introduced us this morning," Charles said. "She makes a fine, businesslike presentation." He cocked his head and smiled. "And she wants it so badly."

"Primaries can be so bloody," Mozart said. "So unpredictable. Things're said, can't be unsaid. When a campaign gets mean and dirty, as this one could get, people digging around in the past—if those of us with cool heads and a realistic attitude don't watch ourselves and be sensible, then it's a tragedy, and there's blood everywhere. *You* know that, Jack. And we have only ourselves to blame for it. Primary campaign becomes an inventory of torts, but when the jury speaks the torts don't go away, as they're supposed to. They fester and the opposition is delighted. We're doing their work for them! They see a division and they move to exploit the division. And the thing about her is, she's a known quantity, so poised and helpful, and so well liked downtown." He shook his head sadly. "Things get torn apart and in the end no one wins."

"Except the winner," I said. I knew what was coming but I wanted to hear him say it. I remembered Carole Nierendorf's description of Mozart's voice, soft and furry as velvet, the velvet bristling with what moved behind it.

"It's a futures market, Jack. It's a commodities exchange. Hog bellies, winter wheat, platinum, politics.

218

Everyone wants to place his bets early, get in on the ground floor before the prices rise. And there's only so much money to go around, things being what they are. I'm talking mainstream money, the sort of money a man's not ashamed to have. What the hell, you want to be on the solid side of things. Am I right? You're an insider, not some renegade dancing around on the fringes. A beatnik. I know you, Jack.'' Mozart turned his head suddenly and yawned hugely. When he turned back his eyes were moist and he was smiling.

''Amen,'' the senator said.

I was watching Charles Nierendorf, his immobile face and heavy torso. He looked like a million dollars and then some. He said solemnly, ''Well put, Elly.''

We were the last people in the restaurant. Sunlight streamed through the dusty window. Dust was in the air, caught in the shafts of yellow sunlight. A waiter was working a vacuum cleaner at the other end of the room, and through the wide door I could see the bartender watching television while he cleaned cocktail glasses. Nierendorf turned, gazing out the window into the street. The drunk was sprawled on the sidewalk in the sun and he was no longer alone. A photographer was taking pictures. The photographer was dressed in blue jeans and a bush jacket and carried a bulky camera case. A plastic card dangled on a chain around his neck. I remembered that one of the newspapers was doing a series on the homeless. I watched the photographer frame his shot, compose it in such a way as to get the curb, the sidewalk, the drunk, and the faded sign, HABERD SHER. He adopted a kind of combat stance and began to shoot, maneuvering in a semicircle, doing a little tango with his feet and shoulders. Once or twice he stopped to adjust the camera setting. He moved in close and then backed up into the street. I was mesmerized, watching him; his energy was palpable, his concentration complete. The drunk never moved, and I wondered if he was dreaming and, if so, the nature of the dream. Then I wondered if the newspaper would have to secure a release. Probably not. The subject was only an old derelict, drunk, down and out, and unlikely to read the morning newspaper; in any case, he would not recognize himself. He was public property as much as any cop or fireman. But the photographer had a prize winner, if his settings were accurate and his composition correct. Now he changed lenses, a long lens for a short one, and, still in a crouch, backed away, out of my view. He would be shooting from this side of the street, everything foreshortened and just the slightest bit distorted, owing to the telescopic lens. I continued to watch the motionless derelict, realizing suddenly that his image was being transferred to film even as I watched, and would be seen by newspaper readers as I was seeing him now, face down, sprawled on the pavement; he looked like a fallen soldier. Of all this, the derelict would have no knowledge; and the thought would not occur to the photographer, who was preoccupied with the fundamentals of his craft, as all professionals are. So it was my story and my story alone, and now I imagined that somewhere on the Gold Coast tomorrow a woman would see the photograph and be moved to pity, would rise from her breakfast table and go to her desk, take out her checkbook and begin to write. Perhaps that would happen; it had happened before. Many times the newspapers alerted their readers to evil and misfortune, and inspired those readers to shake their heads and mutter, What a terrible thing. What a misfortune. And turn the page. I waited but the photographer did not reappear. I knew then that he had gone. He had what he wanted, and if he didn't, a block or two away there were more homeless, women as well as men. There were children also.

Mozart was talking again in his monotonous baritone; the velvet was no longer moving. I listened as I watched the street, thinking again of the photographer with the image of the derelict in his camera; a celebrity derelict, a Pulitzer prize–winning derelict, if the photos were ever published.

". . . it's thrilling, the way our society's opened up, there's so much equality. New opportunities for women, and minorities, and the like. Why if someone had predicted this, thirty years ago, I wouldn't've believed it. Get the men in the white coats! Lock that lawyer up, ha-ha. Haven't times changed in thirty years! That's when I first met you, Jack. Through Pat Bayley, God rest his soul. Remember? We met in the lobby of the Morrison—"

I said, "What was the story, with Pat?"

"Very unfortunate," Mozart said.

"You pleaded him. Why did you do that?"

"No defense," Mozart said.

"There's always a defense. Pat was no bagman."

"Pat was no bagman? Jack, you've been away so long—"

"Not that long," I said. "You sold him out."

Mozart stared at me a moment, then went on as if Pat Bayley had not risen, in that moment, from the dead. "You were an exceptionally mature young man who knew the score; everyone knew you had the world by the tail. You were the sort of young man who inspired the confidence and respect of older men, and that's important and not something to forfeit lightly." He took a sip of coffee, sighing, and the thought behind the velvet began to move again. "That's what I'm saying, Jack. Now we've got this damnable problem. She's so popular and connected. She's the consensus, and it would be a tragedy, tear things apart. Everyone's comfortable with her. We've got a winner, if only we can avoid a family fight. The sort of fight that airs our dirty linen, and only benefits the opposition. That's the sort of thing they're saying downtown. It's in your hands, Jack. That's what downtown thinks."

"And Washington," the senator said.

"Never mind Washington," Mozart said. "This is our own affair."

"Did you know he was sick, when you pleaded him?"

"They had film, Jack. And tapes."

"What's this about?" Nierendorf asked.

"Friend of Jack's," Mozart said. "Man who made a mistake."

"He paid off a federal judge for someone," I said. "Who was it, Elly?"

"That, we never found out. I think it was Pat acting alone, actually."

"I thought you'd know."

"Why would I know, Jack? I just represented him. I wasn't his priest or his wife. I wasn't even a friend, particularly."

"And you never asked me to be a character witness."

"Well," he said, smiling slyly. "You were out of the White House by then. I didn't think, given what we were

221

up against. It didn't seem worthwhile and, to tell the truth, I figured I was doing you a favor. And, hell, he died before he was even sentenced. Went to talk to him at his house one morning, dead in bed. God rest his soul.'' The room was quiet, only the hum of the vacuum cleaner in the far corner. Mozart took another sip of coffee. ''So she's the favorite, Jack. That's the way they see it downtown, and the way I see it.'' I watched him move his shoulders in a helpless shrug, the reluctant messenger of bad news. Mozart said, ''Downtown they asked if I'd have a word with you, since we know each other. See if there isn't a way we can work this thing out. We don't want anyone to take a bath.''

Almost there, I thought.

''Isn't it nice weather?'' the senator put in.

''Well, Jack,'' Charles said. He rose, extending his hand, a firm, confident handshake. I wondered what he remembered about 1959, or if he remembered anything. ''One of these days, maybe we can get together, talk about investment opportunities.'' His voice was soft and when he smiled he showed an even hedge of very white teeth, a banker's professional smile. ''These are boom times, you know. This is the greatest period of growth in the history of our country, but the growth is not across the board. You have to know where to look. In this forest, you need a guide. But what with this and that, there's always something happening on the Street. And we always have room for another investor.''

''You're talking to the horse's mouth, Jack.'' Mozart was on his feet, rocking back and forth on his heels.

There, I thought. There at last. They were offering me a bribe in the contemporary fashion.

I said, ''What sort of investment opportunities?''

''Myriad, Jack.'' He pronounced it my-raid. ''The moment, I'd say we're doing real estate, mostly. The upscale stuff because it's quick, you're in and out. Limited partnership, it's just an excellent way to shelter your money. And make some.'' With his hands he described a building, except it was more the outline of a woman, hubba-hubba in the old days. ''You borrow the money from the partnership, write off the interest. Your exposure's nil.''

''I know how it's done, Charles.''

"Well, good," he said. "Saves a lot of time explaining. Point is, there's no way to lose. Man gets in on the ground floor, steps into the elevator. Hell, you're out at the top."

I looked at Mozart. "Too bad Pat Bayley didn't have an investment opportunity from Charles, the horse's mouth. He wouldn't've needed the envelope with the greenbacks inside." I watched Mozart's eyes shift and I believe he colored slightly, though it was hard to tell; in any event he was no longer rocking back and forth in front of me, but was as still and imperturbable as Buddha. And then I turned to Charles, who had begun to coil: "What do you hear from Carole?"

Charles said blandly, "What does that have to do with anything?"

"Curious," I said.

"She's in Blackford."

"Well, good," I said.

"Yes, it is. It's where she belongs."

"Unmarried?"

"She married some reporter. He's with the media."

So it had worked out after all. "I talked to her on the phone once, a hell of a long time ago."

"What did you talk about?" He was controlling himself with effort.

"We talked about Elly Mozart," I said.

His eyes narrowed and he glanced at Elly.

"Carole's amazing," I said. "She has total recall."

Mozart looked at his watch.

"And your daughter," I said to Charles. "Do you ever see her?"

"Betsy's in Blackford, too," he said. "They're both in Blackford, Virginia." He spoke of them as if they were casual acquaintances, or anonymous casualties who had been left behind in the retreat. Looking at him, at his expensive clothes and hooded eyes and still manner, I knew he was one of those who had mislaid his past, forgotten it, and then caused it to cease to exist. He had edited his own memory, as we all do, but I had the idea he had done it with the ease of one absentmindedly erasing a blackboard after the day's lesson; his history was as scattered and elusive as chalk dust, and as consequential. With such a man, misprision is a sacrament, contemporary naturalness. I had been trying to unsettle both of them, but it was like trying to move granite. I wanted to return Charles to Chicago in the summer of 1959, when we had been apprentices together in the Windy City, and I had had a love affair with his wife. But he had no interest in any of that, and no interest in what his wife recalled of Elly Mozart; probably all lies anyway. And it had nothing to do with the matter at hand. Charles Nierendorf, banker, displayed the professional indifference of a hangman, and yet that was not how I remembered him at all.

He said, "You never married."

"No," I said.

He turned to Mozart. "I don't understand how people get through life without being married. Everyone needs a wife."

I said, "You'd be surprised."

"That's a problem for you, too, Jack, in the campaign." Mozart grinned; more a smirk than a grin. "The bachelor thing. Causes people to worry and wonder."

"And your father," Charles said. "Whatever happened to him?"

"He died," I said.

"People like family men," Mozart said. "Men like themselves, families, children. Stability, that's the key."

I looked at Mozart and laughed. "That's the key?"

"It's the kind of stuff that can be used against you," Mozart said. "And will be, you can count on it. 'Course maybe you don't care, maybe you don't give a hoot in hell. But if I were you, I'd pay attention to Charles's kind offer, which has an expiration date, Jack. It's not open-ended." He frowned, turning; and then back again to me, as if he had forgotten something. "You have a habit of putting a bad face on things, Jack. It's not an attractive trait. The Feds had Pat Bayley cold because he was a fool. He didn't know the first thing about what he was doing, and it wasn't because he didn't have good advice. He did. But he thought he knew better. He was listening to people he shouldn't've been listening to. That's my understanding. And he was arrogant. He thought he saw a certain kind of future, and it was a false future. So the

224

time came, and he took a fall. No mystery there. Anyone could've predicted it. He stuck up his head and someone shot at it and didn't miss.''

"That's so sound, Elly," the senator said.

Mozart said. ''That's about it, Jack.''

Charles said, ''Well!'' and rubbed his hands together. He turned to the senator saying how glad he was to meet him at last, he was surely missed on the national scene, man with a little experience and gray in his hair, ha-ha, and certainly they would have an opportunity to get together in the weeks and months ahead since he, Charles, would be visiting Chicago from time to time to help with the fund raising, not that that should be a problem; people knew a winner when they saw one.

I had not moved, listening to Mozart and then to Charles Nierendorf. I was reluctant to have this end. I wanted to remember everything, because I would think about it for a very long time. I said to Charles, ''And your father?'' Carole had told me about him; he and Charles were particularly close. I suddenly had a desire to see if anything could move the banker.

"He's still in Du Cass, Jack. Full of beans. In great shape; he's eighty years old. Going on forty. I talk to him every week long distance. He's a great guy, my best friend.'' Charles turned to the others, smiling broadly, shooting his cuffs, then giving a high-pitched giggle. ''My old man is a rascal, got a new girl friend, a cupcake of fifty-five, sixty. Not much older'n me, for cripes sake. Did it just to piss off my mother, who's always on his case. He's the sort of guy, never takes any shit from anybody.'' Charles stopped suddenly, apparently affected by his own show of emotion.

Elly Mozart said, ''That's great.''

"She's good-looking, too,'' Charles said. ''And unmarried. My dad doesn't foul another man's nest.''

"Of course not!'' Elly said.

"He's a sweetheart,'' Charles said, giggling again, giving a little kick as he backed away from the table. I thought suddenly that there was something to be said for the ancient father-son rivalry, as opposed to sweethearts together. ''Take care, Jack,'' Charles said. ''Hard times ahead.''

"Give it a thought," Mozart said. "I'd think very carefully, if I were you. And when you've considered it, give Charles a call. He'll be waiting."

Charles Nierendorf and the senator were already halfway across the room, and now Mozart moved to join them. I lit a cigarette, watching them go.

Mozart looked at me with disapproval. "You ought to give those up," he said, and then they were gone.

And in a moment I was on the street, too, alone and angry in the hot afternoon sun. Behind me I heard the door of the restaurant click shut, and the lock turn. The parker sauntered away to fetch my car. The derelict was still collapsed on the sidewalk, so I walked across the street and put a twenty in his pocket, a beau geste, a souvenir from the old days. He did not move, was as oblivious of my twenty as he had been of the photographer's camera. Quite an afternoon, I thought; a graduate-level seminar on *la vie politique*. I took out my wallet and extracted another twenty and tucked that in his pocket; and then a third. Twenty for me, twenty for the photographer, and twenty—twenty for the woman in the Gold Coast apartment, the one who turned the page. I stood looking at the sandy-haired derelict, backing away from the smell. He was baking in the heat, a slender fortyish man with wiry arms and hands as gnarled as tree roots. His fingernails were thick and ragged, and he had a farmer's suntan. And downstate they were preparing the harvest, stuffing the grain into silos, warehouses, Quonset huts, in the ground, anywhere there was space; it would lie there as useless as gold in a vault. I wondered if he was married and then I saw the white circle where his wedding ring had been; so there would be children also. I said aloud, Good luck, farmer. I realized I was tipsy from the wine at lunch and the cognac after. I was too old for cognac at lunch; and too experienced to spend a sentimental afternoon stuffing twenty-dollar bills into the pockets of derelict farmers, trying to put things right. Nothing wrong with a beau geste unless you made too much of it; and if I wasn't careful I'd get the bills thrown back in my face.

It occurred to me then that I'd been stuffed myself, by experts. They were men who knew what they wanted, give them that; and you had to admire the technique; it was a finesse my father would have appreciated. It was as choreographed as a ballet. No good crying about it or getting mad because there was no way to get even; their tables, their cards, their deal. And they were confident they knew their man. We were all professionals, and this was still Boss City. Professionals always understood one another, speaking the common language of the workaday world. If a man yielded it did not necessarily mean that he lost. He would merely have a different sort of reward, an investment opportunity, for example. He would not be a United States senator, but so few were. It was no disgrace, yielding to the inevitable; indeed, there was a kind of dignity and worldliness about it. It was cowardly, though. And fit nicely on a résumé of a modern man who knew the score. It was what they counted on, a practical man looking at practical realities. Hard, cold facts they called them. Hard facts, shrewd men. Fold your hand, your cards are weak.

The sun was so bright the street looked like a Hopper canvas, Hopper's hard edges and lonely sensual people, lonelier in the light than in the darkness; in the threatening darkness you could dream, summon a world, remember or forget, according to your taste. When I turned back, the parker was holding the car door, standing at attention watching me. I could see the bulge of the revolver under his coat, and the sight gave me a chill. I wondered if he had ever shot anybody. I handed him five dollars and he smiled, two fingers caressing the bill of his hat.

"Thank you, Cap'n. But it's been taken care of."

"No it hasn't," I said, pressing the bill into his palm.

"Yes, sir," he said. "Have a nice day!" He tapped the door shut and stepped back, grinning broadly.

And when I pulled away—the afternoon had become very complicated and I decided to revisit the South Side, the university, to stroll in the quadrangle, to discover if possible how much I had forgotten of the beginnings of things—I was careful to keep my eyes straight ahead, ignoring the scene that was surely displayed in the rearview mirror. The moment was arranging itself in my imagination, and I knew it to be true. I did not have to

227

see it with my own eyes in a mirror. The parker stood motionless, alert like a man stalking game. And then he swaggered across the dusty pavement to collect his second gratuity, his hands working through the derelict's pockets, contemporary Chicago naturalness.

2

THE course at Oak Knoll is flat and easy going, golf for middle-aged businessmen and their athletic wives. The front nine is shorter and more interesting than the back, and the fifth hole the most challenging, a dogleg with a great oak two hundred yards out where the fairway swings right. In that part of northern Illinois there are many huge oaks that were growing when Lincoln was living downstate. This one is prodigious and in the late spring beginning to fill with leaves, struggling in a dignified elderly way. The oak is the pride of the course and I remembered it from the last time I had played Oak Knoll, sometime in the 'sixties with Pat Bayley in the Member-Guest, a relaxed afternoon with Pat and two randy, storytelling surgeons. It was the reverse in every way from this April Tuesday, Mozart and I in an electric golf cart, a game arranged by a mutual friend who said that the old lawyer wanted to talk and that he would appreciate it as a personal favor if I would agree to listen to him, Oak Knoll, Elly Mozart, two sharp.

The members bore you to death with their flamboyant descriptions of Five, four hundred and ninety yards from tee to green. The long hitter wants to aim slightly right of dead center and fade the drive; but the fade must be controlled or the ball will land in the rough near the oak or, worse, hit the god damned tree; all the members call the oak the god damned tree. Worst rough on the course, quack grass so thick and high that balls are lost every day. Three sand traps block the entrance to the green, which slopes up and then dips down. The pin is usually in the dip. Behind the green are dark woods and the sixth

229

tee. The fifth is an easy hole for a long hitter with control. A very long hitter can achieve the green in two and with the regulation putts get down in four, a birdie. Because the fairway is so wide and handsome and the turf so soft and inviting, the romantic golfer always goes for the two big shots, for locker room bragging rights, haha. It's a pretty hole to play and the big drive wonderful to watch, particularly if it's yours, the ball rising swiftly ivory white and hard against the deep green of the turf, and then fading and striking the fairway with a big bounce, rolling beyond the oak, coming to rest white as a piano key on the horizon. Hell of a shot, chief. But Five is perverse because it offers such a temptation for the long ball, an appeal to recklessness and bravado; bewitched by theater, the romantic golfer ignores finesse. The truth is, Five rewards caution. Five is kind to the short hitter. Get the drive out straight, second shot in front of the traps, a seven iron to the green, two putts, down in five, par. Meanwhile the big hitter who thinks he's Nicklaus is thrashing around in the murderous rough or one of the three sand traps. Double bogie seven because he thought the drive would look so pretty and he overclubbed it and hooked or, worse, turned the fade into a slice. He forgot that at the end of eighteen it's the score they add up. You can make a great entrance but if you forget your lines in scene two it's a busted performance.

"Is that right," I said.

Mozart nodded. "I've seen a man go out three hundred yards and take nine more blows to get home."

"Because he wasn't reasonable," I said.

"Because he didn't plan ahead," Mozart said.

We were waiting on the tee, stalled by the foursome in front. Two men were searching for balls in the rough, having fallen victim to Five's false charm. They had motioned us through but Mozart had waved courteously; we're in no hurry, take your time. There was no one behind us and Mozart wanted a leisurely Tuesday game. He sat on the bench next to the tee, his legs crossed as if he were at his office desk. He was fascinated by the one-legged player ahead. Mozart explained that he had lost his leg in Korea but had always been a good golfer and saw no reason to give it up; an explosion in Korea was no reason.

"Watch him," Mozart said.

Each shot was an agony. The one-legged golfer backed up to his cart, steadied himself on its chassis, took a huge swing, and fell down. He fell down every time, always on his right hip. He had a detachable peg leg, which he put into the cart before each swing. When he fell down he hauled himself to his feet, using the golf club as a cane. Then he fetched his leg, fastened it, got into the cart, and drove on, always stopping the same distance from the ball. His partners paid him no notice and never helped him up. That was the bargain. The one-legged golfer had a twelve handicap and was valued as a partner for his competitive spirit. He never retreated. His swing was vicious and you could sense his fury and pain and frustration two hundred yards away. When the one-legged golfer waved us through, and Mozart refused, he stood scowling at us before he turned and hobbled off, as if he understood he was being observed and didn't like it.

"Never gives up," Mozart said. "He reminds me of you."

I said nothing to that and didn't believe it. I did not believe in Games as a metaphor for Life, though I knew when I accepted Mozart's invitation for golf that he'd get around to it sooner or later. And I had known a man who had been in the war and nothing that had happened in my life was the equal of what had happened in his, although he did not agree. I believed he was being modest.

"We think you could win, Jack."

"It'll be very close."

He nodded, concentrating on balancing the head of his driver on the toe of his shoe. "That's what our polls say. Too close to call. And the one hope she's got is that you're stalled. You're not moving, Jack. You're dead in the water. You haven't moved a point in a week and here we are, fourteen days until the primary. You've got the message but you can't get it out. You're a man with a bone in his throat. You've got to get the message *out*, to speak and be confident that you'll be heard. If you had her money, you'd win in a walk."

"That's true," I said.

"So near and yet so far," he said, rolling his eyeballs.
I said, "Yeah, Elly."

"She's breathing in an iron lung. And the iron lung's called television. She's paralyzed and the iron lung's keeping her alive because it's plugged into money. Pull the plug and she dies." He grinned, chuckling. "Every hour of every day, somewhere in the state, there she is on the tube in her cloche hat and her pearls and her dog and her husband. 'Give me your hand, give me your voice, give me your vote.' Sound familiar? JFK, nineteen sixty." Mozart looked up. The two golfers in the rough had given up, dropped fresh balls, and hit. They waited for the one-legged golfer, who balanced himself, hit a low line drive, and fell. Now the foursome was headed toward the sand traps, two golfers in each cart, the carts looking like toys as they bounced up the greensward.

"Your turn at bat, Jack. Take it nice and easy and you'll win the hole. It's a beast."

I drove and then it was Mozart's turn. He took his time, wagging the club head and flexing his fingers, muttering to himself. He took a half swing, slashing at the ball, popping it about a hundred and fifty yards. I walked and he rode alongside in the cart.

"Notice the difference in her spots?"

"She doesn't say anything anymore," I said.

"Right. Hand, voice, vote; that's what she says, and that's all she says. And the spots're pretty. We take her to the lakefront and down to Galena and standing in a cornfield somewhere, Bement. Nice music in the background. Maybe a cuddly child or two at her feet with a couple of concerned citizens listening attentively as she speaks. And of course the mutt, Cookie. But you don't hear what she's saying. You hear music or a train whistle or the wind in the god damned willows. But she doesn't talk anymore, noticed that? She doesn't talk because *people don't like her*. They don't like her voice. Shows up in poll after poll. Tin-whistle voice, and people don't like it." Mozart addressed his ball and popped it another hundred and fifty yards. Ahead of us the one-legged golfer was chipping from the apron of the green. It was only a twenty-foot chip shot but he put everything into

232

it, swinging and falling, and rising at once, watching the ball all the while.

"But it'll get us through the primary because the thing is, you're stalled. You're stalled for keeps because you're broke and it's too bad, because you've run a fine campaign, you've made every nickel count. But you don't have money for the spots. You don't have the air force for the carpet bombing. Kid who put our spots together is quite a lad, twenty-five years old. They call him a genius. Can you imagine? Unpleasant boy but shrewd and well spoken. Well-educated boy. Watch his spots and you're reassured. You're reassured that she knows what she's doing and that she's serious and tough, but feminine. As long as you don't hear her voice."

"Might work in the primary," I said. "But you can't run Helen Keller in the general. Speeches, press conferences, debates, every night on the six o'clock news. They'll eat her alive."

"That's correct, Jack. You've spoken the truth. People aren't focusing on this primary. But they'll focus on the general. And when they focus, she'll lose. We can win the battle but we'll lose the war if she's the nominee."

"I'd get her a voice coach, Elly."

He sighed; evidently that was not the reply he'd hoped for. "More complicated than that, I'm afraid. Her husband wants to take charge. And he likes her voice. He thinks it's cute. He thinks she's cute, and the trouble is that we've been holding her back. Let the tiger loose! At least that's what he tells the campaign manager, on the nights that he's fucking her instead of his wife."

I looked at him, but he was staring at the green. There was an argument of some kind. We could hear raised voices, and the one-legged golfer was waving his arms.

"I'd heard there was some sexual tension."

"He's pretty much of an idiot, Jack."

"Heard that, too."

"What you probably haven't heard is that he wants to go on the attack because he thinks she's falling behind. I mean he wants her to get personal, with you. He thinks that unless she does that, she's going to lose."

"There are two theories," I said. "That's the second one."

He nodded. "His motives are not entirely clear, that's true."

"She does that, she loses."

"Perhaps. And perhaps not. You're stalled."

"I'm stalled in part because no one gives a damn. They'll give a damn in a hurry if there's something nasty to put on the six o'clock news. That's free time. I don't have to buy it."

"What the hell's going on up there?"

The four golfers were clustered around the pin. The one-legged golfer moved between two of the players. He staggered on his peg leg and seemed about to fall. He was shouting something. Then he did fall, sprawling on the green. The other three turned and walked off. The one-legged golfer did not move for a moment. You could see his chest heaving. He struck the turf once with his fist, then turned to grab the pin, hauling himself to his feet. It looked to be painful. The other three had disappeared into the woods, taking a cart on the narrow path to the sixth tee. The one-legged golfer waited a moment, clinging to the pin with its little pennant. He looked like a soldier planting the colors. Then after a moment he stumbled off, using his putter as a cane. His partners had left him the other cart. He climbed into it painfully and sat a moment. His chest was still heaving. He had the putter across his lap. Suddenly he rose and heaved the putter into the woods, slinging it backhanded. We watched it rise, glittering in the sun, and then we heard twigs and branches breaking. He shouted something, then sank back into the cart's seat, exhausted. In a moment the cart began to move, very slowly, off the apron of the green and down the path through the woods to the sixth tee.

Poor fellow, Mozart said. He took the game so seriously, each shot worth his life. Everyone understood but it didn't make it any easier. He'd fluff a chip shot or a putt and go on the boil, mad at himself and mad at his partners. He was in pain all the time and took it out on the world. He carried three putters in his bag because he'd always lose one of them, in the woods or in the deep pond on Twelve. When he started to boil there was nothing to do but let him go, blow off steam. He always played in the same foursome, men who understood and respected him; but he could be an awful pain in the neck, poor fellow. However, everyone made allowances.

I was looking at my ball and listening to Mozart, whose voice had fallen as if he feared we would be overheard. The ball was nicely teed on a tuft of grass. I took a big swing and the ball exploded, fading at the end so that it dribbled off the green and out of sight.

"That's a hell of a shot, Jack. That's a fine golf shot, though you took a chance. I hope your lie's good, I didn't see where it went."

"It went off the green," I said.

"That's what I thought," Mozart said.

The old lawyer's third shot was straight, high, and short. He was in front of the big sand trap, a hundred yards from the green, a seven iron for him.

"Do you think you can win it, Jack?"

"No," I said.

"That's my estimate. Funny the way you can feel it. You're stalled. You keep turning the key but the engine won't start, *rrr-rrr-rrr-rrrrrrr*. And it won't start because you're out of gas. You're out of money. It'd be all right if people were paying attention, but they aren't. It's only a primary and the winter's been so damned cold. Everybody's thinking about going to Florida."

"And taxes," I said.

"And there's only two weeks left."

"It's enough," I said.

"If there's money it's enough. Otherwise it's not enough."

"What are you offering, Elly?"

"The money," he said.

"How much?"

"As much as you'll need."

"She won't like it," I said.

"She won't know," he said. He had pulled the cart next to the sand trap and was now standing over his ball, looking at it. He sighed and took an eight iron out of his bag. His ball was sitting high on the springy grass. Mozart moved his heavy shoulders and for a moment he looked twenty years younger, his torso motionless and his eyes steady, concentrating on his lie. Suddenly he swung and the ball clicked away in a high arc. I watched it fade right, strike the back side of the green, and bounce away; we were together in the woods. He replaced the club in his bag and smiled broadly, satisfied. "Normally I'd've taken a seven iron, but an eight felt right. I thought to myself, Eight will do the job. Sometimes you have to go with instinct and ignore experience, and the odds."

"That's what Pat Bayley used to say," I said.

"Pat was a champion," Mozart said.

The sun was lowering. I felt a breeze, damp and chilly from the lake only a mile away. The sun had been so warm, an early spring sun, unseasonable. Mozart had taken the cart around the back side of the green near the path to the sixth tee. He stood there waiting for me, idly swinging an iron. I walked, the turf soft and damp under my feet. I thought he had analyzed the campaign correctly. I was exhausted and my people were exhausted. Many of them were on half salary and I had money for one more payroll. The usual sources were dried up, waiting for the general election. We were stalled because I could not engage my opponent. She had refused to debate. I had done everything I knew how to do, and it had not been enough. Campaigns were waged on the small screen and I was not able to buy my way in, as Mozart had predicted at lunch months before. The kitty was small, and now it was almost gone. I had moved to within a few percentage points, then stalled. And she had sailed serenely on—hand, voice, vote. People had sacrificed for my campaign—and then I remembered the philosopher's answer to sacrifice. I spit on sacrifice, he said.

We moved off into the rough, searching for our balls. Mozart was whistling through his teeth, poking here and there with the blade of his nine iron, and then he began to speak. He said he was retiring next year; he'd have an office but he'd be effectively out of it, "of counsel," except when they needed an old head to put a word in an old ear, ha-ha. His son had come into the firm. They had added half a dozen partners and had branched out. Not so much work at the Hall, he said. His son specialized in taxes and his daughter-in-law in communications law. Can you believe it? She was a living doll and smart as a whip. And they're very lucrative specialties, taxes and communications; and you'd be surprised how they fit, for example when one man's selling a radio station to another. They travel to Washington together, and his son spent his time at the IRS and his wife at the FCC, and at night they met at the Hay-Adams and had a cocktail and dinner with their friends. It makes a nice working holiday for them. And the other day his son brought up the possibility of a merger with a Washington firm, small firm, all young men and of course women, too. Smaller firm than Estabrook, Mozart. I said, Not while I'm alive. And my boy just laughed and a few days later his wife took me to lunch at the Tavern and told me they both want to go to Washington, take over the smaller firm. That's where it's at. And they were going to do it, whether I liked it or not; of course they wanted my consent, and my blessing. It would distress them if I fought it. But you can't stop us, Dad, because my mind's made up, she said. If you fight, you'll lose. I tell you, she's a pistol. So what's a father to do? And as everybody knows, Washington is just like Chicago or any other place: it's who you know. You have to know the right people, get a piece of paper from one part of the town to another without a lot of fuss and feathers. As you know, I can take it or leave it alone. Our nation's capital reminds me of Venice. It's a handsome city but it's dead. Nothing happens there. They collect money and they spend it but they don't make anything of value. They don't *produce*. They love to talk and they love to intrigue. They love to denounce people, and they've got their doge and their nobility and their importance in the world. They're news. It's glamorous but it's two grains of wheat in two bushels of chaff, as the man said. They want the rest of us to go away and leave them alone. Hard to tell that to young people, they don't want to believe it. They don't want to believe what's in front of their eyes. They want to believe the six o'clock news instead. My son and his wife love Washington. It excites them, bless their hearts. So what's a father to do?

"You want to buy them a senator as an anniversary present?"

He looked at me, grinning, and then he laughed out loud.

"Here they are," he said, pointing. He brushed away leaves with his nine iron, uncovering his Titleist and my Top-Flite, both of them in impossible lies. The balls were about a foot apart behind low bushes. A trap was in front of the bushes and the green beyond the trap. The pin was thirty yards from where we were.

"Your go, Jack."

The Top-Flite was behind a tuft of grass in a little ragged trench, barely playable.

"I won't object if you improve that lie," Mozart said.

I swung and the ball ticked the top of the bushes, but had enough lift to clear the trap. I was this side of the green, off the apron.

"My goodness," Mozart said. "That's just a beauty. You're a man who came to play golf." He stood looking at his ball. The bushes prevented a direct approach to the green and the Titleist was behind a fallen branch. "Of course I want to buy them a senator, Jack. And not only them but some other good people I represent and have represented for many years, in good times and bad. They need a senator also. What's the matter? You so far up the ladder that you can't be bought?" He said all that without looking up. "Sometimes I've had a lie like this one, just impossible. Unplayable. So I did what I could." He shook his head and placed the blade of his nine iron behind the ball, just so. Then he reached down and gently removed the branch and threw it away. Now there were only the bushes between him and the green. He said, "Time was, Springfield was all I needed or wanted. Butch Estabrook, too, God rest his soul. They never liked us downstate. We were too big, we muscled people even when we didn't intend to. The big fellow has to be careful where he sits. On the other hand, we had jobs to do and time was always of the essence. And Butch was often abrupt. He frightened people. *Chicago* frightened people, its sprawl and influence. Chicago moved its shoulders and the people on the edges got knocked out of the tree. But what are you going to do about that? Pretend you're a shrimp? Gosh, sorry. We're the engine and the engine makes a racket. The noise bothers some people. It just bothers the hell out of them. Well." He looked at me. "Tough shit."

"I can win without you," I said.

"No, you can't, Jack. You'll lose. Not by much. But you'll lose. And she'll lose too, in the general. Then we've all lost. You, me, her. Three losers. Jesus, I hate to lose. Sometimes you can't prevent it and so you swing with it, *c'est la vie*, and go on to something else. You love the girl but the girl doesn't love you back, so you say all right, there're other girls. And those other girls have also got tits and nice smiles. Win all the time and you know you've bought into an easy game, and who wants that? But if you can prevent it, and still lose, you're a horse's ass. You're selfish, you think you're Jesus Christ. You're a stranger, you're living in another world, because that's not the way we're built here, in this region. You know that, Jack. We don't believe in a perfect world here, we go with what we have; and if a man extends his hand, we shake it or cut it off. There's no middle way. And I'm wondering whether you belong on the first team or in a sandbox, because it sounds to me like you believe in a child's history of the world. Life's dirty, Jack. But of course you know that, too. Or you did. Maybe you forgot." Mozart lifted his nine iron and tapped the grass behind the Titleist, then thought better of it, shrugged, and picked up the ball. He rolled it on the tips of his fingers, removing a speck of dirt and measuring the distance to the pin. Then he rocked back and forth like a man pitching horseshoes, underhanding the Titleist, lofting it over the bushes and the sand trap and onto the fairway, where it bounced twice and rolled onto the green, about eight feet from the cup.

I said, "Hell of a pitch, Elly."

But he was already moving away to the golf cart to fetch his putter. His shoulders were square and his belly looked hard as iron, straining against the cardigan sweater. He wore old-fashioned golf shoes, heavy brogans with cleats screwed into them. In his ensemble he looked like one of the old-timers, Jimmy Demaret or Byron Nelson. All he lacked were plus fours. He was standing behind the cart, looking at the Titleist on the green and smiling slyly. I wondered how long he had thought about what he was going to tell me. I guessed about five minutes. It was an old lecture, he had used the same

239

material for fifty years; not that he had much occasion to use it, the times being what they were. If I turned him down he would regard it as an offense against nature, his own natural law, and he would find a way to exact revenge. And that was what encouraged me to refuse him, to let him know that the game was unimaginably complex, and that there was no natural law beyond unpredictability; the universe was in disorder, and Mozart and I were a misalliance. He had been buying politicians for fifty years. Politicians were his dearest, closest friends; they came to the weddings of his children, and the christenings of his grandchildren. They always needed money so they came to him as a sick person came to a doctor, money a specific against defeat. There were Mozarts all over America, some better, some much worse, a fundamental part of the system. They were owed an article of their own in the Bill of Rights to the Constitution.

He was standing on the green waiting for me. I felt that my life had converged to this moment, that what I would do now would be the sum of my actions in the past. He wanted me to submit to discipline, a novice to his confessor. We had been on the opposite side of things for so long. I hated him for what he had done to Bayley; or what I imagined he did, having no firsthand knowledge of anything. And at that I would be his last prize before retirement, the old scoundrel's final fix. But I wanted the other, too; it also was the sum of my actions, for better and worse. I wanted it as badly as I had ever wanted anything material, in part as atonement for the years I had lived on the margins, not evilly, but carelessly and without force or conviction. It was part atonement and part compensation, though I did not believe I was owed anything. I was not trying to regain something I had lost, but to seize something I had never had. I feared that my goal was beyond reach, and the campaign lost.

Mozart was impatient, standing on the apron of the green and looking at his wristwatch. I stepped up to the ball, not thinking about it, not thinking about golf at all but what I would say to Mozart. I realized suddenly that Charles Nierendorf would be the paymaster, and that meant that when he called my office I would have to pick up the telephone and listen to him and at the end of the conversation say Yes, or anyway not say No, hurriedly of course because it would be late in the day and I was scheduled to meet young Mozart and his wife and some boys from Chicago at the Hay-Adams. Probably it would be the young Mozarts, the boys from Chicago, and Charles Nierendorf himself, the eight of us jolly at cocktails while we discussed the problem at the FCC and who did I know over there? Can you make a call, Jack?

I tapped the ball, too weakly except that the green was fast. The ball was mis-hit and I groaned to myself, then looked up to see it jump and curl erratically toward the pin; and it dropped.

"My goodness, Jack!" Mozart cried. "You're a rascal. You're in the wrong business. You should be a golf professional. That's a par five!"

"Birdie four," I said. I could not believe it. I was grinning, elated. So that was how things worked out when you didn't pay any attention to them, didn't worry them, merely did them. The disorderly universe was not always malignant, only unpredictable. Frequently it was benevolent, usually when nothing was at stake.

"My, my," Mozart said, not acknowledging the error. "You just step right up, square yourself away, and bingo. I'd've sworn you didn't even have your mind on the game. I'd've sworn you were a million miles away. You don't need any help from anyone. You're a self-reliant fellow, Jack."

"That's what my father preached, self-reliance."

Mozart smiled. "Did he practice?"

"Not that I ever saw," I said.

Mozart concentrated mightily on his own putts, and took three of them. We walked off the tee and got into the cart and began the short drive down the path to the sixth tee. The woods were densely packed, the light pale and sullen. I realized with relief that we could not play eighteen; it would be dark soon; and it was chilly. Mozart was silent, steering the little cart down the winding path; he was irritated with himself for his three putts, and with me for taking so long and then holing the shot. I looked up, observing the crowns of the shagbark hickory and ash so black and twisted, anarchic against the April sky. It was quiet except for the hum of the electric cart and the crunch of gravel. High up in one of the hickorys something caught my eye. It glittered dully in the light, something balanced on the branches, its man-made linear symmetry incongruous. I shaded my eyes and looked at it, knowing at once it was the one-legged golfer's putter, stuck where he had thrown it in rage. It looked harmless enough now, and a good wind would bring it down. I supposed there were putters all over Oak Knoll, in trees and under bushes, and in the water at Twelve. The putter looked so fragile and insignificant, balanced on the thick limbs of the hickory, like some-thing left over from a flood. I turned away, then looked back, and the putter was lost to view, concealed again in the tops of the trees.

Standing on the sixth tee, we looked down the steep sloping fairway at the foursome approaching the green. It was as if we had stadium seats, watching the playing field below. Six was a short hole, two hundred and fifty yards. The one-legged golfer was leaning against his cart, preparing to chip. The club moved and the ball went wide and dribbled into a sand trap. He fell and then rose, painfully, and slapped the pitching wedge into the golf bag. He leaned against the cart a moment, his chest heav-ing. Then he got into the cart and slowly drove it around to the back of the green and into the sand trap. His com-panions waited for him on the green; they were ready to putt. The one-legged golfer got out of the cart, his club in his hand, and steadied himself. He looked from the pin to his ball and back again, calculating the distance. He swung, falling, the sand spraying in a fan, the ball moving a few feet and coming to rest. It was difficult for him to rise, the club head sinking into the sand. At last he stood, swaying; the one-legged golfer looked disori-ented. He patted his trousers free of sand, got into the cart, and moved it forward so that he could lean against it and try again. Balanced, he swung, fell, and the ball was lost in the spray of sand. When he looked up, he saw that he had lifted it over the lip of the trap and onto the green's apron, a trifle. He drove the cart out of the trap and parked it, alighting with an aluminum rake that extended like a telescope. He leaned against the back of the cart and carefully raked the sand, back and forth a dozen times until the tire tracks and his own marks were erased, and the trap was as he found it. Then he collapsed the rake and replaced it in the cart, fastened his peg leg, fetched the putter, and hobbled onto the green. His companions had played out and now they stood silently, watching him. He took his time lining up the putt. At last he putted, lagging the ball about six feet beyond the cup. It took him two more to get down and when he moved violently to backhand the putter into the bushes, one of the men said something; a blast of rough laughter gusted up the fairway. The one-legged golfer wheeled on his friends, raising his fist, his face scarlet—and then, hesitating and lowering his fist, he made a little agonized gesture and limped back to the cart, laying the putter on the seat. The others sauntered away. He sat a moment, his head bowed, his chest heaving. I watched the one-legged golfer mark the scores on the card. "You win," I said to Mozart.

3

A few years later my mother died, quietly enough though she was not at peace. She missed my father every hour of every day, and her last years were spent inside her own memory, grown caustic but not unreliable. I think she was happy to let go. I was not surprised that her funeral instructions were the same as his, that she be cremated and her ashes taken to Big Lake and scattered on the water near the cabin we had rented during the war. After he died she had gone alone and never spoken of it, except to smile and say that the wind was high that day and my father, irascible to the last, had refused to come out of his urn in any orderly way.

We held a memorial service in Chicago, at the Presbyterian church on the Near North Side that my mother attended occasionally when she and Victor had lived near Lincoln Park. A few friends, widows, came in from Lake Forest and Winnetka. No one came up from Florida. The service was brief, we few clustered in the front pews. We sang a hymn, the minister read a lesson, and I gave a brief eulogy. Of course Marie was there and Brother Sam also, though we spoke only a few perfunctory words to each other. Immediately after the ceremony he departed by limousine to O'Hare. He had an important conference in the Far East, a currency manipulation of some kind; whatever it was, it couldn't wait. Sam had gone to Washington in the twilight of the previous administration as an assistant secretary of the treasury, then returned to his old firm. He was now the senior partner, an international lawyer, an adviser to governments. He was especially close to the authorities at Seoul and at Singapore. He

244

reckoned that his government service, though brief, was worth half a unit a year to his firm. When I asked him what a unit was, he replied a hundred million dollars. Naturally he retained an interest in wills and trusts, though the bulk of that work was handled by a young associate, who herself was shortly to go on leave to work for a while at the Justice Department. It was the young associate who confided to me that Mother's will was a fucking disaster; it would be probated in Illinois, for Christ's sake, where estate taxes were horse cock.

My mother's will stated that her ashes were to be disposed of "as soon as it is practical and convenient," which meant in her vernacular at once. Marie offered to go with me to Big Lake—she wanted to see it, she had heard so much about it—but I said thanks, no thanks. I believed it was a mission best accomplished alone; and she had her own business to attend to. People depended on her. So the day after the memorial service I took the urn and drove north to the Little Fort River Valley in the vicinity of the Wisconsin line. It was a lovely soft April day, all the birches and elms maturing beautifully. On the way up I had the idea I would call Carl Fahr. I had not seen him in many years, but I knew he was living in his house on Egg Lake because I had received a note a few days before. He had seen my mother's obituary notice in the newspaper and had written to say how sorry he was, how fondly he remembered her, what good times they'd had when my father was alive; all my old friends are gone, he said.

Somewhere west of Libertyville I turned in for gas and called Carl from the pay telephone. I recognized his voice immediately, but he did not recognize mine. There was a ghastly pause and he said Oh! as if the wind had been knocked out of him. I said hello again and gave my name, and that seemed to settle him. It took him a moment to recover and then he said, My God, Jack, you gave me a scare. You sound like your father. I thought it was him and I wondered, well, I didn't know what to think. You sound exactly like Victor, Jack.

He said, Give me a minute.

I said I was sorry, I had no idea.

Goodness gracious, he said, and then he laughed.

I said I hadn't meant to give him a scare.

Whew! he said.

I didn't realize, I said.

It's good to hear your voice, Jack, Carl said.

I explained that I was nearby and asked if I could come over and see him and he said of course, delighted.

He met me at the door, a tall, stooped old man. He was walking on metal canes, having had two hip operations. His skin was so pale it was almost translucent. I remembered him as fine-featured, a delicate, debonair man, but the years had accumulated in his bones, in his long jaw and cheeks, his forehead, and his loose sardonic mouth. You could see the skull beneath the skin and he had enormous ears with great hairy lobes. Yet when he spoke it was with the same youthful voice, and his handshake was firm.

We went onto the porch, where his houseman had laid out a tray of drinks, tomato juice and bouillon and vodka, several kinds of whiskey, and wine chilling in a bucket. The houseman emerged from the kitchen to ask if everything was all right, Carl. He smiled at me and Carl made the introduction, the son of his oldest friends, in the valley on a visit. Ernst was about my age, though he moved with the spring of a younger man; he had an unpronounceable German surname and bustled away after checking the tray a second time, and pouring himself a glass of wine. Ernst looks after me, Carl said. He's been my friend for ten years, longer; it's almost eleven years now. He smiled at my evident surprise.

He said, "You look like Victor, too."

"You mean, now."

"Yes," he said.

I shook my head.

"Victor never understood," he said.

"Victor never understood a lot of things."

"Your mother was different."

"She was very fond of you."

"And I of her. Of them both." He turned to the kitchen door and called for Ernst. When there was no response he turned back and asked me to make the drinks.

I made myself a Scotch and poured a glass of wine for

Carl. The wine was from a small vineyard in Minnesota, Minnesota Chardonnay. I wondered where it came from exactly, the southern farm country or north in the direction of the Iron Range. Then I decided that it was from the château country around Minneapolis, Wayzata or Hamel, one of those.

I asked if Ernst wanted to join us.

Carl laughed and said, No. On Sundays he watches the football games, all afternoon. One damned game after another.

We sat on the porch with our drinks on the railing and looked over Carl's lake, which seemed to me very much changed since the war. It was smaller and no longer egg-shaped. But when I asked Carl about it he said it hadn't changed as far as he was concerned. There were a few houses that I didn't remember and at the far end someone was water skiing, in a wet suit because the air was chilly. The sky was clear and the trees pale with color and as I looked around, at the tray of drinks and the comfortable porch furniture and the curvy, lazy lines of Carl's old house, I thought it was one of the prettiest places I had ever seen. I wondered again about the lake and whose memory was faulty, mine or Carl's. He looked at it all with an easy sense of proprietorship natural to anyone who had sat on the same porch for fifty Aprils. A newly green lawn stretched from the porch to the edge of the water, where the boat house was.

I said, "Maybe you're right."

He said, "It hasn't changed in any real way. Someone builds a house and you think, Oh, damn. Then in two years or three years your eye gets used to it and it's as if it were always there, except that one." He pointed across the lake to a house that was higher than the firs surrounding it; it had a flat roof supporting an enormous dish antenna. "That nightmare," he said. "They ought to do something about those things." That seemed to stir something in his memory, for he suddenly frowned. "I keep writing your office, Jack. And there's never any satisfaction."

"Tell me what it is," I said.

"The Social Security checks. They're late again. There was a late one in February and another in March."

"Did you get them?"

"Eventually," he said. "Late."

"I'll look into it," I said, taking out a notebook I kept for that purpose and making a note to myself.

"I know you have more important things to do."

"It's the damned bureaucracy," I said.

"It's a mess. Washington is a mess."

I could not suppress a smile. There was always a mess in Washington. I would have to wait a moment to discover which particular mess Carl meant—taxes, inflation, corruption, the deficit, the Russians.

"I voted for you, Jack. In the general election and in the primary, though she was a very plucky young woman. I liked her. She spoke her mind, straight from the shoulder. It got kind of dirty, I thought." He smiled. "Reminded me of the old days."

Dirty wasn't the word. "Yes," I said.

"I wish you could do something about the foreign aid. We're giving away our wealth, just giving it away, and there's no appreciation."

I leaned forward, curious. I hadn't heard anyone complain about the foreign aid budget in years. It was what they talked about in the 'fifties and early 'sixties. And it wasn't much more now than it was then, including inflation. "It isn't a lot of money, Carl."

"You voted for it, last session."

"That's right, I did. And I probably will again."

"It's all beyond me," he said. Then, "You handled her well."

"Thanks, Carl."

"She was out of line, raking up the past in the way that she did."

"The voters thought so."

"It's just politics, but still."

I did not know how to reply to that.

"You were tough, too. It was quite a show. I think Victor would have enjoyed it. For a while there, he was the center of attention."

"Victor would have enjoyed it?"

"I think so. You know Victor."

I said, "Victor was complicated."

"Whoo-ee," he said, expelling his breath in a great

248

rush, then smiling. "It must have been hard on Iva, though."

"I don't think she knew," I said. "She didn't keep up with politics, even my campaign."

He nodded. "Goodness, Jack. You gave me a fright when you called. I'm sorry I reacted so. Your voice was Victor's voice to a T and I thought . . . well, I didn't know what to think. I thought it was possible that I had died, and." He fluttered his hands, angel's wings.

"I hadn't any idea my voice sounded like his."

"Identical," he said. "It gave me the willies. You don't look anything like him, though, not really. You favor your mother."

I said, "It's Sam who looks like Dad."

"Where's he living?"

"East," I said.

"And he was in the government, too, for a while."

"For about five seconds," I said.

"Well, that's the idea, isn't it? Get in and get out."

"Sam's idea," I said. "Not mine."

"You boys never got on, did you?" I shrugged and he did not pursue it. He said, "I'm glad you're here, Jack. I'm so damned sorry about your mother. I would've come to the service, but." He nodded at his canes. I didn't say anything for a moment, watching the boats move at the far end of the lake. Something turned over in my memory, but I couldn't recognize it. I said, "She wanted me to take her ashes to Big Lake, just as she did with Dad. Odd; they hadn't been up here for years. I think the last time we were all here together was that summer during the war, that time you and Victor got into it about my fish."

He looked at me, slowly shaking his head. His hand went to his ear and I noticed he was wearing a hearing aid. "I don't remember. What was that?"

It was incredible to me that he would not remember, the incident was so vivid in my memory. I said, "A fish I caught. My first fish, a bass. A very small bass. You said it was under the limit; he said it didn't matter whether it was under the limit or not, I had caught it and it was mine."

Carl nodded.

"It was quite a bone of contention," I said, consciously using the archaic phrase in hopes that it would stir his memory.

"This fish," he said.

"Yes," I said, understanding suddenly how absurd it all was.

"And what did you have to say about it?

I said, "I said, 'Throw it back,' that it didn't matter that much. And it didn't, either, except later."

"And Victor didn't want to."

I said, "Not on your life. 'Let the god damned kid have the god damned fish, Carl,' " giving as good an imitation of my father's voice as I could, then immediately regretting it, because a shadow crossed Carl's face. But he smiled and leaned forward, evidently enjoying himself.

"And I wanted to stick to the rules."

"That's right," I said.

He laughed suddenly, throwing his head back. "Sounds like me. I was a great stick-to-the-rules man, back then. Sounds like Victor, too. Yes, that's Victor all right."

"Do you remember what happened?"

He shook his head. "I don't remember at all. But I can guess."

"Guess," I said.

"We kept the fish."

I laughed. "Right."

"Victor was irresistible," he said, and turned away to stare at the water, sparkling in the sun. He took a dainty sip of wine, holding the glass by the stem.

"And that night I got a mysterious fever and you went for the doctor."

"I remember *that*," he said. "Never forget it. We were drunk as owls, Victor and I. Old Doc Pafko was scared to death, thought I'd run him up on the beach in the Gar Wood. Made us call him a cab to get home. Charged Victor double for the house call." Carl laughed, a wintry old laugh. "Ten dollars instead of five."

We were silent a moment, watching the sun play on the cold blue water. The water seemed almost furry, rippling in the breeze. I lit a cigarette and blew a smoke ring, and then the memory came back to me: watching the boats from my parents' apartment in Florida, after my father had his stroke, and we had argued, and I had gotten so drunk and called Carole Nierendorf. It was the week of the summit.

He said, "I don't remember the fish, though." He was still staring at the water, framed between the boat house and a giant blue spruce. "What was the fever about?"

I said, "I don't know. Nerves, I guess. Maybe the fish was bad."

"All I remember is that you were fine the next day. God, Victor was worried though."

"He was?"

"Worried sick."

I said, "I'll be damned."

"They were afraid of polio, and he felt responsible."

"He did?"

"Of course. He felt responsible for everything."

I looked at him. "Victor?"

"That was Victor's problem," he said.

"Victor's tremendous concern for everyone," I said.

Carl shrugged and did not reply. I had irritated him with my sarcasm, and I moved to make amends. "It was a long time ago."

"Sure was."

"And a pretty small fish," I said. I got up to refill Carl's glass and my own.

He said behind me, "God, I've lived a long time."

"And you're not done yet."

"No, I'm not," he said. And then, imitating Victor, "God damn it."

I handed him his glass and cleared my throat. "Real reason I'm here, Carl. It's a kind of sentimental thing, and don't hesitate to say no. But I thought it'd be nice if we got into the Gar Wood and drove over to Big Lake so that I could do what Mother asked me to do. Like the old days, coming around the point of land—" Carl frowned and I stopped talking, knowing suddenly that it was a foolish idea and that I'd be letting myself, and Carl too, in for disappointment. It was another beau geste, like stuffing twenty-dollar bills into the pockets of derelict farmers. I said, "I suppose it's ruined, though.

Spoiled. Bungalows everywhere, gas stations, fast food.''
I smiled. "Slot machines in the roadhouses.''

"It's changed some," Carl said slowly. "I was waiting for you to come up here during your campaign, and disappointed when you didn't. You'd recognize it. It was always a pretty little lake. It was pretty when the Indians had it. And it still is.''

"Next time," I said. "Cabin still there?''

"No, that's long gone. Some people from Winnetka bought the property, tore it down, and put up a big house. Nice house, not like *that*." He pointed at the vertical house with the dish antenna, rising above the firs. "Funny thing about the one-armed bandits. The new people didn't like them, didn't like the trade they brought, didn't like the image. So they elected a sheriff who'd enforce the law. That was a while back. Now the one-armed bandits are around again. People like them. I mean the new people who replaced the new people. They like the slot machines and double nassau on the golf course. Sheriff isn't a member, so he doesn't get around the back nine much, watch the money change hands. So the slot machines are back, just like the old days, because people don't want them out.''

"Syndicate still here?''

"Sure, but you never see them. We're into the second, third generation. Some of them are pretty rough, except for the people from Winnetka. He's heavy-duty. Quiet people, keep to themselves, pay their taxes, and support the sheriff.''

"Well," I said.

"So that's everything to date at Big Lake.''

I said, "I remember it was about twenty minutes in the Gar Wood, here to there.''

"About that, full throttle." He seemed to pull into himself, his neck bending until his long jaw rested against his collarbone. Then he looked up, lifting his chin as he did when he wore the yachtsman's cap so many years before. I could see he was thinking about the boat, and about my mother, and considering my request, though perhaps all he could see was an urn. I wondered whether he had been with her when she came up with my father;

252

but she had not mentioned it, so I suppose he hadn't been.

He rose slowly and put his glass on the tray, moving forward to steady himself. He swayed a little when he stood, the way old people do, blinking once or twice to accustom himself to his feet. He reached around the tray to take a key from a hook. He said, "Come on."

I said, "That's great, Carl. Thanks."

But he was already moving off the porch onto the lawn, moving with surprising grace, very erect, manipulating his steel canes. The lawn was long and sloping and he stepped carefully, watching for the sprinklers nestled every few yards in the young grass. It had been years since I'd seen a built-in sprinkler system. There was one huge blue spruce at the bottom of the lawn near the boat house and we passed through its shade on the way to the water. The tree was as high as a flagpole and well remembered from my childhood. At dusk it had a truly blue cast. A few feet from the boat house Carl paused, rooting around in his jacket. He brought out an old iron key and stood contemplating it, and the blue spruce, the boat house, and the water.

The door's window was so dusty that I could not see through it. Carl worked the lock this way and that until finally it gave and the door swung open. The Gar Wood was cradled in its slings, motionless. There was a launch on the lake whose wake was lapping at the shore and the boat house pilings. We went inside and Carl pulled on the overhead door. He pulled once or twice without success and then, cursing, stepped aside so that I could do it. When the door rose at last the interior was filled with spring light, probably for the first time in . . . it could have been forty years.

The Gar Wood was covered with a fine film of dust, the brightwork rusted and the mahogany desiccated. The hull was green where it touched the water. The slings that held it aloft were frayed and the boat dipped, bow down. Next winter's ice would seize it fast and crush the mahogany like an eggshell. It took me a moment to understand what I was seeing, it was all so unexpected.

Carl said, "There she is."

It made me angry to look at it, so neglected and beaten

up, allowed to go to seed. Its defeat seemed willful and unnecessary, a calculated act of contempt. It was vandalism of the sort that happens occasionally in art museums, a canvas slashed with a razor blade or defaced with ink. But that was never the act of the curator or the owner. There were two dead birds floating in the water, birds that had gotten in somehow and were unable to get out. Carl prodded one with a cane and it ghosted away.

"She hasn't been out in a long time," Carl said.

"I can see that," I said.

"Someone came by about, I don't know, two, three years ago, scraped the hull."

"It was longer ago than that," I said.

"Do you think so? Perhaps it was. Her engine still worked at that time. He fixed it up. I could hear it on the porch."

"I'll bet you could," I said. "It must have been quite a sound."

"Purred like a cat. He wanted to buy her but I said, Hell, no. She's mine." Carl tapped a cane on the deck, hollow little taps. "The Gar Wood was made to last," he said.

I leaned forward, wondering if the leather still gave off its pungent smell. It didn't, all I smelled was dampness mixed with fish and algae. On Carl's seat was a flat cushion, but when I looked at it carefully I discovered it was his yachtsman's cap, still crushed around the visor, it too covered with dust. I could barely make out the gold braid. I remembered that he used to call it his sixty-mission-man cap, after the bomber pilots in the war. A crumpled Pabst can floated in the inch of water that covered the floorboards.

"Nice lines, hasn't she? Never a boat like the Gar Wood. When they made her, they broke the mold."

"I wish you hadn't shown her to me."

"Boat's more than sixty years old," Carl said.

"It's one of my earliest memories," I said.

He looked at me curiously. "Is that so?"

"The boat, these lakes, the cabin, during the war. Before things got so messy."

"Well," he said. "I don't know what you mean by that. But now you've seen it."

I said, "Why, Carl?"

"Too much trouble," he said, and turned away.

"You could sell it, give it away. You could've put her in dry dock, arranged for someone to look after her. You could have done a hundred things. But you let it go to pieces. I don't understand that."

"I said it was too much trouble and that's that." He was standing in the doorway now. The sun caught his fine white hair and turned it into a kind of fuzzy halo. But the expression on his face was not angelic, or saintly. He tapped a cane loudly against the door frame. Time to go. "I have better things to do with my time and money. I guess you're the sort of man who likes to hang on to things. I'm not. Never was." He continued to beat the cane against the door frame in a steady tattoo. "You want it, Jack? It's yours."

"I don't want it, Carl."

He looked at me with the suggestion of a smile, the wiseguy's cold superiority. "You're just telling me how great the boat is. Your earliest memory, you said. Now you don't want it. I always thought you liked this boat."

"I did," I said. "I thought it was the handsomest boat I ever saw, coming around the point, bow high, unstoppable. But it was yours. And it still is. But it isn't the same boat."

He backed out of the doorway. He was full in the sunlight looking back at me. He took the heavy key out of his pocket and paused fractionally before saying, "There were dozens of these boats in the lakes in the old days. Now this is the only one. And there won't be any more." He motioned me out of the boat house. "I know what you're looking for, Jack. But you're not going to find it here."

4

In the silence and half light of late afternoon I worked on correspondence, mostly notes of thanks to mother's friends. When the receptionist rang to announce that they were here and did I want to see them now, I had to think a moment, remembering who they were and what I was supposed to do with them. My mind was elsewhere, focused on the correspondence, struggling to make each note specific and consoling.

Then I said, Yes, show them in, make them comfortable, fetch them Coca-Cola from the refrigerator. It was Saturday and the office was empty except for me and the receptionist. And now sixteen seniors from a government class of a prep school on the North Shore, in Washington for an on-site inspection. They had been in town for a week, and I was the last monument on their itinerary. Mozart had asked me to do it, since one of the students was the granddaughter of a very old friend and client.

Appreciate any help you can give me, Jack. Appreciate anything you can do for these fine young people, seeing Washington for the very first time. It'll be something they'll remember all their lives, talking with their United States senator in his office on Capitol Hill. Hearing about the government from one of their own, a man who knows the score, an insider who's worked his way up. There's so much cynicism today. People have lost faith. The young have. So you give it to them straight from the shoulder, Jack. They'll never forget it.

I had arranged a briefing at the Pentagon and a tour of the Supreme Court and the Library of Congress. Mozart wondered if the vice-president would be available and I replied that normally he would be, certainly, except that week he was visiting NATO installations in the Low Countries. The director of the CIA was likewise unavailable, alas. Perhaps one of the news people, Mozart suggested, a network personality or syndicated newspaper columnist. The youngsters were naturally interested in the news media, and the school had mentioned the columnist who had been receiving so much attention, Gobelin. Surely I could arrange a meeting with this Gobelin. Impossible, I said; such interviews were booked months in advance, and Gobelin was frequently out of the city, on tour, speaking. His lecture fees were enormous. I mused to Mozart that years ago students were content with a visit to the basement of the FBI, where one of Hoover's heavies fired a machine gun and explained about the capture of John Dillinger and Ma Barker, public enemies. Times have changed, Mozart said.

I served the fine young people Coca-Cola and their two chaperones glasses of beer. I drew their attention to the pictures on the wall, and the souvenirs here and there; the office was filled with memorabilia, tangible evidence of public life. Part of one wall was covered with cartoons from Illinois newspapers of various aspects of my career—the good, the bad, and the ugly, as I explained to the students. Schmidt-Rottluff's *Zwei Mädchen* was home in my study, but the photograph of Katrina Lauren was on the table behind my desk next to Mary Lincoln's letter to Iva Jackeson, getting and spending in Washington. The desk itself was plain government issue; it had no history at all. I said that normally the office would be astir, phones buzzing and quorum bells ringing. But the Senate was not in session and because it was Saturday there was only the receptionist outside and me in here, working on private correspondence. I indicated the pile of letters.

When the youngsters were settled I made a little speech about how the Senate worked, explaining that some of the archaic rules were better suited to the century before than the present one. There was a tremendous resistance to change because of the fear of unintended consequences. So much had gone wrong so unexpectedly. Many of the members wanted change but there seemed to be no consensus. Yet despite everything the place

257

seemed to work and the nation's business get done, more or less. The longer you were around, the more you came to appreciate the rules, which were dense but fair. I explained about committee assignments and the seniority system. The Senate wasn't a place for quick-change artists, except that lately it had become a training ground for presidential candidates. The Senate was a superb place to begin a run at the presidency; the temptation had become almost irresistible; it was a feature of the changing times. It used to be that you had to wait around for twenty years to become a ranking member of an important committee but that wasn't true anymore, because so many members were retiring, burned out and frustrated, or running for the presidency. Some of them began running for President during the first year of their first term, and you could always spot the signs. They had positions on everything. They were earnest and helpful and seldom in town. They had more answers than there were questions, and they got a haircut every week.

I looked at the clock on the wall. I had been talking for fifteen minutes. Another five minutes would do it and then they could leave and I could finish my sad correspondence and go home for a drink and dinner, put some music on the stereo, and finish another pile of required reading—draft legislation, the *Record*, various journals, and research papers—and then, later, anticipating my chronic insomnia, Conrad's *Youth*. The story reminded me of Karcher and Karcher's theories of the uses of adversity. I was suddenly very hungry.

The two young teachers stood near the door, warm beer in their hands, eyes glazing. It was warm in the high-walled office, and the atmosphere heavy. The students sat quietly listening. One pretty girl was taking notes on a yellow legal pad. Everyone seemed tired and dispirited at the end of the day. I looked out the window when a bright light caught my eye. One of the young hopefuls was being interviewed on the sidewalk by a television personality. They both looked so composed. The senator moved his hands easily as he spoke into the camera. I could almost read his lips as he answered questions. In the harsh artificial light it looked like high noon though it was only dusk, the eastern sky dark and benign.

I motioned the students to the window and we all stood a moment watching the interview, live. I said that this, too, was the way the Senate worked. It was a fundamental part of the system. It was necessary to collaborate with the media in order to make yourself visible and have an effect on things, and demonstrate to people that you were alert and on the job. That was crucial. Without the media you were just another tree crashing in the forest. I gave a brief biography of the senator in question, who in many respects was on the right side of important issues. Many hopefuls did interviews from that particular location on the sidewalk, the Capitol dome in the background, nicely lit now that dusk had come. A little group of tourists was watching the interview, respectful looks on their faces; they would remember the moment and take it home to tell to friends. Suddenly the lights went out, causing unexpected gloom, dark as a jungle with the dome's moon shape beyond. The interview was over, and for a moment no one moved. The network personality and the young hopeful approached each other and shook hands. The senator put his free hand on the other's shoulder, squeezing. The reporter laughed and wagged his finger, a friendly rebuke. I interpreted the scene for the students: There had been an awkward or inconvenient question, one the senator had not anticipated or had stumbled in answering. Probably it wasn't important, from the look of things on the sidewalk. The reporter began to explain something, using his hands and body as an agile golfer does when describing good form, the way to achieve the sweet shot. He was giving the senator advice on the technique of the live interview. The two men stood together companionably, as if they had just come from the locker room after eighteen holes. The senator nodded in agreement as he listened. He was listening hard, one professional to another. He was a quick learner, that one; but he would never be more than a hopeful. The technicians packed their gear into the back of a station wagon, NewsCenter 5. The senator got into the front seat with the reporter, and the technicians squeezed in back. The show concluded, the little group of tourists wandered off.

The students resumed their places.

There was one last thing to say.

As they thought about life, and what they would do with it, they should consider a career in government, public service. Washington was a great city, dynamic, hospitable, livable, and beautiful. It was particularly beautiful in April, the fragile cherry blossoms along the Potomac; the aroma was lovely, it broke your heart. Washington was exciting, and good to its young. Advancement was steady; there was something new every day. Public service was a great challenge. There was a wonderful career to be made in the Senate, and the way to begin was as a member of the staff, a senator's office staff or a committee or subcommittee staff. There was something for everyone, economics, foreign affairs, the environment, the military. The pay was competitive and the benefits excellent. Congress was government on the ground floor; everything came together in Congress. There was unbelievable growth in the staffs. It was a growth industry, owing to the fantastic complexity of things and the shortage of solutions. It took a moment getting adjusted to the process; you had to adjust, as you adjusted your eyes to a sudden change of light.

As I spoke I looked at the pretty girl making notes, listening hard. I wondered if she was Mozart's client's granddaughter. If she was bright and hard-working there would be a place for her in Washington, in the Senate or elsewhere. Her connections would smooth the way. She was certainly a disciplined note taker, a no-nonsense sort of girl. When she looked up at me I saw that she had large blue eyes and long lashes. She seemed to be listening with her eyes as she continued to write, even though I was silent.

I had suddenly lost my way, distracted by the correspondence piled on my desk. I had written a different letter to each of mother's friends. There were a dozen letters in all, painfully composed. They were self-conscious letters, as difficult to read as they were to write. But they had to be written. As I wrote them I saw myself alone and distressed on the edge of Big Lake, smoking a cigarette in the last moments of twilight, Chicago's faded industrial glow on the southern horizon. I struggled with my own memory, as one must, and found in this a kind of consolation, a specific gravity, as I buried my mother at last, her ashes falling, then dispersing on the hard surface of the water.

I heard a restless movement, and then someone coughed.

I looked up and smiled broadly. Yes, it was a fine career. The essence of public life was compromise. That was what made the government go, gave it its very existence. It was exquisite, the give-and-take making a beautiful balance. Balance of this kind was breathtaking, like viewing an aerialist or a great painting. In its symmetry compromise was more beautiful than defiance, which was inharmonious. It was immature. It was arrogant. In the Senate as in life you yielded, conceding ground; and your opponent did likewise and from that struggle came something durable and true-speaking. And you lived to struggle another day, always within the rules. There was nothing to compare with a career in Washington. There was great camaraderie all around, though it was not like the old days. In the old days everyone knew one another; it had been a kind of love. That was the way it had been when I first arrived in Washington, thirty years before. In those days everyone was on a first-name basis. The government was like a small family concern, back then; people looked out for each other, and it was good if you had connections. Of course connections never hurt in any walk of life. I had arrived an apprentice from Chicago, but Washington had taken care of that. It was a great city, always giving more than it received. It gave and gave and gave and gave and expected nothing in return except loyalty.

About the Author

WARD JUST is the author of nine previous works of fiction, including *The American Ambassador*. He lives with his wife, Sarah Catchpole, in West Tisbury, Massachusetts.